ALSO BY KIMBERLY MULLINS:

Notebook Mysteries ~ Emma (Book 1)

Notebook Mysteries ~ Decisions and Possibilities (Book 2)

Notebook Mysteries ~ Changes and Challenges (Book 3)

Notebook Mysteries ~ Unexpected Outcomes (Book 4)

Notebook Mysteries ~ Haunted Christmas (a novella)

Notebook Mysteries ~ Suspicions (Book 5)

Notebook Mysteries ~ Parisian Intrigue (Book 6)

Notebook Mysteries ~ A Party to Remember (a novella)

Stand alone novels:

Divided Lives (K.R. Mullins)

1897 A Mark Sutherland Adventure

Notebook Mysteries

Notebook Mysteries

Changes and Challenges

KIMBERLY MULLINS

NOTEBOOK MYSTERIES - Changes and Challenges

Book 3 of the Notebook Mysteries Series

Copyright © JKJ books, LLC 2022

First edition: March 2022

Mailing address for JKJ books, LLC: 17350 State Highway 249, STE 220 #3515 Houston, Texas 77064

Library of Congress Control number: 2022900493

ISBN 978-1-7360104- 8-8 (hardcover)

ISBN 978-1-7360104-7-1 (paperback)

ISBN 978-1-7360104-6-4 (ebook)

This is a work of fiction. It is based on historical events within Chicago during the time period 1881-1883.

Edited by Kaitlyn Johnson, Strictly Textual; Cover Art by Miblart

CHAPTER 1

1885 PRESENT DAY, CHICAGO

Emma rolled over in the bed and reached out to brush the brown curls off his forehead. "Dear-one, you need to wake up sleepy head."

"Sun's not out yet," he said in a muffled voice, lying on his stomach with his face turned toward her, partially buried in the pillow.

"What has that got to do with anything?" she teased.

He opened his eyes and turned on his side, pulling her to him, murmuring, "Good morning, Emma."

"Good morning, Jeremy," she said as he turned on his back, pulling her on top of him. She sank into him with a sigh; a little while later, they came up for air.

"You need to get moving," she reminded him.

"I thought I just had," he commented wryly.

"Oh, you! Out," she said as she pointed at the bookcase and not the door.

She stayed in bed and watched him rise slowly, wrapping his long lean body in a robe. He leaned over to her and said, "See you at breakfast."

"Definitely," she said. He moved the bookcase aside to reveal a door to his room.

CHAPTER 2

Things have definitely changed in the past two years, thought Emma as she settled back on her bed. It began with a request from Mr. Carlyle to protect his granddaughter, Millie. He believed she was being taken advantage of financially. The case had turned suddenly. Millie was discovered to be the mastermind of a smuggling organization and was responsible for multiple murders. Her death by hanging had brought the case to a dramatic end.

"Unfortunately, or maybe, fortunately," Emma mused, "Mr. Carlyle died of natural causes before he could hear his granddaughter's guilty verdict."

Then, a surprising thing happened after the funeral; a lawyer contacted Emma to attend a reading of Mr. Carlyle's will. *The will,* thought Emma, *offered many complications and opportunities.*

The day of Mr. Carlyle's funeral, after they returned home, Emma had been working on lace designs in the sitting room when Dora called her from the foyer. "Emma, a note was delivered for you." She walked into the foyer to take the note, reading it quickly.

"What is it?" asked Dora curiously.

"It's from Mr. Burns, Mr. Carlisle's lawyer. It looks like I'm invited to the reading of the will tomorrow," she said absently.

"Why is it so soon and why invite you?" asked Dora, perplexed.

"The timing must be at Mr. Carlyle's request," Emma murmured thoughtfully. "He might have left me a little something. I did adore his library and it would be nice to have something to remind me of him."

CHAPTER 3

1883 LAWYERS OFFICE

*E*mma woke early that morning, determined to be on time for her appointment with Mr. Burns. She rode her bike over to his office, placing it on her shoulder as she entered. She saw a large man in a blue suit speaking to a gentleman sitting at a desk. *Mr. Burns*, she thought.

The large man straightened when he saw her, folded his hands in front of him, and assumed a solemn expression. "Miss Evans?"

"Mr. Burns?" He acknowledged her with a nod of his head. "Call me Emma, please," she offered.

"Call me Andrew." Mr. Burns looked at the man sitting at the desk and said," Jason, please help Miss Evans."

Jason stood up, motioned toward the bike, and said, "I can take that for you."

She thanked him as he took it from her and moved it to another room.

Mr. Burns offered his elbow and escorted her into his office. As they entered, she found it was a very sober room, with a heavy desk, leather chairs, dark floor rugs, and official-looking framed documents on the walls. She looked around, curious to see who else would be at the reading. When she saw she was alone, she looked at Mr. Burns and asked, "Will anyone else be here?"

"No, I've already notified persons that have small bequests. They will not be here for this communication," he said absently, putting on his glasses as he moved to sit behind his desk. "Please, have a seat."

Emma sat in the heavy brown chair facing the desk. Her eyes darted around the room and finally settled on the lawyer. She watched him pull paperwork from his top desk drawer and was a bit startled when he abruptly began to read.

Emma didn't understand what she was hearing at first. Something about her being the sole inheritor.

She shook her head and asked in astonishment, "I was left what?"

The lawyer removed his glasses and rubbed the bridge of his nose. "Mr. Carlyle contacted me after Millicent's arrest and made the changes to his will at that time. He left the bulk of his estate to you."

"But why me? I'm the one who caused Millie's arrest. I would have thought there would have been some animosity," she said, shaking her head, not understanding.

"When Mr. Carlyle started the investigation, he was suspicious and believed his granddaughter was involved in something nefarious. I think he sent you in to uncover if she deserved her inheritance. There at the end, he had a feeling things were not going to turn out well and wanted the money to go to something positive," he said patiently.

"Okay," she said, rolling her shoulders. "I never turn down a challenge. Where do I sign?"

Mr. Burns smiled, glad there wouldn't be an argument. He stood and shuffled the papers to her side of the desk. As Emma signed, he commented, "There will be some time before the money is officially released. There will be a probate hearing and, once that is completed, I will contact you about the dispersal."

She thanked him and left the lawyer's office in a daze, walking her bike instead of riding it. As she made her way down the sidewalk, she kept thinking, *So much money and so much responsibility.*

"Hey, Em!" a voice called.

Emma didn't hear it; she was wrapped up in her thoughts. "Emma," Jeremy said, touching her shoulder.

Startled, Emma whirled to defend herself and grabbed the hand placed on her shoulder. When she realized who it was, she said, "Jeremy, sorry. I was distracted."

He pulled her in close and murmured, "I could tell." He stepped back and looked down at her. "What happened at the lawyer's office? Get a nice book or small gift?" Emma had told him she was invited to the reading of the will.

She leaned close and tilted her head to speak into his ear. "He left me everything. Don't get too excited," she added when she saw his expression. She explained how the inheritance would work. "It is an added responsibility. I will have to set up a charity to manage the money. He wants me to give it away to people who need it."

"It's still amazing," he said, dazed at the size of the estate Emma now owned.

"Yes," she agreed, not thinking about the money, but about the responsibility.

"Any plans yet?" he asked, knowing her propensity to be organized.

She smiled wryly. "I'm working on it. Can you and Cole come by tomorrow night to meet and discuss the inheritance with the team?"

"Only if I can get you alone after," he said as he leaned in for a kiss. They both enjoyed the interlude.

"Want me to see you home?" he asked.

"No, I'm okay. I think I'll ride the rest of the way," she said as she climbed on her bike.

"I'll be on my way, also. I'm working a case at Citizens bank downtown. I'll be there all week if you need anything," he said.

"Okay, see you tomorrow," she said.

He leaned in for another kiss. "See you tomorrow," he confirmed and waved her off.

She rode to the boarding house, parked her bike in the back, and entered through the kitchen door. Dora heard her coming and ran over to hug her. "Sister, how did it go?"

Emma shook her head and sat down at the table with Tim. He had his books opened and looked up. "Hi, Emma." He noticed she looked distracted and asked, "Everything all right?"

Looking at them both, she said, "Well, looks like we have another opportunity to bring the team together." She went on to explain her conversation with the lawyer. "I think a team meeting to discuss forward steps would be appropriate."

Dora and Tim looked at each other and then at Emma before nodding in agreement. "I asked Jeremy if he and Cole could be here tomorrow after dinner," Emma said.

Making notes, Tim said, "That should work. We'll let Jake and Thomas know to be here."

Emma went to bed early, thinking about the new responsibility and what it would mean. One team member was on her mind, someone who hadn't been around for a while, because of her. *I miss him,* she thought decidedly. *It's time to bring him back to the team.*

She got up extra early to make his favorite treat: strudel. She was sliding the trays out of the oven when Dora entered the kitchen, wrapping a headband around her hair.

"You're up early this morning," she commented.

Emma glanced over. "Yes, I thought we might need a dessert tonight and, since I invited everyone without telling you, I thought I'd help out."

"Thanks for doing that. I appreciate it," Dora said sincerely as she started to get breakfast organized. There was a soft knock on the door and Dora let in a yawning Amy, who greeted them and quickly began to get organized for the day. Dora noticed the box sitting on the table. "Hmm, dessert for tonight, you say? If that's so, who's the box for?" Something occurred to her as she waited for the answer. "Is it for Tony?" She knew it was his favorite.

"It is," Emma said as she added strudel to the box and used a string to hold it closed. "I want to approach him about coming back to help with cases and be an active part of the team."

"Does he know you're coming?" Dora asked suspiciously. She had concerns about Emma's abrupt way with Tony.

"Yes, I sent him a note and asked to see him before work this morning," Emma said, finishing up the box.

Dora exhaled a breath she didn't realize she was holding. Another thought occurred to her. "Does Jeremy know about this?"

Emma frowned over at her. "Jeremy knows Tony and I are still close."

"You haven't been close for a while," Dora reminded her.

"Well, that last case was involved," she said wryly. "But I plan to change that, with this," she said, indicating the box.

"You're putting a lot of faith in a pastry," Dora said with a laugh. "You might mention it to Jeremy," she suggested.

"I might," she said as a compromise.

Emma cleaned up her work area and stored the extra strudel for the evening meeting. She helped get breakfast on the table and spent the morning working on some lace designs, watching the time so she could meet Tony at the museum before they opened. The clock chimed, she gathered up her things and headed to the kitchen. "I'm headed out to see Tony." She kissed Dora on the cheek on her way out.

"Don't forget your magic pastry," Dora teased.

Emma grabbed the pastry box and sent her a grin as she headed out to get her bike. The wind was refreshing on her face and she enjoyed the ride. She was lifting her bike on her shoulder when she saw Tony sitting on the steps.

She put it down and rolled it over to where he was sitting. "Hi, I thought I would meet you inside," she said, taking extra time to settle her bike against the stairs and adjust the pastry box. When she finally glanced back and saw he was smiling, his hair falling into his eyes. Her fingers itched to adjust his hair instead, she just stared for a long moment and lifted the box in her hand. "Your favorite."

"Yes," he said quietly. She didn't notice he wasn't looking at the box. He averted his eyes when she looked toward him.

"Why don't we walk over to the park?" he suggested.

"That would be nice," she said with a quick smile.

"I can walk the bike." He stood and took it from her as they moved onward. A comfortable quiet settled around them. They found an empty bench to sit on and opened the box of strudel.

She let him eat one before starting a conversation. "Tony, we miss you and the team would love to have you participate as a full member."

"I miss seeing and talking to you, and I miss the family. I also miss the excitement," he admitted.

She laughed at that and commented, "We're never short on that!"

"I guess the question is, can we be as close as we once were, but not be together?" he asked laconically.

"Tony," she said, touching his hand and looking deep into his eyes, "I want to be close. I want to share what's happening in my life and hear what's happening in yours."

He set his other hand on top of their clasped hands and squeezed. "I do, too. I've missed this so much." For over an hour, they sat and talked about their lives and what had happened since their breakup.

"So, Mrs. Smith?" she teased.

He turned red and said with a smile, "I like her. She's taken me to her tailor and shown me how to dress. I'm enjoying her company."

"I've noticed," said Emma, touching his new collar. "Very dapper. She seems good for you. I don't see her missing an event because of an ongoing mystery."

"No," he murmured. "She wouldn't do that."

"You never mentioned what's up with Mr. Smith?" she asked consideringly.

"He passed away some time ago," he said simply.

Emma looked worried and Tony noticed, saying, "Now, stop that. He died of natural causes; he was older and had a heart condition."

Emma smiled brightly. "Well, I am a bit busy, so I may not be able to investigate that."

He laughed and continued. "I've also been studying art history and the museum is paying for school. I'm learning how to tell if paintings are authentic—the types of paints used, the cracking and wear on a picture which could indicate when it was painted. I'm especially excited about eventually traveling and seeing Paris. Philip and I have been invited there this year to authenticate some paintings."

"Paris, oh, that's wonderful! I hope to get there one day. You must tell me everything when you get back," she said wistfully.

"I will," he promised. He turned serious for a moment and looked at her searchingly. "I assume that you and Jeremy. . ." His voice trailed off.

"Yes, we're together now. Tony, it was after we broke up, I promise," Emma said softly.

He nodded, believing her, and asked, "Do you see it going long term?" He knew how she felt about marriage.

She thought about that and said, "Right now I do, but I try not to think that far ahead."

"This is true. Have you told him you're inviting me to rejoin the team?" he asked.

"Tony, you were always welcome," she said, distressed.

"I know, but I needed some time to find out what I wanted, separate from you."

"Yes, we operated so much as a couple, it was hard to find where we started and stopped as individuals," she said.

"To get back to the initial question, will you tell him?" he asked, feeling he needed to know the answer.

"I'm a little confused about that," she admitted. "Dora brought it up, too. I just don't typically run things by him, work- or case-related. We do have some overlaps when additional resources are needed by us or Pinkertons, but no communications like that."

"Emma, I think you should realize that this will go past work issues; it's personal. I would rather not have any drama tonight at your meeting," he stressed.

"There is that," she conceded. "Okay, I'll head over after and mention it to him. I won't be asking permission," she warned.

"I didn't think you were," he murmured, watching her. *I can do this*, he thought. *We can be friends again. What the future holds, I just don't know.*

"Tony, are you happy?" she asked, concerned by his intense expression.

"Me? Yes, I am. I feel I'm on the path I am meant to be on," he replied in a steady voice.

"Yeah, me, too."

They finished the pastry, enjoying their time together. They talked quietly as they walked back to the museum. Before leaving, she asked, "Tonight?"

"Tonight," he confirmed, and they parted.

She didn't look back as she rode off, so she did not see that he waited until she was out of sight before slowly climbing the stairs to the museum.

CHAPTER 4

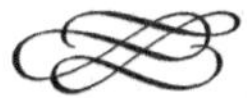

*A*s Emma was riding to the Pinkerton offices, she thought absently, *I'll need to confirm that I can go by and see Jeremy at the bank.* She was also thinking about her and Tony's conversation. *How to approach this topic with Jeremy?* She arrived at the Pinkerton office and placed her bike on her shoulder, climbed to the top of the stoop, and entered the office building.

She set it down to close the door behind her, noticing how quiet it seemed. It was close to lunch and there wasn't anyone at the outer desk. She started down the hallway as Cole exited the office, in the process of putting on his black jacket. He glanced toward the door and saw her standing there. "Emma, what can I do for you?"

"I hoped to stop by and see Jeremy at the bank, but I wanted to be sure it is safe to do so," she said.

"I don't see why not. We are trying to be preemptive, so we have extra people stationed and there's not a confirmed threat of a possible shooter or robbery. Just don't distract him," he warned, shaking his finger at her, then spoiled the severe words with a smile.

She blushed and grinned. "I'll try not to." She picked her bike back up and accompanied him down the stoop.

She waved at him, watching him go, and climbed on her bike to head toward the bank. As she approached the building, she rode close to the windows, peeking in. Jeremy stood inside, speaking with an older gentleman. Three other Pinkerton employees were posted nearby, watching the bank area. They noticed her in the window and called over to Jeremy. He glanced her way and waved her in.

Emma nodded, heading toward the door. She jumped off her bike and parked it in the bushes to the left of the entryway before entering and waiting while Jeremy completed his conversation. He walked over to greet her and leaned in to kiss her cheek, saying, "Hello, Em. What's going on?" He added quietly, "Don't stay around very long. We're expecting some action this afternoon."

"Just something quick, I invited Tony to rejoin our investigation group. I wanted to let you know," she said, unsure of what tone to take.

Jeremy gave her a long look and said, "Emma, I know you and Tony would like to stay close and I know you're committed to me. I appreciate you telling me, but you don't need my permission to add members to your team."

She smiled. "I love you, Jeremy."

He said back softly, "I love you, too, but you need to go now!" He walked her swiftly to the door.

"Jeremy," one of the men called, indicating a man just coming in, armed. Jeremy pulled Emma to the right side of the door.

Emma drummed her fingers on her lips. "Jeremy, I have an idea." He listened quietly and nodded, then motioned to the men to spread out. The tellers and manager were told to duck behind the counters. The gunman burst through the door with his weapon drawn. Emma was ready for him; she leaped from a crouched position, wrapping her arms around his legs. As he collapsed in surprise, Jeremy used his arms to strike downward, forcing him to drop the gun to the floor. The Pinkerton men jumped on the now unarmed man and restrained him. Jeremy retrieved the gun and helped Emma to her feet.

"Great response, Emma. Thanks for the assist." He grinned and offered her a hand up.

She accepted it and bounced a bit as she was pulled to her feet. "Glad I could stop by," she said, grinning back. "Coming over tonight?"

"Wouldn't miss it," he said and went back to directing his men to remove the assailant from the bank. Emma retrieved her bike as she exited and headed home to arrange the meeting.

Dora met her at the kitchen entrance from the dining room. "I heard you come in. How was Tony? Will he be joining us tonight?"

"He will," Emma confirmed.

"Good." She paused before continuing. "And Jeremy?"

"Oh," Emma said nonchalantly, "I went by the bank. He said it was my team and my decision." She didn't mention what happened after the conversation. Dora was a worrier and Emma didn't think she needed the additional stress.

CHAPTER 5

That evening, Emma was sitting with Dora, Tim, Thomas, and Jake when they heard a knock at the front door. "I'll get it," she offered. She went into the foyer and opened the door to find Jeremy and Cole there. As she invited them in, Jeremy leaned in for a kiss, while Cole waited patiently.

Cole gave them a minute, then cleared his throat. Jeremy stepped back from Emma with a smile.

Cole said, "Emma, we appreciate your help today at the bank. I understand," he said looking at Jeremy and then back at her, "that the takedown was your idea."

"I just thought catching him unawares would make it less likely someone could get hurt," she explained. She leaned into their group and said, "Let's keep that between us." They nodded, understanding she didn't like to share all of her adventures with her family. "Follow me, we're in the kitchen."

As they joined the others at the kitchen table, there was a knock on the kitchen door and Jake said excitedly, "I'll get it." Dora smiled as he answered the door.

Tony entered the room, hugging an enthusiastic Jake as he

smiled at the group. "I hear there is strudel available at this location."

That made everyone laugh and any tension caused by his presence melted away.

"Tony, hi." Jeremy made the first move, standing and sticking out his hand toward him. There was only the slightest hesitation as Tony accepted the gesture. They weren't friends, but they could work together. Tony sat by Jake, who excitedly began chattering about the pictures at the museum until Emma commented, "Let's get started." She went on to explain how the inheritance would work. "It will be a self-supporting charity. We have enough money to set up a management company can choose projects to support."

Tim was making notes as Emma discussed the money, other properties she'd inherited, and how Mr. Carlyle wanted it distributed.

He looked up and said, "Emma, I think you'll need to meet with his business manager and find out how the money is currently being managed. I'd also recommend a thorough audit of all of the money and property."

Emma was drumming her fingers on her lip and Jeremy noticed with a tilted smile. She looked at Tim and asked, "Who would you recommend for the audit?"

"I have three New York City companies I can recommend," he said, jotting down the names and handing her the paper.

She was studying it when Dora asked, "Emma, how are you thinking the money should be managed and distributed?"

The amount of money left to her was more than she could handle alone. "The manager I mentioned would report to a board to vote on different projects to be funded. Then I think a vote from the group and finally a co-signature from the manager and me to release the money."

"Who are you thinking of for the board?" asked Dora,

although she already had an idea of who would be asked to participate.

"I was thinking of," she looked around the room at each person, "Jeremy, Dora, Tim, Jake, Tony, Thomas, and Cole."

"Speaking for me and Dora," commented Tim, holding Dora's hand, "we would be honored."

Jake looked on and said, "Emma, you really want me on the board?"

"I do, Jake. You bring a lot of positive things to our team, and I think it'll be the same on the board. Will you join us?" she asked in a serious voice.

"I will," he said, looking very happy at being included.

She glanced over to Tony and asked, "Tony?"

"It sounds like an amazing project. I want to be included," he said.

She turned to Thomas, who nodded. "I've always looked out for you, and I think looking out for more people is a good thing," he said.

"Last but not least, Cole and Jeremy, will you be joining us?" asked Emma.

They looked at one another and then to Emma, with Cole responding, "We will do it."

Emma flashed a grin at the whole group, knowing her team was amazing.

With that, the board was in place, and Emma said, "I'll be approaching the person I think will work as a manager soon. If they accept the position, then I'll schedule my trip to New York to meet with the business manager, Mr. Beeker. Agreed?" They all agreed on the path forward.

CHAPTER 6

The next morning, Tim and Emma met separately in the study to review what she would need to speak with Mr. Beeker about. Reviewing his notes, Tim looked up to comment, "Emma, I'd like to participate in the audit. I know you can take care of the initial meeting, but I think you need someone you can trust to help guard the charity's interest."

After a moment, she said, "I agree. I'll go to the initial meeting in New York with Mr. Beeker and get the auditors set up."

"That will allow me to get organized here so I can make the trip," confirmed Tim.

"You'll be able to stay at Mr. Carlyle's house," she suggested.

"That sounds good. I'll review my schedule and give you some dates," he said, wondering if he could get Dora to come with him.

As they completed their business, Emma headed out of the study and up to her room, mulling over the candidates to lead the charity.

We'll need an extremely efficient business person who is personable and honest, she thought. She opened her notebook to review the list of potential people who could fill the role The one person who kept coming to the top of that list was Clair. She already operated a charity that was making a difference in women's lives by protecting them from abusive men. *This would give her a new direction in her life, but is it something she wants?* Emma asked herself.

Clair had become a very close friend of Emma's over the years. They were two very different people—Emma, the daughter of an engineer, business owner, and detective, and Clair, who didn't know her father and owned and operated a bordello. What brought them together was their shared past event and their common goal of helping people in trouble. Emma thought decisively as she marked other people's names off her list. *There's no better person to sift through the many requests and know which are truly deserving of help than her.*

A few days later, Emma arranged to meet Clair at their regular restaurant, where they discussed business monthly or just enjoyed each other's company. She entered the office space of the restaurant; management allowed them to use it for their private conversations. She saw Clair across the room, sitting at the round table set up with an afternoon tea. She wore a beautiful light blue afternoon dress with a bustle and a white lace shirt peeking out of the jacket opening, giving the appearance of a very lovely lady of leisure. Seeing Emma, Clair stood and circled the table to embrace her. "Emma! I was so worried about you after reading the news and hearing from Thomas about what went on in your last case."

"Yes, I was worried about me also," she said wryly. She got to the point quickly. "Something has come out of that case that I wanted to talk with you about."

Clair raised her eyebrow questioningly.

Emma smiled and continued. "That's actually why I asked you here today." She recapped Millie's case for her and said,

"Mr. Carlyle left me his entire estate and asked that I do something of value with it. I started thinking about you."

"Me? What could I have to do with this?" Clair asked in astonishment.

"Let's sit and discuss it. I see you ordered a lovely tea," said Emma warmly.

Clair nodded distractedly. They moved to sit at the table, enjoying their tea before Emma continued the discussion about the inheritance.

"I'll need to set up a trust to manage the money and determine what causes we want to help. I also need a manager to guide that trust and communicate with board members." She reached over and touched Clair's hand. "I would like that person to be you."

Clair was stunned at Emma's request. She sat for a long moment taking in what this could mean. What it could mean for her and Thomas.

"We would, of course, work a salary out and continue investing so the money can build and continue to be used for good," stated Emma.

"What about my current business?" asked Clair, taking the offer very seriously.

"It's your business, but my suggestion is that you hire a manager—someone you trust—and give them the opportunities you were given. You wouldn't have to sell it, but you could start limiting your time there."

"You've given me a lot to think about." Suddenly worried that Emma might be ashamed of her business, she asked, "Would you want me to hide my past in this new role?"

"No, not at all," said Emma, looking Clair in the eye. "This is about taking chances on people and giving them opportunities. I think you'll be the perfect person to offer them the help they need. I also think you would be able to tell the sincere proposals from those that are not."

Clair teared up and could not speak for a moment. She cleared her throat and said, "I'll need to discuss this with Thomas, and I may finally say yes to his question."

Something occurred to Emma, and she said in an excited voice, "Would that question be 'Will you marry me?'"

Clair blushed. "Yes."

Emma jumped up and went around the table to hug Clair. "Where will you have the wedding?" she asked excitedly, planning.

Clair interrupted her with a grin and a laugh. "I should probably tell Thomas first."

They sat back down and continued discussing their men.

After a few moments, Emma ventured a question that had bothered her. "Can I ask you something personal?"

Clair smiled and waited. Their relationship had always been close.

"How were you able to own your business and the house? You had mentioned a benefactor when we first met."

"Well, that is a very personal question, and I was just thinking of him when you mentioned giving a chance to someone. It was my father."

"But I thought. . ." said Emma, remembering what Jeremy had told her he'd learned from the census records.

"Yes, it's true I didn't know who he was most of my life. A lawyer contacted me to let me know my father was dying and he had no other children to leave his estate to. He wanted to help me get what I wanted, and what I wanted was to purchase the house and run my own business. I was able to work out a deal with the previous manager. She was eager to move on."

"And the shelter you run?" Emma asked.

"It was his house," she said simply. "I kept it and turned it into something useful."

"It's that kind of thinking we'll need to build the charity," said Emma, knowing she had chosen the right person.

"How soon until we know if the charity will happen?" asked Clair, wanting to make plans of her own.

"I will be headed to New York to confirm the money and the selling of large assets," Emma said.

"Alone?" Clair teased, knowing who Emma was seeing.

"Well, no," Emma admitted. "I thought of asking Jeremy to come with me."

Clair stopped teasing and asked in a more serious voice, "Do you have any questions for me?" Emma knew she meant questions about Jeremy and their private time together.

"I do." They spoke in low tones, sharing secrets.

CHAPTER 7

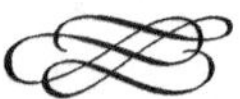

Emma met Jeremy later that evening at a nice restaurant for dinner. She brought up the subject of New York. "Jeremy, I have to go to New York to get the final settlement for the will. I'll also need to review the list of assets and the house in New York."

"When will you be leaving and where will you stay when you get there?" he inquired, thinking about the trip.

"I'll be setting it up for next week, and I'll stay at Mr. Carlyle's house. I need to meet with staff as well as Mr. Beeker. I told them to retain the staff until we can work out the next steps."

Jeremy reached out his hand and covered hers. "Emma, I'd like to go with you." Before she could say anything, he continued, "This time, I'd like to share a compartment with you."

"With you, as a couple," she murmured. She tilted her head at him, considering his suggestion. "I want to have you go with me as a couple, but you are aware that I do not want to get married."

"I do know that," he acknowledged. Emma had always been honest with him.

"And you still want to be with me as a couple?" she asked, knowing it could be a dealbreaker.

"I do. Emma, I love you in whatever form that takes, married or not married. It doesn't matter to me as long as we're together," Jeremy said.

"But if we get involved that way and you change your mind about marriage or kids. . ." she said with downcast eyes, worried she'd hurt him.

"Emma, look at me." He waited until she met his eyes. "I won't. I love you and we'll be on the same path together," he promised.

"Jeremy, I love you, too. I would love for you to go with me to New York," she said, tears welling up in her eyes.

He laughed and said, "Now that's settled, let's eat." They finished out their evening with a long walk home.

CHAPTER 8

*E*mma contacted Andrew Burns, the lawyer for the estate, and had his office arrange the tickets for her trip to New York City. She sat down with her family the night before leaving to discuss her plans.

Dora commented, "It's remarkable that Mr. Carlyle left the money for such a wonderful purpose."

"Yes, and I think Clair is wanting to change her life. This could do it." She had told Tim and Dora her choice for manager and Clair's response.

Tim said seriously, "She certainly knows how to deal with money." He asked, concerned for Emma, "I know you've made this trip previously, but would you like some company? Someone, to go along with you to speak with Mr. Beeker?"

"Jeremy is coming with me on the first trip for introductions and review of the New York City property," said Emma evenly, not displaying any emotion.

Dora squinted at Emma; she knew that tone. Emma was hiding something. She gave her one last long look but decided to not interfere, for now.

"Good. I know this is your project, but I think taking someone is a good idea. He could also offer observations of Mr. Beeker," said Tim, relieved Jeremy would be accompanying her.

Emma wanted to tell Dora that Jeremy was going to share her compartment but decided it was better to keep quiet.

CHAPTER 9

"You are going to New York with Emma?" asked Cole, pacing by Jeremy's bed.

Jeremy watched him out of the corner of his eye as he answered. "Yes, to help with the business side of things from Mr. Carlyle's will." He continued working on folding his shirts and putting them into the suitcase

"Hmm, is that the only reason?" Cole asked, finally standing still.

Jeremy smiled absently and continued to pack. "No, I like being with her."

"Jeremy," Cole said rather forcefully, waiting until Jeremy looked at him. "I don't want her hurt."

"Honestly, Pops," he dropped down on the bed beside the carpet bag, "she's the strongest woman I have ever met. Nothing happens to Emma that she doesn't want to happen."

"She is a rather independent woman, isn't she?" Cole said thoughtfully

"She is that. Pops, I love her so much. I would never hurt her," stated Jeremy simply.

"Maybe I should speak with her about you," he gently teased. Jeremy smiled a crooked grin in response.

CHAPTER 10

The next morning, Jeremy helped Emma down from the hired cab and handed the carpet bag to her. They made their way to the train and into their private compartment. As they closed the door behind them, Emma removed her hat and patted her hair. Before they could sit, a knock sounded at the door. She answered, finding the steward outside.

"Is there anything you need?" he asked.

"Right now, just privacy," she said as she slipped him some money.

He recognized her from previous trips and grinned. "That shouldn't be a problem."

Emma turned back to Jeremy after she closed the compartment door, leaned against it, and said, "Off on another adventure we go."

Jeremy grabbed her and pulled her to him for a long, thorough kiss. When they came up for air, she placed her hand on his chest and pushed back playfully. "Well, enough of that for now. Let's get settled." They unpacked in the compartment and pulled out books to relax with on the long train ride.

Jeremy patted the seat and said, "Come sit with me."

She sat and leaned into him. As the train started to move, she sat up to remove her jacket. "Would you mind if I remove my boots?"

"No, go ahead and get comfortable," said Jeremy, who had already opened his book to read.

One day turned into another, with Jeremy and Emma sharing the compartment, food, and books. They got to know each other more intimately and, as they pulled into the Buffalo station, Jeremy leaned over and kissed her, saying softly, "I love you."

"I love you, too."

They exited the train, carrying their bags, and moved to the daily train that would take them to New Jersey. They settled into their new compartment, with Emma laughing at Jeremy's antics. They completed the trip with a prearranged carriage ride from New Jersey into New York City. Jeremy looked over at Emma and asked, "Do you find it odd we're staying at Mr. Carlyle's house?"

"No," she said, shrugging. "It's mine until I sell it. Mr. Burns mentioned that some of the help will get retirement pensions and others will hopefully be offered jobs with the new owners."

"Tell me about Mr. Carlyle's man of business, Mr. Beeker. You met him on our last trip. Can we trust him?" Jeremy asked, curious about the man managing such a large amount of money.

"I had Tim check him out. He has an established business and Mr. Burns didn't have any concerns with the way the estate has been managed."

"Okay," Jeremy said, pondering, and decided he would look the man over when they had their meeting.

The carriage pulled up in front of the familiar large stone home. Jeremy just shook his head; he had forgotten how big it was.

Emma smiled faintly and said in a wry voice, "I guess I don't have to go in the back door this time."

Jeremy acknowledged this with a smile as he jumped down from the carriage. "Here, let me help you down," he said. He turned and reached to assist her from the carriage. The driver handed down their bags, which Jeremy took and thanked him for. They completed the transaction and approached the door.

The butler must have been watching for her because the door opened before they could knock. He looked down from his tall height and said, "Welcome back, Miss Evans."

She said formally, "Thank you, Mr. Cummings."

"Won't you come in?"

They nodded and entered the foyer. Jeremy placed the bags on the floor and looked around. Emma glanced at Mr. Cummings and said, "We are very sorry for your loss."

"Thank you, Miss Evans." He nodded in acknowledgment. "How long will you be with us?" he asked in a solicitous manner.

"About a week. We're here to review the books for the estate. We do appreciate you staying on until we get things settled," Emma said sincerely.

"Mr. Carlyle took good care of us and we will stay as long as we are needed," he said as he cleared the emotion out of his voice. "Would you like to see your rooms?"

"Please," she said and saw the sideways look Jeremy sent her. She didn't return it as they followed Mr. Cummings up to their rooms, located next to each other. They each went into their separate rooms. Emma laid her bag on the bed and sat next to it, studying the large room. She heard a door open and glanced toward it, but didn't see any movement.

"Psst." Emma looked to her left and saw Jeremy had entered her room through a side door.

"Interesting feature," he said suggestively.

She laughed and asked, "Mr. Cummings tell you about that?"

"He was the sole of discretion," he reassured her. "He just mentioned it as a feature of the house and thought I might want to know. How can I not take advantage?" he asked as he pushed her back on the bed. He quieted her giggling by kissing her thoroughly.

They "rested" and made their way slowly downstairs for lunch. Afterward, they met the rest of the house staff in the study to let them know they would only sell the house to someone willing to take on the current staff. There were sighs of palpable relief from the younger members. Emma said to the group, "Please let Mr. Cummings know if you would like to stay on with the new owners." With that final comment, Emma and Jeremy exited as Mr. Cummings took over the meeting.

Jeremy and Emma took the rest of the day to settle in and enjoy a quiet evening at the house. The meeting with the accountant, Mr. Beeker, was scheduled for 10am the following day.

CHAPTER 11

The next morning, Emma and Jeremy arrived at the office and were met by Mr. Beeker. Emma introduced Jeremy to him, and they shook hands.

"Emma, I didn't expect to see you so soon and under this circumstance," he said in a solemn tone, offering her his elbow. "Will you both accompany me to my conference room?"

The room they entered was large and had a long narrow table surrounded by ten chairs on each side. Those chairs were empty. "Have a seat, please," he said, indicating the two chairs toward the end of the table. He sat across from them and opened his logbook, saying, "Mr. Carlyle's organization is run by agents within this office. We'll have each one come in to discuss the investments and strategies they are managing."

As the day progressed, agent after agent explained their part in the organization. Emma's head began to spin with figures. This was far bigger than she'd realized, and she knew she couldn't do it alone. She would need to be able to interact with her business manager routinely. After the interviews were finally completed, she looked at Mr. Beeker and said in a serious voice, "Our home base is Chicago, and it will be difficult to be kept apprised of the financial situation from that far away."

He looked thoughtful and said, "I have thought about that and most of my staff is willing to relocate. We would leave a small contingent here to give us access to local investments. "

"I like that," said Emma. "I've selected my charity manager, and it would be nice if the business and the charity were in the same building."

Mr. Beeker nodded his head in agreement. "I would also recommend a board to vote on the direction of the money and the accountability."

"Yes," she said, "I had thought of that, and I've selected a board I trust. I'd like to get some money released as soon as possible so I can get the offices going and an initial budget set up."

Though he was surprised at the speed of her decisions, he thought quickly and said, "We can arrange a bank account and a line of credit in Chicago. We'll also need to scout locations for our offices."

"I can help with locations and building availability," suggested Emma.

That statement made something click for Mr. Beeker and he said, "That's right, your father is Ellis Evans. I have seen some of his work here. We would, of course, appreciate the help. Purchasing or a long-term lease is what I would recommend."

She nodded, liking that idea. "I agree. We can review what's available and make the decision together. I'd also like to include the charity manager." She looked through her notebook and asked, "Can you give me an update on the status of Mr. Carlyle's property here in New York?"

"I've given that some thought and, as you asked, I inquired about selling Mr. Carlyle's house." She nodded. "The offer is here," he said, handing her the contract. She looked at it and handed it to Jeremy to review. He went through the documentation on the house and nodded that he thought the offer was good.

"I would like to remove some things from the house-books and some carpets, painting, and books. Will that be a problem?" she asked.

"No, I don't see a reason that should be a concern."

"We will also need to have access to the house until after the financial matters are settled."

"Of course."

"Could you send me a copy of the paperwork? I'd also like to review it with my lawyer in Chicago. Have they said if they will take on any staff who may not want to retire?" she inquired.

"Yes, you can take that one with you for your lawyer. As to the staff, I made the deal contingent on keeping any staff wanting to stay," Mr. Beeker replied.

"How will the money be handled once a decision is made?"

He went on to explain the sale of the house. They also reviewed setting up lines of credit for the charity and how the bills would be paid through the business offices.

"Mr. Beeker—" she started.

"Geoff, please," he interrupted.

She smiled. "Geoff, I will be arranging for a third-party audit of the books."

He looked surprised but not upset. *A good sign,* thought Emma.

Geoff commented, "That is a good idea. We're ready. Do you need suggestions on what companies you might want to use?"

"No, I have someone who can either manage the work or will arrange for the third party to manage it," said Emma.

"I am looking forward to working with you," he said sincerely.

"I am also, but I want to confirm the numbers first," she said cautiously. She was holding off on final approval until the audit was completed.

"Are you meeting with the auditors while you are in town?" he asked, curious about the timing.

"I am," she confirmed. "I'll select one and let you know the timing."

They shook hands and said their goodbyes. After they climbed into the waiting carriage, Emma said, "Jeremy, you've been very quiet. What's your impression of Mr. Beeker?"

"I didn't see anything in his behavior that showed he was hiding something. He answered your questions and seemed open to the audit," he said thoughtfully.

"Yes, I noticed that also. I'm glad you saw what I saw," she said consideringly. She leaned over and kissed him softly on the lips. "Thank you for coming with me today."

They talked about the meeting on the way back to the house. As they arrived, Mr. Cummings let them in, saying, "Miss Emma, there was a note delivered for you." He handed it to her.

Emma opened it, reading silently.

"What is it?" Jeremy asked, noticing she seemed very happy.

She looked up with a smile. "Mark's parents. I let them know we were in town. They would like us to have dinner with them." Jeremy and Emma had met Mark a few years ago when he tried to pick their pockets. Emma had offered to send him books if he stopped the criminal activities. He agreed and they started exchanging books through the mail. Thinking out loud she said, "We need to go to a bookseller before heading over."

"When are we expected?" Jeremy asked.

"Tomorrow night, so we have time to get the books in the morning," she said.

"So, we have tonight alone?" he asked, moving toward her in a vaguely menacing manner. She laughed and eluded him by dashing into the living room. "Think you are safe there? I can still get you."

Mr. Cummings smiled and quietly stepped away to give them some privacy.

Emma let him back her into a corner, saying, "Well, I could always pull my knife on you or—"

Jeremy interrupted her with a deep kiss and suggested in a low voice, "How about a nap upstairs?"

"I do think I am a bit tired. . ." They both laughed and went up to their separate rooms.

That evening, Emma and Jeremy went to dinner at Delmonico's, enjoying a good steak dinner and a quiet pleasant conversation.

CHAPTER 12

The next day, they headed out to a local bookseller to find *Twenty Thousand Leagues Under the Sea: A Tour of the Underwater World,* a classic science fiction adventure novel by French writer Jules Verne. They kept looking and found *Frankenstein; or, The Modern Prometheus* by English author Mary Shelley that told the story of Victor Frankenstein, a young scientist who created a hideous creature in an unorthodox scientific experiment.

After purchasing the books, they spent the rest of the day speaking to various accounting firms. Emma wanted to choose the best fit for the audit. She was drumming her fingers on her lips and reviewing her notebook. She looked up toward Jeremy, lowered her hand, and asked, "Jeremy, what did you think? Which one do we pick?"

"I think we saw the same things today. The companies Tim recommended are all good and appear to be very thorough. I would say when you choose, make sure the reports and findings are sent directly to you," he suggested.

"I was also wondering about the payments for this. I'll need to get the account set up to pay them myself, that way it's not coming directly from the company being audited," she commented thoughtfully.

"Yes," agreed Jeremy.

Emma made up her mind and sent a note to the companies she had interviewed, confirming her choice. She asked them not to contact Mr. Beeker. She would take care of that herself.

The evening came quickly, and they dressed for dinner with Mark and his parents. They took a carriage to the family's apartment and found it in a working-class neighborhood. It was nicely looked after, and the family lived on the third floor. Jeremy knocked and, while they were waiting, they could hear running shoes on the floorboards.

The door opened quickly to reveal Mark. "Emma! Jeremy!" he shouted.

"Mark! How are you?" asked Emma, happy to see him again.

"Mom!" he called out loudly over his shoulder. "Emma and Jeremy are here!"

"I can see that," his mom said wryly, coming up behind him. "Come in, come in."

They entered the small hallway of the apartment, following her and Mark to the living room. The furniture was older looking but in good condition. The side tables were full of novels and textbooks. She knew from Mark's letters that his parents worked for the school system as teachers. Her husband joined them, and the introductions began with Mark's father saying, "We'll start. I'm George, and this is Elizabeth."

Emma smiled broadly. She pointed to herself, "Emma," and then to Jeremy, "and Jeremy."

Mark interrupted the introduction when he saw Emma was carrying a package. "Are those books?" he asked eagerly.

Laughing, Emma held the package up. "What, these?"

"Yes!" he said in an excited voice. "What are they?"

"Give them a minute," said Elizabeth. "Let them sit down."

They moved to the sofa with the family filling in chairs around them.

Mark looked so expectant that Emma gave in and handed him the books. They watched as he tore the paper off. *Twenty Thousand Leagues Under the Sea: A Tour of the Underwater World.* "Wow. Have you read it?" he asked, already flipping through the pages.

"I have," commented Emma.

"I have also," said Jeremy.

"There is a second one," reminded George.

Mark looked like he didn't want to put the first down, but he was curious. He picked it up and tore the paper off of the second book and exclaimed, "*Frankenstein*! I have heard this is really good."

"If you notice, it was written by a female author, Mary Shelly," prompted Emma.

"Oh?" Sounding disappointed, he put it down and picked up the first book again.

"You know," said Jeremy nonchalantly, "there is a monster in that second book."

"Really?" Mark asked, starting to sound interested. He retrieved the book to give it another look.

"A very unusual monster," commented Emma.

"What is unusual about it?" asked Mark curiously.

"Well, you'll have to read to find out," she commented. "It's really good. You'll have to write me your impressions."

Elizabeth tapped him on the shoulder and said, "Why not put it away for now and you can read it later."

Mark nodded and got up to take them to his room.

"I have to admit," said George, "that I enjoy reading the books you've sent. In fact, Mark has set up a lending library for the neighborhood. He's also quick to let people know if they haven't returned the books promptly."

Emma and Jeremy smiled. She responded, "We're very glad

you found an outlet for his energy, something other than criminal enterprises."

"Did you find out anything about how he got involved in pickpocketing?" asked Jeremy, curious how a kid from a good family with money would get into trouble.

"The Whyos gang," started George as Mark came back into the room and sat on the edge of his dad's chair. "They were recruiting the local schools and this one likes adventure," he said, patting Mark on the back.

"It sounded like fun," Mark said defensively.

"Was it fun to get caught?" Elizabeth asked, an edge to her voice.

"No, definitely not," he answered, holding up his hands in response.

"Mark, has the gang approached you since you stopped working for them?" asked Jeremy.

He avoided his eyes and his mom walked over to him and took him by the chin, saying, "Mark, Jeremy asked you a question. I think you should answer it."

As she released his chin, he admitted, "They have."

"Have they been threatening you?" asked Jeremy.

"No, not really, just offering candy and other things. I didn't accept anything," Mark said, hoping the conversation would end soon.

"I'll leave the 'other things' until later. Are you still talking to them?" asked Jeremy.

"No!" He lowered his tone and continued, "No, I'm not. I stay after school and help with classroom stuff and I take my books," he looked at Emma, "to read. When I know they're gone, I leave with the teachers."

"Smart," approved Jeremy and looked over at his parents. "I'll have the local police keep an eye on the school grounds."

"Thank you," said George in a relieved voice.

The conversation went on to more casual topics as they

moved into the dining room for dinner. The food was good and the conversation was full of books. The evening wrapped up and they hugged each other as they were leaving, promising more letters and books.

"Emma," inquired Mark as they were leaving, "can I come to see you and Jeremy in Chicago one day?"

They looked at one another and nodded. "Yes, we would love for you and your parents to visit."

"We'll plan something," Elizabeth promised.

"Jeremy, could I speak with you for a moment?" George asked.

"Yes, of course," he said and they both stepped away down the hall, speaking in low tones. Jeremy and George finished their talk and shook hands.

Jeremy took Emma's hand as they said their goodbyes.

"That was lovely," commented Emma on their way to the house, enjoying their carriage ride home.

"Yes, such nice people," commented Jeremy.

"What did George want to talk to you about?" she asked curiously.

"He wanted to confirm that I'd follow up with the local police on the activities around the school," he said absently.

"That's good. Do you foresee any problems?" she asked, worried for Mark.

"No, I have several officers I trust to check into it for me," he said as he heard her breathe a sigh of relief. "There was something else."

"What was that?" she asked.

"He wanted to know if things don't get better if we could help them relocate," he said, waiting for her response to the request.

"Of course," said Emma immediately, liking the idea of having Mark and his family closer.

They went silent, each thinking about Mark and his family.

CHAPTER 13

The next morning, Jeremy headed to the police station to talk to his contacts and ensure Mark would be protected at school. He arrived back at the Carlyle house in time to pack for the trip home; they would be leaving that night.

Jeremy sat on Emma's bed, watching her finish packing. "Any problems with getting help to watch the school?" she asked, still folding her blouses.

"No. The officer I spoke to, Mac—Steven Mackenzie—will look into it. He's going to take a personal interest because his nephew goes there also," he said in a distracted voice.

"Well good." She sat next to him and said, "We've completed all of our tasks."

He nodded and seemed to make up his mind about something. He said, rather abruptly, "Emma, I love you so much, and I don't want to be apart from you when we get back home."

"Me either," she said laying her head on his shoulder. "Let me think about how that might work."

"If anyone can figure this out, it will be you," he teased.

They descended the stairs and said goodbye to Mr. Cummings and the other staff. Emma promised she would keep them informed about any new owners. She gave them her contact information, and they headed out to the station via carriage.

The travel home was bittersweet, knowing their time together would be limited. Emma would continue to work on how she and Jeremy could be together in a more permanent manner. In the meantime, they would have memories of their stolen moments together.

They arrived back in Chicago, descended the train's stairs, and walked slowly toward the waiting carriage. The trip home was made in almost complete silence. When they stopped at the boarding house, Emma found herself with tears in her eyes.

"None of that now. This isn't forever," Jeremy said, reaching over to wipe her tears.

Emma nodded. "I know. I'll see you soon."

"Yes," he said quietly and hopped down to help her out of the cab. He handed the carpet bag to her and climbed back in, waving as he was pulled away.

She was a little down as she went into the house, but she shook it off.

"Emma," called Dora from the kitchen. "Is that you?"

"It is," Emma called back.

"Come in here and tell me how it went."

"On my way," she said. She left her bag in the foyer and started to unbutton her jacket as she made her way to the kitchen. As she entered, she saw Dora was in the middle of making Brotchen rolls.

Tim sat at the table with his books opened. He smiled broadly as she entered, saying, "Emma, it's so good to have you home. It's been quiet without you." He winked at Dora.

"Tim's right, we've missed you," she said as she finished up the last of the Brotchen rolls and placed a towel over them to allow them to rise. She moved around the table to hug Emma. "Sit. Tell us about your trip."

"It went well. I was glad to have Jeremy there with me," she said, looking down at her notebook. She didn't notice the look Dora and Tim shared. She glanced up from her notes as she started to describe the financial company she had met with.

"Were you able to meet with the audit companies?" asked Tim.

She confirmed that she had met and named the company she had selected.

"That's a good company," Tim said approvingly. "You were able to confirm there is no connection between the auditors and the financial company?"

"I didn't disclose what audit companies I interviewed with Mr. Beeker. Jeremy and I interviewed each one, and the one I selected had no past audit experience or other business dealings with Mr. Beeker," she said in a business-like manner. She looked closely at Tim and said, "You're right, it's a good idea to have you there to oversee the audit."

Tim looked thoughtful and said, "I'll have one of our more experienced temporary accountants help to manage our business while I'm gone." He looked over at Dora. "Can I tempt you into going with me?"

Dora said, "Yes, but I have the same issue with coverage here."

"Well, maybe not," said Emma slowly.

"What are you thinking?"

Instead of answering her, Emma looked over at Tim and asked, "That boarding house next door. Is it still available to purchase?"

Tim nodded and said, "They haven't had any buyers."

"Make them an offer," she said decisively. "I have my money from the Baker office job, and I have all of my savings." She had already given some of her savings to help with the expansion of the bakery and liked the idea of owning more property.

Tim had the cost of the house along with their amounts in

savings. Dora sat quietly contemplating this new business venture and said, "Please include me also." They always made an effort to keep the boarding house business separate from the other business, but this decision would mingle Tim, Dora, and Emma's money.

Tim ran the numbers and said, "We can do it. If you both are okay with it, I'll make the offer tomorrow."

"Is there anyone living in the house currently?" asked Dora.

"No, it's empty and will require some repairs," said Tim. He had already investigated the details.

Emma looked at Dora and said, "I know the boarding house is your domain, but may I make some suggestions?"

"Yes," said Dora cautiously.

"I assume you'll want to manage both?"

"Yes, I'd like to use my experience to get them organized."

"There would be no one better for the position," teased Emma, knowing Dora enjoyed her work. "I think we can all pull together on this. Papa can review the structure for any additions or renovation recommendations." Something occurred to her. "Dora, won't that be too much responsibility if it requires you to cook here?"

"I hadn't thought of that. We would need double staff. And I think it's time to consider a full-time cook and helper here also." Dora seemed a bit troubled by that.

"Dora, that would mean you would manage the boarding houses, but wouldn't have the cooking or cleaning responsibilities," said Tim.

That brightened Dora up and she said, "I like that." She looked over at Emma. "Do you still have the contact information for Mrs. Spencer?"

"Yes, she's decided to stay in Chicago. She has no reason to work, but you might be on to something. The last time I saw her, she indicated she was bored," Emma commented.

"You mentioned she was a talented cook and with the case

resolving her son's murder, I hope that she might be open to working for us," said Dora, thinking out loud.

"She cooks beautifully. I think she'd like that," said Emma.

"So, that would give me Mrs. Spencer there," Dora said making notes.

"What about Bessie for Amy's role there?" asked Tim.

"Bessie? Hmm, that might work. Harold is still trying to save money and that would give them some stability." Harold and Bess were current boarders, saving to have a family. "I'll approach her," Dora said continuing to take notes. "I'll put some figures together to see what would be fair."

"What about your position here?" asked Tim.

"Let's get both houses organized and then we can get an additional cook," she suggested. *Amy might want to move into that position.* She would have to talk to her.

Tim agreed and moved forward quickly with the purchase. He went in with a lower offer than they were asking because the house would need some modifications to be converted into a boarding house. The offer was accepted readily.

CHAPTER 14

*E*mma took over watching the renovation details while Dora and Tim went to New York for the audit. She had arranged for them to stay at Mr. Carlyle's house. The house was still owned by the estate and would not move to the new owners for another month. Mr. Cummings had been notified of the guests and the reason for their visit. Tim would oversee the movement of items that Emma had made a list of and had also arranged an audit space with Mr. Beeker. He and Dora would be away for three weeks.

Before they left, Dora had contacted and interviewed Mrs. Spencer for a future new role and a temporary role while she was out of town. Mrs. Spencer agreed and reviewed the menus and duties with Dora and Amy. Amy would help guide her while Dora was away. Living in would not be necessary, as she owned her own home and enjoyed her privacy. Tim also had his temporary help set up. The person would work out of his apartment and keep in contact with their workers until Tim returned.

While the renovations were underway, Jeremy stopped by. Emma took him on a tour of the new house.

"Nice. Is Dora okay with the changes?" asked Jeremy.

"Yes, she's excited, and it's another investment for us," she said, looking around.

"What about the current boarding house. Any changes there?"

"I've been thinking about that," she admitted as they walked over to the original boarding house. "We have Molly moving out to the new house, and we also offered a larger room to Bessie and Harrold at a higher price. Harrold is doing well, and he and Bessie enjoyed the boarding house environment."

"So, who does that leave living here?" he asked.

"We're keeping Jake here and I was thinking we could ask Savannah if she would like to move in also."

"So, a house of specialists?" he teased.

"I think it would also allow Tim and Dora to have extra rooms for children," she commented softly.

He smiled broadly and asked, "Are there any announcements?"

"Not yet." She laughed. "They're just working on it." She opened the door, and they entered the foyer. She nodded toward her right and asked, "Sitting room?"

"That would be nice," he said. The room was empty, and it would give them a few private moments. He sat down, thinking about the changes in the boarding houses. He rubbed his chin and said contemplatively, "That leaves the room next to yours still open?"

"Yes," said Emma, looking at him. "What are you thinking?"

"Remember that door at Mr. Carlyle's house, between our rooms?" he asked in a low voice.

"How could I forget?" she whispered back, leaning into him.

"I was wondering if we could put one in your room, connecting to the one next door?" he asked.

"I'm not sure," said Emma doubtfully. "A door would be rather obvious."

"Not if," he paused and raised his eyebrows, "we hide it behind bookshelves that we could fashion to slide out of the way when we wanted to be together."

"I like that idea," she said, smiling at his ingenuity. She pulled out her notebook, saying, "I can draw up the plans for us."

Jeremy watched her draw and offered comments on how it might work. "We'll need to reinforce the wall before we add a door."

They spent the day adding to the drawings. "What type of mechanism would you use on the bookshelves—to make them slide more easily?" she asked, showing him her drawing.

"Maybe some types of wheels or rail," he suggested.

"Hmm, I'll have to ask Papa about that," she said, oblivious as to what that would entail.

"Hmm," he mocked, "maybe not your Papa."

"Oh, sure," she said, blushing. "We can work on it privately."

"What's the next step?" he asked.

"We have to be up front with Dora and Tim," she said in a firm voice.

"How do you think they'll react?" he asked.

"I'm not sure," she said, tapping the drawings in her hands, "but they know to expect surprises from me."

"This is true," he said. "Yes, that's something we should probably do in person." He pulled her close. and said, "Come here, I have something else to confer with you about."

CHAPTER 15

The renovations were going well as Emma continued to monitor and document their progress. About a week into Dora and Tim being gone, Mrs. Spencer had settled into her job as a cook at the boarding house. She and Amy were getting along very well. So well, in fact, Mrs. Spencer developed a habit of staying after dinner was cleaned up to talk with her.

After dinner one evening, Jeremy was in the sitting room reading while Emma worked on her lace designs. A knock sounded at the door and Jeremy said, "I'll get it." He put down his book and stood up to walk to the door.

He came back in and Emma looked up, asking, "Who was it?"

"Telegram, two of them," he replied, holding them up.

"Two?" she asked as he handed them to her. "Looks like one from Tim and one from Dora."

Emma opened the one from Tim first, curious about the audit. She read out loud, "The audit is going well. Nothing in the books is out of the ordinary so far." She looked at Jeremy and smiled. "Excellent news. I'll follow up with an official confirmation to Mr. Beeker. It's time to start shopping for an office location."

"That's good. Who's the second note from?" he asked.

"Dora," she said. "I wonder why two notes." She opened the second envelope and her expression changed abruptly. "Oh no!" she exclaimed.

Jeremy walked over to look over her shoulder, asking in a concerned voice, "What is it, Emma? Is something wrong with Dora?"

"No, it's not that. I contacted Mark and his family to let them know Dora and Tim were in town. I thought it would be nice if they got together," she explained, accidentally crushing the telegram with her stress.

"Yes, that does sound nice, so what's wrong?" he asked, seeing her distress.

Emma continued, "Dora said they've sent several notes to Mark and his family but have not received any contact back."

"Emma, there could be any number of reasons for that," he reasoned.

"Yes, that's true," she noted, calming down.

He could see she was still troubled and suggested, "I'll reach out to Mac and see if he can go by their place."

She took a deep breath and let it out slowly. "Okay, I guess I've been worried since we spoke with them about Mark still seeing those men at his school."

"I'm sure they're just busy and not able to answer Dora's notes. I'll send a telegram now," he said as he grabbed his jacket.

"Thanks, Jeremy," she said, relieved.

"Anything for you." He kissed her quickly on the way out. He made his way directly to the telegraph office to send the note, making his way back to the boarding house to say goodnight to her before heading home.

CHAPTER 16

It would be several days later before Jeremy's contact sent a note back. When he received the reply, he sent a cab for Emma with a note to meet him at the Pinkerton office.

Emma arrived at the office and raced up the stoop. As she entered, the agent in the outer office motioned to Jeremy's office. She nodded and went to the door, entering without knocking.

Jeremy was in a serious conversation with Cole when she entered. They stopped talking when they saw her and Jeremy walked over to greet her. "Emma, I'm glad you could come right over."

"Jeremy, what's happened? Did you find out something about Mark and his family?"

Jeremey smiled slightly; Emma was always thinking ahead. He abruptly got serious, saying, "Emma, we had Mac check out Mark and his parent's apartment. They weren't there."

She sat down heavily in a chair near the desk. "Could they tell if they left voluntarily or were taken?"

"Mac said he couldn't tell. He did say it appeared that they left in a hurry or there could have been a scuffle. Chairs were found turned over, items on the floor."

Cole asked, "Would it be normal to find their home like that?"

"No," she said and looked at Jeremy with raised eyebrows.

He nodded and said, "Agreed. They appeared to take pride in their apartment. It was very neat and clean while we were there. Also, Mac checked with their school, they haven't reported to work in more than a week."

"Jeremy, tell Mac to make sure the place is secure. We also need to find out who owns that building," Emma said.

"What are you thinking?" asked Cole.

Looking over at him, she said, "I'm not sure, but at a minimum, we need to verify their rent is paid until they're located and their items secured." She looked at Jeremy and asked, "Was the lock broken?"

"No," he responded, "that didn't appear to be the case and the door was closed and locked when he got there."

"That doesn't mean they weren't taken," she stated, drumming her fingers on her lips.

"Agreed," said Jeremy.

"It could be either at this point," commented Cole.

Emma asked, "Jeremy, do you think the Whyos went after Mark in his home?" She didn't let him answer and continued. "Did Mac say anything about the situation at the school?"

"The Whyos gang is a possibility. It's odd," he mused, "that they're going to such lengths to get to Mark."

"Mac's note also said that, since the family's disappearance, there's no one hanging around the school," said Cole.

"Where do we go from here?" asked Emma, feeling like she needed to be doing something.

"We think," said Jeremy, nodding at Cole, "that I'll go to New York to see if I can find out what's going on."

"Okay. When do we go?" she asked, thinking ahead to what preparations they would need to make.

Jeremy turned to Cole. He got the silent message and stepped quietly out of the office. Jeremy waited until the door closed and turned to her. "Emma, I'm going alone."

"Why do think I wouldn't be going?" She was completely confused by this turn of the conversation. Jeremy never told her she couldn't do something.

He wanted her to see reason. "Because you need to stay; you have responsibilities here." His voice softened. "You know Dora and Tim are counting on you." He could see that she was going to interrupt him, and he said quickly, "We don't actually know if anything has happened."

She still looked defiant but said out loud, "What do you plan to do?"

"Go there," he said simply. "I'll look around and try to find out what might have happened." He could tell she was upset at not being included and said, "Emma, I know you care about what happened to this family. I do also, trust me to look into this."

They stared at each other for a long moment, before Emma said with a sigh, "Jeremy, I do trust you. I'll stay here." She narrowed her eyes at him and added in a mildly threatening manner, moving a hand toward her hat, "You will let me know what is happening."

"I will," he promised with a smile. "No need to pull your knife." He drew her to him and gave her a long kiss.

She pulled away and laid her head on his chest. "How long will you be gone?"

"With trains, over two weeks," he commented. When she didn't say anything, he said, "I will miss you."

She snuggled closer. "Me, too." She thought of something and said, "You can stay at Mr. Carlyle's house."

"Thank you, that would be nice," he commented, smiling

into her hair.

"I'll contact Mr. Cummings to expect you." She sat up, pulling out her notebook to take notes.

"Also, a telegram to Dora and Tim might be a good idea," he suggested.

"I'll do that," she said. "I'll head over there now."

Jeremy said regretfully, "Yes, we need to get going. I'll stop by the train station to get my tickets." They shared a long kiss and slowly separated. They walked out together and parted at the stoop.

Emma went directly to the telegraph office. She opened her notebook to read off her note, *Tim, thanks for update on audit. Good news. Renovations go well here. Jeremy will be in NY in a week. Notified Mr. Cummings to have room ready. He will be checking in on Mark and family's possible disappearance.*

They would have questions, but the note should relieve them that someone was looking into the situation. She sent a second note to Mr. Cummings: *Mr. Cummings, Jeremy will be arriving for 1-2 week stay. Please assist him as needed.*

She thanked the telegrapher, made her payment, and headed home.

That afternoon, Emma was with Jeremy at the train station. "Send me a telegram when you arrive," she reminded him. She remembered the package she was holding, "Oh, and this is from Mrs. Spencer—sandwiches and other snacks."

"Thank you," he said, grateful for the food.

As they parted, she watched him board, then turned away to go home. As she was leaving, she noticed two Pinkerton men also boarding the train. "Curiouser and curiouser," she muttered, quoting Lewis Carroll. Jeremy must be taking this disappearance more seriously than she thought.

Jeremy, though, was watching from the train and saw his men arriving. *Emma missed them*, he thought. *Good.* He had the men with him, as a contingency, to help if Mark's family was taken.

Emma was in the carriage on the way home, thinking about the agents she had seen boarding the train. Jeremy hadn't indicated he was taking Pinkerton personnel with him. "But," she mused, "it was a smart thing to do if he runs into trouble." She wasn't bothered he hadn't mentioned the agents; he was taking the lead on this case.

She did have responsibilities here, and sometimes life required one to stay home and let other people have the adventure. "Growing up," she supposed.

CHAPTER 17

This trip is less entertaining than last time, Jeremy thought, opening his book to read. He laid it on his chest, thinking of their plans. When they arrived, Mac would meet them, and...

He dozed off with the rocking of the train.

CHAPTER 18

*E*mma visited the neighboring boarding house to check on the work being completed there. Bags clanged with tools as the workers were finishing up for the day.

Hearing her name called from the stairs, she looked up and saw Mara descending from the upper floor. She was dressed in pants, a loose shirt, and had a cap pulled over her blond curly hair.

Emma smiled broadly. "Mara, how are you?"

"I'm really good," she replied, happy to see Emma. They had met when Emma was helping out Mr. Marella on a case involving Mara's family a few years before. The case ended on a positive note, and her family was happier after secrets were revealed. Marco, Tony's brother, and Mara had started seeing each other soon after the case ended.

Chicago 1883. Emma hadn't expected to hear from Mara after the case came to a close. It had been over a year since she had talked to her. The note she had sent over asked Emma to meet for lunch. Emma confirmed the date, time, and location, then went into the meeting with a bit of trepidation, wondering what Mara might want. *Was she going to be angry or confrontational?*

Emma had gotten to the restaurant first and sat at a table, enjoying the bright sunny day. The windows were open, and wind teased the curtains. The tables were set with bright blue and white tablecloths. She ordered a tea service while she waited.

The tea had not yet arrived when she saw Mara in the doorway. She was dressed in a yellow and white afternoon dress, just showing her boots as she walked. She appeared to be very cheerful. Seeing that helped Emma release some tension.

Mara walked right over and said, "Emma, thank you so much for meeting me."

She stood and greeted her with a kiss on the cheek, saying, "I was surprised to get your invitation."

"Yes, I could see you might feel that way," she said with a slight smile. "Please, sit. I would like to talk with you."

"All right," Emma replied curiously.

They both sat as the tea service was delivered. They took a moment to order their lunch. As the waiter left, Emma looked toward Mara with eyebrows raised in question.

Mara started abruptly. Emma could see she was nervous and waited to hear what she had to say. "I wanted to speak with you about working with Mr. Marella's crew. I want to learn how to be a plumber."

Emma laughed out loud. "You know, I thought you wanted to talk about what had happened last time we saw each other."

"No, Emma," she said as she reached out and touched her hand. "That's the best thing that could have happened to our family. Dad and Grandfather are so close now. They are rarely out of each other's company."

"That is so nice to hear. So many times, my cases end with someone being hurt or taken to jail. I do like this better. How is your father doing?" Emma asked, honestly interested in the wellbeing of Mara's family.

"He's so much better now that he doesn't have to hide anything. I think Grandfather has gotten him to talk about what happened in the war. It has been good for him and us," Mara stated, tearing up a bit.

"I am so glad," Emma said simply. She thought for a moment about her original question and murmured, "Okay, how to approach getting you on as an apprentice." She drummed her fingers on her lips. She thought about how to approach Michael, then looked Mara in the eyes. "I think you should meet with Michael one-on-one, without Marco. Show him this is your idea and that it's for your future."

Mara tilted her head at the comment and replied, "I see what you mean. This is for me. I always wanted to be useful and learn a skill." She considered the advice and said, "Okay. I'll try that. Thanks so much for helping me. I so want to be skilled at something useful."

Emma smiled; finding someone so like-minded was nice. They continued discussing their futures and things they would like to achieve as their lunch arrived.

Soon after, Mara took Emma's advice and approached Michael at a job near her home. Emma had indicated that it was the best place to see him about being an apprentice plumber. Michael was surprised by the request, but with Emma in their lives, he was aware girls were changing, wanting to do more. He talked to her for a long time and tried to work out if she was serious or doing this to be around Marco. He watched as he talked to her. She wasn't giggling as though hiding a secret and her clothes were sensible.

Mara stated clearly that, though she enjoyed Marco's company, that he had nothing to do with this. She suggested a trial period and, if she worked out, then she could start her apprenticeship. He considered this and asked for a few days to think about it. He also wanted to speak to Marco about how he would handle working with Mara.

That evening at the apartment, the Marella family sat around the living room, having enjoyed a nice dinner. Michael looked at Marco consideringly and called his name.

"Yes, Dad?" Marco said absently, reading the paper.

"I'm thinking of taking on another apprentice plumber," Michael said nonchalantly.

"Anyone I know?" he asked absently, not looking up from his paper.

"Marco put down your paper and pay attention. I have something important to talk to you about," requested Michael, wanting to see his expression when he told him about Mara.

Marco abandoned his paper slowly and said, "Okay, I'm listening."

"Mara came to see me today," Michael said laconically.

"Why would she do that? Is she okay?" he asked, suddenly worried.

"She's fine," he reassured him. "She wants to begin an apprenticeship to work as a plumber."

Marco suddenly smiled. "That would explain many of our conversations. She's always asking the technical details of my job."

"What do you think? Could you handle working with someone you're courting?" he asked, ready to tell Mara no if it was against Marco's wishes.

Marco considered this for a moment and said, "I would have to be professional at work. No courting?"

Dad nodded. "And there will be a trial period, so if you think you can't handle it, we can end it at that time."

Marco mulled that over and came to a decision. "Dad, I can handle it. If this is something she wants, we should help her achieve it."

Michael liked seeing how much his son had matured. He

nodded and said, "I'll send her a note now and tell her to begin working with us on Monday."

Marco checked his watch. "I need to get organized for tonight." He was meeting Mara soon to take her to the dance.

A little while later, Michael knocked before entering Marco's room.

"Come in," called Marco.

Michael entered and saw Marco getting ready to go. He said, "Marco, Mara sent a note saying she was looking forward to working with us on Monday."

"Good," Marco said as he finished brushing back his hair and did a final check on his clothes. He walked into the living room with Michael.

Mrs. Marella smiled approvingly. "You look nice."

The other boys, Enzo and David started teasing him. "Yeah, Marco, you look SOOO nice."

"Thanks, Ma," he said, pointedly looking at his mother, ignoring his brothers.

"Don't stay out too late," she cautioned.

"I won't." He leaned in to kiss her on the cheek on his way out.

Marco headed to get the wagon so he could pick up Mara for the dance. He pulled the wagon to the front of her house, jumped down, and walked to the door. Before he could knock, Christopher pulled open the door, asking excitedly, "Marco, how are you?"

"Is Mara ready?"

"Christopher, let Marco in," called Mara's dad, James Saunders. He entered the door and met Mr. Saunders in the Foyer.

"Mr. Saunders, hello," said Marco, watching how he seemed to smile more easily.

"Mara will be a moment. Would you like to come into the sitting room?" he asked.

"Thank you. Mara mentioned you're working in the garden

much more lately," said Marco, showing a genuine interest as he sat down opposite Mr. Saunders.

"Yes. We're evaluating new fertilizers, looking at what a plant needs, such as nitrogen and phosphate, to flourish."

"Where are you getting your information from?" asked Marco, wondering about this business of working with dirt.

"We are looking at these," Mr. Saunders said, indicating the stack of magazines and books next to him. The pile included the magazine *Amateur Gardening*, the books *British Apples* by A. F. Barron, *The Garden: Its Art and History* by Jacob von Falk, and *Handbook of Tree Planting* by Nathaniel H. Egleston.

Marco heard a soft voice call his name and turned around. When he saw Mara, he stopped and didn't say anything. "Marco, are you okay?"

"You're beautiful," he said simply.

She blushed prettily and turned to her mom, who stood at her side, to kiss her goodnight. They said goodbye to her family and went out on the porch.

"I was expecting pants," he teased as he walked her to the wagon.

She stopped and turned to him. "Marco, I'm sorry I didn't tell you, but I wanted to do this on my own."

He nodded and said, "I love that independent spirit in you, Mara. I just hope there'll be a place for me also."

She leaned in to kiss him. "Always," she murmured. They kissed for a long moment.

They broke apart laughing and Mara said, "We should head to the dance."

"Yes," he said, feeling content as he helped her into the wagon.

CHAPTER 19

Mara started her trial with them the following Monday. She worked hard and was professional. Marco took the situation seriously and kept his attitude professional as well.

At the end of the three-month trial period, Michael decided it was time for a meeting with Mara. He asked the boys to head back home, saying they would follow behind.

Mara entered the room where Michael was working. "Did you want to see me?" she asked, nervously pulling off her hat.

Michael smiled, trying to put her at ease. "Mara, I wanted to speak with you about your work."

"Yes," she said, afraid to say anything more.

"You've been doing a wonderful job, and I want to take you on as a full-time apprentice," he said warmly.

She opened and closed her mouth, before saying, "You do?"

"I do," he confirmed. "So, we'll need to sit down and map out our plans for you to learn the business." He cautioned, "It won't happen all at once. There will be steps to follow."

"I'm ready," she commented, eager to begin her new career.

"I want you to come by on Sunday evening, and we'll begin

setting up our strategies and learning opportunities. You'll watch and learn, the next steps will include you doing the work with supervision, and then you'll work independently," he explained.

"I understand," she said in a serious voice.

"Now, we need to talk about Marco," he added. "I won't interfere with your being together, but we want to keep the same atmosphere we have had the last three months at work," he said in a kind but firm voice

She replied in the same tone, "I agree, Mr. Marella. I appreciate this opportunity."

"You know," he said, giving her a long look, "you remind me so much of Emma. I just had to give this a chance."

That made Mara smile since Emma was her role model. They walked out together, heading home, talking softly.

Marco and Mara continued to work together for the next two years and were together when they were off of work.

They were sitting quietly in the park one day when Marco turned to her and asked, "Mara, I waited to ask you to marry me, I know you wanted to complete your apprenticeship before we made any plans. Will you marry me?"

She looked at him, wanting to blurt out a yes, but she hesitated. "I know the wait was hard. You understand that I want to continue to work?"

"Yes," he said, knowing how important that was to her. There had been too many times in her life where she felt helpless, unable to support her family. She didn't want to be put in that position again.

She continued to ask questions. "And that cooking and cleaning will be split between us?"

"Hmm," he said with a smile. "I figured that might be the case. I spoke to Emma about a room in the new boarding house we're working on, to see if there was space for us. She said there was."

She grinned and asked, "Thinking ahead?"

"Of course," he said, still aware she had not answered his question.

She looked up at him, eyes shining, and said simply, "Yes."

"Yes!" he said exuberantly. He pulled her over for a long kiss. He pulled away and grabbed her hand and they headed home, almost running to tell both families. They were overjoyed with the news.

Marco sent a note to Emma confirming that they would take one of the extended rooms when it was ready.

CHAPTER 20

1884 BOARD HOUSE RESTORATION

"How is it going up there?" Emma asked, pulling out her notebook.

"Really well. The water piping is just about done. They're removing and reinforcing some walls up on the second and third floors," Mara said professionally.

"For the extended rooms," commented Emma, watching Mara turn red. She followed up with another comment. "I hear there's a wedding coming up."

Mara was still blushing but appeared to be very happy. "Yes, as soon as the boarding house is completed, we'll have the wedding at my family home and then move in here. We'll be sending out invitations soon and would like you and your family to attend."

"We will be there," Emma said sincerely.

"I'm so happy that your family bought this boarding house. It will be lovely to live here," she said, thinking of Marco and their future.

"I'm glad we'll have you and Marco as tenants. It'll be nice to have friends close by."

"Well, back to work," Mara said, picking up her tool bag and heading to the kitchen. Dora had left definitive instructions about the renovations in that area. Emma followed to make notes and sketches to send to Dora for her review and approval.

CHAPTER 21

NEW YORK CITY

eremy exited the second train in Buffalo with the two Pinkerton employees following. He had prearranged a carriage to take them to New York. They arrived and stopped by the Carlyle house to drop off their bags.

Mr. Cummings greeted them at the door. "Mr. Jeremy, we are happy to have you back. Will all of you be staying with us?" he asked, looking at the men accompanying him.

"No, just me. The men will be at a local hotel. Would you mind if we leave our bags here? We need to look into something that can't wait," Jeremy inquired.

"Yes, I will take them and put them away until you return. Should I tell Miss Dora that you have arrived?" Mr. Cummings asked.

"You may tell her and let her know I'll see her this evening."

"Of course." Mr. Cumming gestured to the two-footman standing in the foyer to move their bags.

"Could you also see that Officer Mackenzie at the 3rd precinct gets this note?" Jeremy asked.

"Of course, sir," he said and took the note from him. "I will have it sent over now." He snapped his fingers and the footman across the room walked over quickly to take the note.

Jeremy and the Pinkerton men left immediately. Their carriage stood waiting for them, and Jeremy gave him Mark's apartment address. He also notified Mac to join them there.

As they arrived, Jeremy told the driver he would no longer be needed and paid him. He and the two Pinkerton men climbed down from the carriage and headed into the apartment building, finding Mac waiting outside the unit.

He saw them approaching and he put his hand out in welcome, saying, "Jeremy, good to see you."

"You, too, Mac. Can we go in?" Jeremy asked, shaking his hand firmly.

He turned and opened the door. "Yes, I had it re-keyed so it would be secure until the family returned."

"Thank you for thinking of that," Jeremy commented as they entered the apartment. He looked around the long hallway and into the living room. It was much different than the last time he'd been there. Mac was correct when he said it was in a disarray; chairs were turned over, and papers lay scattered on the floor.

One of the Pinkerton men took the time to evaluate the door. "Jeremy, this doesn't appear to be a break-in. There was no splintering of wood on the doorframe." He looked over at Mac and asked, "Do you still have the original lock set?"

"I do." He pointed to a side table. The Pinkerton detective looked at it, saying, "There are no scratches that would indicate it was picked and no other damage."

They continued through the rooms, looking for anything that might tell them if the family was taken or if they had left of their own free will. Jeremy wished he had looked closer when they were last there.

Emma would have remembered everything, he thought wryly. He checked the closets and saw that their clothes were gone. If the family didn't leave of their own volition, then their abductor was smart enough to make sure the clothes appeared to be taken from closets and drawers.

Jeremy moved down the hall and into Mark's room and immediately noticed the one thing only he and Emma would have known to look for. He scooped up the incriminating items and rushed back into the living room. "They were taken."

"How do you know?" Mac asked curiously.

"These," he said, indicating the books he carried. "Mark would never leave his books, especially ones he hadn't read." Jeremy knew this was the one thing that would have gone with them. He wondered if Mark had done this deliberately, knowing he or Emma would not miss that detail. *Smart kid.*

"Okay, so what next?" asked one of the Pinkerton detectives.

"First," said Jeremy, "I need you and Paul to go door to door asking if anyone heard or saw anything. Also, find out who they pay rent to. Hopefully, that leads us to the owners."

As they left, Jeremy turned to the officer. "Mac, is that person still hanging around the school trying to recruit kids?"

"He's back since I last checked for you. I've been keeping an eye on him and, so far, he hasn't done anything I could take him in for," he commented.

"When is he usually there?" asked Jeremy.

"Early, when school starts."

"Okay, so we meet with him first thing tomorrow. Until then, let's keep it quiet. Agreed?" Jeremy asked Mac.

Mac agreed readily as they waited for the Pinkerton agents to complete their sweep of the building.

After Paul and Joe returned, Mac asked, "Did anyone notice anything out of the ordinary?"

"Not much. They didn't hear anything unusual."

"Interesting. This is definitely a professional kidnapping and not a spur-of-the-moment event," Jeremy said thoughtfully.

Paul opened up his notebook and said, "We did get the

manager's name and went down to his apartment, but he didn't answer."

Jeremy said, "We'll check in with him tomorrow." They formed a plan for the morning and split up. "Mac, thanks so much for your help."

"When a family is involved, I want to help," said Mac sincerely. "I'll meet you tomorrow morning near the school, the alley at Barnard Street." With that, he headed back to the police station.

Jeremy hailed a cab to return to Mr. Carlyle's for their bags. Once there, he turned to Joe and Paul. "Be here at 9am. You have the location of your hotel?"

They confirmed the time and the location, then made their way out of the house with the assistance of Mr. Cummings.

After Mr. Cummings showed them out, he returned to Jeremy and said, "Miss Dora would like you to see her after you get settled."

"Thank you, Mr. Cummings. Is she in the sitting room?"

"No, sir. She is in the kitchen," stated Mr. Cummings.

"Kitchen?" inquired Jeremy with a smile. He should have known.

"Yes, I believe she is working on different recipes with our chef," he said.

"Of course. I'll go see her as soon as I put my bag up and wash my face," said Jeremy.

"Follow me to your room," said Mr. Cummings.

Jeremy did as he was told. After he was refreshed, he went downstairs to see Dora. *It is a large house,* he thought as he strolled down the grand staircase.

When he reached the foyer, Mr. Cummings reminded him, "Through the dining room."

"Thank you," commented Jeremy and he headed to the kitchen. As he opened the door, he noticed the room was large and white. He immediately saw Dora and someone he assumed was the chef sitting at the table.

Dora was in a conversation about how to make macarons. "Jeremy," she said, seeing him enter. "Come here."

He went over and kissed her on the cheek as a hello.

"It's so good to see you," he said. He looked around and inquired, "Where's Tim?"

"The audit takes up most of his days. He'll be here this evening," she said matter-of-factly.

"How is it going?" he asked, hoping to avoid delving into any questions about Mark and his family.

"Really well, from what I understand. Tim says the investments are sound. They're sending out runners to the companies being invested in, to confirm facts. It takes time," she said.

"Yes, I can see that," he said thoughtfully. "Emma said the boarding house renovations are going well."

"I got a telegram from her detailing them and some other news." She pulled the note from her pocket and read aloud, "*Marco and Mara are engaged and want a double room at the boarding house.*"

"That's great!" exclaimed Jeremy.

"Jeremy, this is Chef Jacques Bernard. We've been sharing recipes," she said with a smile, indicating the man sitting beside her. "This is Jeremy Tilden; he is visiting with us for a few days."

"So nice to meet you. Your food is wonderful," Jeremy commented sincerely, remembering the meals from his prior visit.

Chef Bernard bowed his head politely. "Thank you."

"Jeremy, let's move into the sitting room," Dora said in a tone that brooked no denial.

He nodded and followed her out of the kitchen. She kept her serious expression as they sat down and asked expectantly, "Why are you here? Are Mark and his family in trouble?"

"I can't share much," he said, and she looked trouble at his response. He qualified his statement by saying, "I don't know much yet. I have two men here with me and an officer from the police department. We're investigating and I promise I'll share information as soon as it's safe to do so."

"You sound like Emma," she muttered. "I understand and will try to be patient."

Hoping to distract her, he said, "Tell me about your trip. What have you seen since you've been here?"

Dora's face changed immediately, and she said excitedly, "Jeremy, they finished the East Street Bridge! We were able to walk across it. It's amazing!"

"You know, when Emma and I were here last, we didn't think to check on its completion. You'll have to show me," he suggested.

"I wish Jake were here so he could photograph it," she said.

"That would have been wonderful. I'm sure we can get him a visit soon," Jeremy suggested.

"Yes, I'll have to bring him back here at some point," she said, liking that idea. She missed seeing him daily.

"Would he be okay with the change in schedules?" Jeremy asked, knowing that Jake liked things to be in a certain order.

"If I keep his schedule about the same, with food and sleep, he should be just fine," Dora commented.

They continued to enjoy each other's company until Tim came home that evening. They were helping set up dinner in the dining room when they heard someone in the foyer.

Tim entered quickly, saying hurriedly, "Sorry I'm late."

She went over to him and asked, "Long day?"

"Long enough," he said, rubbing a hand on his neck.

He noticed Jeremy and walked over to him. "Welcome. Nice to see someone from home. Emma let us know you would be arriving. Anything to share on Mark and his family?" Tim knew some parts of the investigation process were kept quiet to protect the people involved.

"Nothing in particular yet," Jeremy said. "We have some leads to follow up on in the morning."

"How did you prevent Emma from coming with you? I can't imagine she was happy about it," Dora said with a smile.

"No, not at first, but she realized she had responsibilities to you both and your businesses," he explained.

Tim started asking questions about the renovations. Before Jeremy could answer, Dora put her hand on Tim's and said, "Let's eat first and talk about that after."

He nodded, realizing how hungry he was. They sat down at the table as Dora let Chef Bernard know they were ready for dinner. The macarons were brought out for dessert.

With dinner over, they moved into the sitting room. Tim couldn't wait any longer and said, "Tell us about the renovations."

Jeremy smiled. "Emma has Michael Marella's team working on water and gas piping. As I understand it, the larger rooms are almost ready."

"How many?" asked Tim. He didn't know about this development.

"It looks like two. Emma sent a telegram over this morning. It seems Marco asked Mara to marry him and would like a joint room," explained Dora.

"Like ours," said Tim. Jeremy wished he could bring up the idea for him and Emma, but this wasn't the time.

Dora smiled. "Yes, it'll work well because Mara doesn't want to have to cook and clean with her current workload."

"I understand that. They'll be good tenants. The second boarding house is filling nicely," Tim said.

"Yes," said Dora, "one less worry."

They talked about the audit and then relaxed with their books. It was a nice, quiet evening.

CHAPTER 22

The next morning, Jeremy woke early and was able to get breakfast from the chef before Paul and Joe arrived Standing, he started to the foyer, when Mr. Cummings entered to announce that Paul and Joe were waiting in the foyer. Jeremy thanked him and exited the dining room. He greeted them and said, "Let's head out." They climbed into the waiting carriage and went to meet Mac at the school.

They arrived about a block away from the school at the predetermined location. Mac stepped out of the alley and gave them a description of the man they were looking for. He was disreputable-looking, with a rumpled brown jacket and badly cut hair.

"What's the plan?" asked Jeremy as they got a visual on the man.

Mac looked over and said, "I'll get him." He did just that; he had him by the collar before the man in question knew Mac was there. He hauled him over, asking Jeremy, "Where to?"

"The Sutherland's apartment," said Jeremy. "It's the best place for this discussion." Everyone nodded in agreement. They transported the now quiet man in a carriage to the apartment.

"Recognize this place?" Jeremy asked as they entered.

"Why would I?" he asked belligerently.

"Because you know where Mark and his family are," stated Jeremy.

CHAPTER 23

CHICAGO

Clair arrived at the boarding house for the first time in her and Emma's association. Emma had some guilt over the fact she hadn't invited her there before now. She thought she was watching out for Clair's feelings and those of the people at the boarding house. But that was probably not true; if she was honest with herself, she felt uncomfortable with Clair's occupation. It was fascinating but only from a distance. It was time to have her at the house.

Emma was making notes in the dining room when she heard a knock on the door. "I'll get it," she called out. She made her way to the door, knowing who was there. She opened the door and said graciously, "Clair, please come in."

Clair smiled and looked a bit nervous as she entered. She wore a lovely deep green dress with a matching hat. She removed it, patting her hair. "Emma, it's so good to see you. Thank you for inviting me over."

Emma looked her in the eyes and said sincerely, "No, I should've made this happen much sooner." She reached out and touched her hand. "Clair I'm sorry this invitation wasn't made long ago."

Clair hadn't realized the meeting would affect her emotions and had to wipe a tear off her cheek. "Well, I'm here now, that's what's important."

"Papa's in the study waiting for us. He has a list of buildings and properties for us to review." She saw Mrs. Spencer come out of the dining room as they passed. Emma paused, looked over, and said, "Mrs. Spencer, could you bring the tea service into the study?"

"I'll bring it in a few moments," she said quietly

"Thank you, Mrs. Spencer. This is Clair Edwards. Clair, this is Mrs. Spencer. She will be our cook at the new boarding house next door," Emma said. She noticed both Mrs. Spencer and Clair were very tense. *What is wrong between these two?* Emma asked herself. "Clair is our guest, and we will be polite to her."

"That's okay," said Clair, visibly upset. "Maybe I should leave."

Mrs. Spencer said to Clair, "I'm sorry, you are welcome." She looked down at her feet, seeming bothered by something. She looked up at Clair and said, "You don't recognize me?"

Clair blotted her eyes, ready to say no, but she took a moment to look at her more closely. "Aren't you Susan Single-ton?" she asked in amazement.

"I was," Mrs. Spencer confirmed quietly.

Emma was confused and looked between the two. "Do you know each other?"

Mrs. Spencer said, still looking at Claire, "In a previous life, when I was much younger."

"So was I," said Claire ruefully. "I believe you had a son?"

"Yes, I left the life because I wanted to keep him. He was murdered."

"Was that one of your cases, Emma?" Clair asked.

"Yes," Mrs. Spencer answered for her.

"I am sorry for your loss," said Clair sincerely.

"Thank you," she said graciously. "I'll go get the tea now."

"Thank you, Mrs. Spencer," said Emma quietly.

As they watched her go, Emma turned to Clair and asked in a low voice, "Was she?"

"One of the girls? Yes. She was already a bit older when I started and had her son by that time. She was always in the kitchen helping out. It looks like she turned that into a way to get out. Good for her," Clair said sincerely.

"Yes," said Emma. *People are so complicated,* she thought to herself. She motioned to Clair to follow her. As they entered the study, they saw Papa bent over his desk, reviewing drawings.

"Papa," Emma called. "Clair has arrived."

He looked up and smiled. "I finally get to meet you." He strode over and took her hands in his. "It is so very nice to meet you. I've heard so much about the things you have accomplished."

Clair seemed shocked at the statement but responded calmly. "I've heard about you also. It's very nice to meet you. I understand you have some recommendations for the location of our new venture."

He smiled and said, "I do. Come over and see. Emma, you know most of these buildings." They eyed the drawings and Papa started going over the list.

"Emma and I figured you needed a space with a large meeting room, an office for you, and a secretary. Clair, have you thought of what other staff you may need?" Papa asked.

She looked consideringly over at him and said, "I was thinking we would need at least two secretaries and an assistant to help me and one to help with scouting charity investigations in the field."

Papa said admiringly, "Clair, that's perfect thinking. You're right, all requests must be investigated to make sure they are deserving of the help."

"Papa, how about a space with two floors? We'd be able to have the financial people with us, too," explained Emma.

He nodded and said, "I like that idea. Clair, what do you think?"

"Yes, I think that's the right idea. Is there a building we could own outright that maybe had four stories?" asked Clair, thinking ahead.

"Yes, I think I have the one." Papa flipped through his list. "The address is 3339 Smith Street. Would you both be interested in seeing it?"

Emma looked at Clair and back at Papa, saying, "We would."

"Great. Let's go." He started out of the room just as the tea service was delivered.

"Papa," Emma suggested gently, "how about we have our tea first?"

"Oh, sure, we can do that," said Papa, looking a bit distracted. They went back into the study, sat down, and enjoyed their afternoon tea and cakes.

As they finished, he asked impatiently, "Now may we go?"

"Now we can go," Emma acquiesced.

They toured four buildings that day, but the last building Papa had picked was a new one with four stories located downtown. He had been involved in the building design and pulled the structural drawings to review. He wouldn't let them pick a building unless it had been reinforced to withstand a fire.

"Can we go in?" asked Clair.

"Yes, I've notified the owner we would be here today," he said, opening the main door. They examined it from top to bottom, letting Clair take the lead.

"We would need to remove some walls and move a few things around," said Clair.

"Yes. You'll also need a kitchen space on the two floors," said Papa.

"Yes, that is a good idea," said Clair thoughtfully. "I like this building. It has everything we need and is in the right location."

"You will have an assortment of art and rugs. I am having

these shipped from the Carlyle house. You will have first choice for the space here," said Emma.

"That is wonderful," she said thinking of all of the design choices in front of her. She looked over at Emma. "What about the financial people? Will they have to approve this before we purchase?"

"I think we should notify Mr. Beeker to come and review it. But I say, if we think this is the one you want, we make an offer today," she said firmly. Clair must be able to make decisions for the charity.

"Papa, can you send the financial information in a telegram to Tim?" asked Emma. He nodded and she looked to Clair for confirmation. "And ask the owners to hold it for us?"

"It shouldn't be a problem. I know the man," said Papa, pulling out a piece of paper to make a note.

"I'll also send a note to Mr. Beeker to come to Chicago to review the building," said Emma.

"What if he doesn't like it?" asked Clair, worried.

"I think he'll like it, but if not, we can rent the other floors out," Emma pointed out reasonably. "Okay?" she asked, looking first at Clair, then Papa.

They both answered, "Yes."

Papa had arranged for their carriage to wait for them. "Can I drop you off, Clair?" he asked.

Emma replied for her. "You can drop off both of us, Papa. I want to speak with her."

"Okay, I'll see you at home," he said absently as he helped them both down at Clair's stop.

They waved bye to Papa, Clair and Emma walked together arm in arm down the street. Emma stopped and asked, "Well, did you say yes?"

"I did," she admitted.

"That is wonderful," Emma said sincerely. They continued to walk. "Have you figured out where you and Thomas will live?"

"We've thought about it and I'm thinking of a house near the business, once we make the offer for the building," she said.

"That sounds like a plan, and it would put Thomas close to the bakery," observed Emma.

"He still enjoys the work, and I would never ask him to stop," Clair said.

"It sounds like things are coming together for you."

"Yes. One other thing I've decided: I'm selling my business to my general manager. She'll pay me monthly until it's paid off. It will remove me from the day-to-day running and allow me a fresh start."

Emma hugged Clair's arm. "I'm glad you made that decision. It sounds like the right thing for you to do."

They hugged and parted ways with Emma to the telegraph office and Clair to her business.

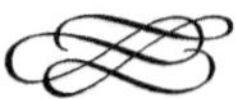

CHAPTER 24

As they entered the apartment, they sat the man down, and Jeremy moved over to start securing his arms and legs to the chair.

"Hey, that's too tight."

"Yeah, a friend of mine taught me how to make sure you can't get out of these." Thinking of Emma, he said, "You're lucky she isn't here. She's rather fond of knives." Jeremy moved in front of him and said, "Who took them?"

"Took who?" he asked, not looking him in the eyes.

"We are not playing that game. We'll start with the facts." He ticked off on his fingers. "One, you hang around schools to entice children to join your pickpocket teams. Two, I know you continued to hound Mark, but he told you he wanted out. Three, you wouldn't take no for an answer."

"So, what? That doesn't mean I took the three of them," he muttered.

"Three?" Jeremy jumped on that. "We didn't say there were three."

Cornered, the man started talking. "Listen, I'm a low man on this operation."

"What operation?" asked Mac, stepping closer.

"The kids are just part of it," he admitted. "They're the lowest level and, as we spot kids that we can move into other things, then we take them."

"Why Mark?" Jeremy asked.

"He was a problem; that could lead to other kids telling us no. We wanted to grab him as an example to any others trying to get out," he said.

"Why take his parents?" asked Mac.

"He was too protected. He was always with someone," complained the man.

Smart kid, thought Jeremy.

"So, we followed him here and planned to sit on him and get him to listen to reason," the man continued.

"What went wrong?" asked Jeremy quietly, knowing something must have to move from intimidation to kidnapping.

"The parents fought back, and we couldn't take the kid without them."

"Why move them to another location? Why not use this one?" asked Mac, knowing it would take planning to move them without being seen.

"A note arrived saying visitors were coming," the man said simply.

Tim and Dora, Jeremy thought.

"We had to get them out before anyone else got involved."

Jeremy was losing patience and raised his voice. "Where are they? Are they okay?"

"Define okay," the man muttered. When he saw their expressions, he admitted, "They are pretty banged up."

"Where are they!" Jeremy demanded again.

"I can't say," the man said plaintively.

"Can't or won't?" asked Mac.

"I honestly don't know where they are."

"Who would?" Jeremy demanded.

The man mumbled.

"What was that?" asked Mac.

He shrugged.

"Okay," said Jeremy, taking a deep breath. "Where do you think they are?"

He looked away, not answering.

"Hey! Answer him!" demanded Mac.

The man finally said, "Listen, I didn't have anything to do with this after they were moved. But I think I know where they might be."

"We're listening," said Jeremy.

"They probably have them in the East Street Bridge," he said, staring at Jeremy.

"What do you mean in the bridge? The bridge is a bridge, not a room," said Mac.

"Well, my brother-in-law worked on the building of the bridge and he worked on this room they called an anchorage. It has spaces that are 50 feet tall," the man said.

"Stand him up," Jeremy said to Joe. "You're going to draw out a map to this location and then you are going to sit here with this nice man," indicating Paul, "until we retrieve the family."

"Oh," he added casually, "and any moves to escape, Paul has authority to shoot you. Understood?"

"No-no problem," he stuttered.

They untied him, keeping their guns aimed as he drew up the location to the anchorage and how to get there. "It's located inside the base of the East Bridge at Cadman Plaza West at the intersection of Hicks Street and Old Fulton Street in Brooklyn. To get there, walk down Cadman Plaza West toward the river, past the overpass. The anchorage entrance is to the right."

He handed it to Jeremy, who looked at it and then at Joe, saying "Tie him back up and use the method from earlier. We don't want him escaping."

Jeremy folded up the map up and nodded to Mac and Joe to

go on their way. They took a carriage across the bridge to the location indicated on the map. As they were dropped off, they pulled their hats low over their faces. Mac had removed his police jacket and hat. They made their way to the entrance and stayed out of sight.

"Okay, how do we handle this?" asked Joe.

Jeremy said, "We wait for someone to come out, then grab them. We're unsure how far they are into the anchorage."

They didn't have long to wait; a man was approaching a door carrying a bag that looked to have food in it. Mac made hand signals for them to spread out and, as the figure walked up, Mac put a gun to his head and said, "Where are you headed?"

"Nowhere," he said, standing very still.

"Now, why don't I believe that? You have a family locked in there?"

"How do you. . ." he stuttered in surprise.

"How do I know that? I just do. Tell us who's in the space, how far in they are, and if any are armed."

He took a long look at Mac and then at the three guns pointed his way and gave all the details. They put cuffs on him and tied him to a tree. As Jeremy was about to place a gag in his mouth, he said, "Wait. There is a password." He told them and the three approached the door; they knocked and gave "hidden" as the password in a low voice.

The man who answered didn't look at who he was letting in and said absently, "Got the groceries? People are getting hungry in here."

Mac grabbed him from behind and held him with an arm around his neck. Jeremy and Joe had their guns drawn, and Jeremy asked, "Where are they?"

"Down there." The man pointed with his hand.

Jeremy nodded and Mac knocked the man out with the butt of his gun. They laid him down and approached the back of the area quietly. They could see two men and the family there. George and Mark were tied up and Elizabeth was lying on a cot. Mark saw them enter and averted his eyes so as not to give away their position.

Jeremy gave a hand signal to have the men spread out. They had the two men guarding the family covered. There were guns, but they were abandoned on the table and not close to the men. They must have considered the area well protected.

Once Mac and Joe were in place, he said loudly, "You are surrounded! Put your hands up."

The men went for their guns, but Jeremy shot the leg on the table. When the table collapsed, the guns scattered on the floor. The men froze where they were and lifted their hands above their heads.

Jeremy kept his gun trained on the men as Mac and Joel collected their weapons and moved them out of reach. Once all were securely tied up, Jeremy directed them to untie Mark and George. George immediately went to check on Elizabeth.

"How is she?" asked Jeremy.

She opened her eyes, moaning, holding her bruised face. "Are you okay?" asked George softly.

"Yes, I was very dizzy when they first hit me, but I'm mostly okay now. I figured it was better to pretend to be worse than I was," she explained, sitting up slowly.

"That was smart," said Jeremy, watching them hug each other.

Mac stated, "We need to get everyone out now. I'll take these men in for kidnapping and you'll be questioned at your home. Do you understand?"

They nodded.

"I'll escort the family," Jeremy said.

Mac had arranged for two carriages—one to transport the kidnappers and one to move the family. As they rode home, Elizabeth cried softly in George's arms, relieved to be safe.

Mark waited as long as he could before asking, "How did you figure it out, Jeremy? That we were taken and hadn't run away?"

Jeremy looked over at him and said, "Your books. You left them behind."

He grinned. "I hoped you would notice that. "

"I did and I found it very clever, but I think Emma would have found it faster than I did," he teased.

"I think you're right," Mark said seriously.

"Jeremy, I think we're ready for that move to Chicago," George said firmly.

"I agree. I'll take care of your tickets and see about getting your belongings shipped."

"Jeremy, can I get my books to take with me?" asked Mark anxiously.

That made him smile. "Yes, I think we can arrange that," he commented.

Jeremy would provide protection for them while they packed up their apartment and made their statements to the local police.

CHAPTER 25

CHICAGO

A telegram arrived at the boarding house late that afternoon from Jeremy. Mrs. Spencer opened the door and took the message from the waiting delivery boy.

"Emma, there's a telegram for you," she said as she walked into the dining room, handing it to her.

Emma was working at the table on the documentation for the building they had chosen for their office space. She took the telegram and said absently, "Thank you, Mrs. Spencer."

Emma opened the envelope and started to read. "It looks like we have company coming."

"Is there room here?" Mrs. Spencer asked, wanting to help.

"Yes, we can set up something in the third-floor rooms," Emma said.

She sat drumming her fingers on her lips. She would like to have more details, but those would have to wait until they arrived. *Funny, I thought I would be upset not to be involved in the adventure, but what I am is relieved that everyone's okay.*

Emma continued reviewing the two boarding houses, knowing it would be another few weeks before the renovations were completed. Water and gas pipes were just about done upstairs, and the kitchen remodel had started. The kitchen was the biggest project and was driving the schedule because of the delivery of a new stove and the building of new cabinets. There was also additional support and wall removal for the expanded rooms.

She made a list of the new housing situation that would be in place once the boarding house was available.

<u>New Boarding house</u>

2nd floor: Harold and Betsy, Marco and Mara

3rd floor: Mark, Mr. and Mrs. Sutherland and two open rooms.

4th floor: Molly, her boys, and two open rooms

<u>Current house:</u>

2nd floor: Dora and Tim and two for future

3rd floor: Jake, Thomas (Temp), Emma and one open room

4th floor: Savannah, Papa and two for future

We'll have some openings, thought Emma, *even with Mark and his family. We will have to put notices in the local paper to fill those rooms.* She would have to review that with Dora. She closed up her book, thinking it had been an active day. So many good things had happened.

A few days later, Emma got another telegram from Tim. They would be in New York for another week to finalize the details and head home. She could expect them in about two weeks.

The house should be completed at just about that time.

CHAPTER 26

She spent the next few days working with Amy and Mrs. Spencer to get the rooms ready for Mark and his parents. They opened the windows and aired them out. The sheets were changed, furniture dusted, and floors mopped.

A week later, Emma had a wagon waiting at the train station. She stood inside the station and watched the train arrive. When she saw Mark and his parents disembarked, she called, "Mark!"

He looked around when he heard his name, saw her, and ran toward her. She grabbed him in a tight hug.

"Mark, I am so glad to see you," she said, pushing back his hair on his forehead.

"Me, too. You should hear how Jeremy found us," he said excitedly, wanting to share the story.

"Let's talk about that at home, okay? Right now, I bet your parents want to get settled," she suggested, standing with her arm on his shoulders, waving at them.

"Emma, we're so glad to see you," they said as they approached her.

"As am I," she said sincerely. "Hi, Jeremy," she said softly, kissing him hello. She turned back to the group and said, "I have the wagon with me, so we can get everything at once."

"Where is it?" Jeremy asked, wanting to be on their way.

"Thomas has it over there to the left."

They spotted him and waved. He moved the wagon closer and they put the family trunks and bags into the back.

"Mark, can you ride back here with me and Jeremy? George and Elizabeth, why don't you climb up with Thomas?" Emma suggested.

When all were settled, they started on their way to the boarding house.

"Are we staying with you, Emma?" asked Mark.

"For now. I have rooms set up. We'll talk with your parents to see if you want to stay at the boarding house or find an apartment of your own."

George heard the question and turned to say, "We'll make that decision once we find jobs."

They sat quietly the rest of the way. All were grateful the family had made it safely to Chicago.

Once there, everyone helped take the bags up to their assigned rooms. George and Elizabeth exclaimed how nice it was.

Emma said, "We have breakfast, lunch, and dinner for the family. That includes you."

"Emma, we don't expect to live here for free," George protested.

"Why don't you get settled and we can talk about the long-term plans. Okay?" she suggested.

"Yes," they said gratefully.

She showed them the lavatory and told them snacks were available in the kitchen until the dinner hour. Mark's family convinced him to wash up and rest a bit before dinner. He would have liked to tell Emma all about their adventures, but it would have to wait. They knew Emma wanted some time alone with Jeremy.

Once their door was closed, Emma looked at Jeremy and said, "Want to go to the study for a bit and discuss things?" she asked with a smile.

"That would be wonderful," he said, liking the idea of some time alone with her. They headed downstairs and she closed the door of the study before running into his arms.

"I missed you," she murmured.

"I missed you too," he said, and they kissed long and slow. It would be a while before they came up for air. They finally broke apart with a laugh.

"Okay, tell me about the adventure," Emma said as she sat on the couch, eager to hear what happened.

"Emma, I'm sorry I had to go on my own," he said, sitting down next to her, hoping she wasn't mad she had been excluded.

"No, Jeremy I'm not upset," she assured him. "I realize I have responsibilities here and there will always be more adventures."

"True," he said and started to tell her what had happened and how they found the family.

"Really, a room inside the bridge? I'd like to see that," she said, awed.

"You will. We'll go back sometime and I'll show it to you," he promised.

She got serious. "We have the family out of harm's way here, but what about the kids still there?"

"Mac has made it his personal goal to give those kids an opportunity to get out," he explained.

"How will he do it?" she asked.

"He's planning a watch and raid, where they take the kids for indoctrination," he explained.

"Will it work?" she asked, concerned.

"For a while," he admitted. "The Whyos are integrated

enough to look like they support the cleanup, but I expect it will start again. Gangs like them depend on the lower part of the organization to eventually move up into the other jobs."

"I hope it works out. Maybe some afterschool programs through the charity? I'll ask Clair to look into it," Emma suggested.

Jeremy nodded, settling back on the couch, and asked casually, "Have you given thought to our living situation?"

"Oh, yes. I've mapped out the houses. Let me show you." She went to retrieve her maps from the desk drawer and laid them out for him to review.

He examined the plans and asked questions on how it would work. "This is doable. I think I can do this myself with some help."

"We'll have to get approval from Dora. The boarding house is her domain," she cautioned.

"Then we speak to Dora," he agreed. They settled down and enjoyed each other's company.

Dinner that night was full of stories of Mark and his family's adventures.

After dinner, George said in a grateful tone, "Jeremy, we need to thank you for notifying our school about our family emergency."

"It was that," said Jeremy wryly.

"Will you look for work teaching?" asked Emma.

"Yes, my administrator said he would send a letter of introduction for me. I'll go over to the local school administration tomorrow and find out what my options are. I'm hoping they approve Elizabeth working also," said George.

"Do you expect trouble getting Elizabeth approved?" asked Dora.

"They don't normally let married women work as teachers. I was able to convince them to let me continue working in New York," commented Elizabeth.

CHAPTER 27

Things worked out for George and Elizabeth; both found jobs in the Chicago education system. Jeremy arranged for their furniture and other belongings to be sent down by train. They wanted to make sure the family was happy with the forced decision. They would store the furniture in the new boarding house until their future living arrangements were settled.

Another week went by, Dora and Tim had sent a telegram saying the audit was completed and they were on their way home. Emma was relieved. Dora's job was harder than she'd thought it could be, and she didn't even have to cook.

She went to the train station with Jeremy, this time in a carriage to pick up Dora and Tim. They got off the train—Tim first, followed by Dora. She appeared happy to be home. She ran up to Emma and said, "I'm so glad you're here to get us. I just want to get home."

"How are you, Tim?" inquired Jeremy.

"Good, really good. We can discuss more information later," Tim said, wanting to get them moving. They kept the conversation light on the ride home.

"Mr. Cummings says to send his regards," Dora told Emma. "I also got recipes from the Carlyle's chef to try here."

"Wonderful, you'll have to show me," Emma said.

Jeremy commented with a laugh, "Just make sure you make those macarons!"

"I will," said Dora. She looked over at Emma and explained, "They are wonderful little cookies."

As they arrived at home, Tim kept looking at the boarding house under construction. Dora noticed and said, "Tim, why don't we get washed up and change clothes, then we can take a peek at all of the changes."

Tim was reluctant and finally agreed. "Emma, can we meet down here in twenty minutes?"

"Definitely," she agreed.

They all met downstairs and headed over to review the changes in the new boarding house. Emma brought her map to show them the room layout. Tim was eager and said, "Let's take a look."

It had been over a month since Tim and Dora had seen the house. When they left, the walls were damaged and the floors were covered in debris. What they saw when they entered was a finished house. Floors polished and clean, walls painted and finished.

Emma looked over at Dora and said, "Kitchen first?"

"Please," said Dora readily.

Tim smiled at Emma and nodded. They followed Dora into the kitchen. Dora pushed the door open and stood still for a moment. Emma cast a worried glance toward her through the continued silence.

Dora abruptly turned around and gave Emma a long hug. "It's perfect."

"I'm so relieved you like it." Emma knew it was the one room that had to be right.

Dora walked around, looking at the cabinets and long

expanses of workspace, and observed, "We'll still need a kitchen table and. . ."

As she continued to list out their needs, Tim and Jeremy indicated they were heading upstairs to observe the work that had been completed up there.

Tim yelled down from the top of the stairs, "Emma, can you explain the layout up here?"

Emma yelled up, "I have a map! I'll bring it up." She headed upstairs with Dora.

She showed them the layout she had selected, and Dora and Tim reviewed it closely.

"I like the idea of making some of the rooms bigger and having more long-term people in residence, but if it's two rooms, the rent will be higher," worried Tim.

Emma nodded, saying, "I've asked the boarders about an increase and they agreed. They would like the extra space."

Dora was thinking about the next steps. "We'll need furniture. A dining room table, couches, and chairs for the sitting room and beds."

Tim said, looking at the budget Emma had provided, "We have that covered since the house was abandoned."

"Dora, we can hunt through thrift shops and redo the furniture instead of buying new," suggested Emma.

"I like that idea; it would be a mix of things," said Dora.

They continued the tour, testing the gas lights and plumbing. All were working well. "The Marella's did a good job," said Tim.

"They always do," commented Emma. "And just think, we'll have Marco and Mara living here if something comes up." The group laughed and continued with their review.

Mrs. Spencer and Amy made a nice dinner, and the group met in the study afterward to discuss business. Emma asked the first question, as she pulled out her notebook. "The audit?"

Tim had his accounting books for the charity out. "It went

well. I sent runners out to every investment to confirm they were in place. We certainly didn't want a Little Dori here."

"No," agreed Jeremy, "I'm glad you had the runners go and investigate, so many investments were paper-only businesses."

Tim continued, "We went over the paperwork in detail and met with bank officials. The investments are solid. I've also arranged for the capital we need to start the charity. I have the books organized and I believe we're ready to set up a meeting and a one-on-one review with Clair."

"That's wonderful. Papa, Clair, and I have toured several buildings and found one we would like to make an offer on. Papa has the owner waiting for us to do a final walkthrough, which we saved for when you both got back home," said Emma.

"Mr. Beeker should be here in a day or so to confirm the building arrangements," Tim added.

Dora said with a serious expression, "Emma, we appreciate you staying and helping keep the projects moving forward." Emma smiled and reached for her hand.

Mr. Beeker arrived a few days later and confirmed the space would be fine for what the staff needed. He met with Clair and discussed the charity and how it would run before heading back to New York to start the relocation.

CHAPTER 28

*L*ater that week, after Tim and Dora got settled back into their normal routines, Jeremy and Emma asked them out to dinner. It was a pleasant evening that ended at Jeremy's house. Cole had gone to visit Papa at the boarding house.

They were telling stories to one another and enjoying the evening. Jeremy nodded at Emma, indicating for her to bring up the topic. "Jeremy and I would like to discuss something with you," she started.

Dora looked excited and squeezed Tim's hand in anticipation.

Emma noticed and said bluntly, "It isn't that kind of topic. We aren't planning to get married." This statement caused Dora to go still.

Emma took a deep breath before she continued. "What we want," she looked to Jeremy, "is to be together and we want your support to have him move into the boarding house."

Jeremy took it from there. "We're very committed to one another and know we'll be together for a very long time, and I would like to move into the room next to Emma."

Tim laughed suddenly and said, "Is that all? That will be easy to arrange. We will have the room once the new boarding house is open."

"Well," said Jeremy, "we would also like to make a few changes between the two rooms."

Emma chose that moment to pull out her drawings and showed them the design of an additional door and a bookcase to hide it on both sides, allowing access to Emma's and Jeremy's rooms.

Dora looked confused and then blushed profusely when she understood what they were saying. "But if you do that, what if. . ."

"I get pregnant?" Emma completed the question for her. She was ready for it. "We talked about that," she said. Jeremy took her hand. "We agreed we would get married if it comes down to that. I don't think it will; I just don't feel that I'm meant to have children."

Dora touched her stomach, wishing she was pregnant. It had been years and she was unsure if they would ever have children.

Emma noticed and said sincerely, "It will happen for you. It just takes time."

Tim was looking at the drawing. "We'll have to do this work ourselves to keep it quiet."

"Yes, I thought of that. I'm pretty handy with tools." Jeremy would do anything to protect Emma's name.

While they worked on the design, Dora pulled Emma to her side and said, "What if someone finds out? You know it could be bad, you would be ruined."

Emma tilted her head and said, "From what I have seen, marriage seems to be a fix for things like that. If we get caught, we will consider our options. I am not worried for me but I do not want to affect our businesses."

Dora nodded and didn't say anything further. Once Emma made up her mind, there was little that could change it.

"I can help with some of the final touches. I worked with Tony's family on the job," Emma said.

The two couples agreed. Jeremy would move in and they would keep it quiet. They also chose not to tell Papa or Cole what the actual arrangements were, only that Jeremy was moving in.

When Papa heard this, he decided it was time to give his girls their space. He mentioned his idea to Cole, and he agreed that Papa would move in with him. The "brothers" were together again.

Tim and Jeremy worked on strengthening the wall between the rooms before adding the door. Tim looked at the design again and asked, "Jeremy, what gave you this idea, to attach the rooms?"

Jeremy said, "Well, in Mr. Carlyle's house, they had connecting rooms and it seemed convenient."

"It is that," said Tim, chuckling.

They got the wall strengthened and started cutting a space for a door. Once completed, they finished the woodwork around the entrance and added the door. The bookcases were stationed in each room and Jeremy moved in. Papa moved out at the same time.

Everything was coming together; the new boarding house was completed. Mark and his family had decided to make their home at the boarding house, selling the furniture they weren't using to Dora. Dora and Emma bought additional furniture as well: couches and chairs for the sitting room, dining room table, buffet, kitchen table, and assorted beds and desks.

Tim, Dora, and Emma continued to run the boarding houses, their temporary business, and also kept taking on cases for both the Pinkertons and private clients.

CHAPTER 29

1885-BACK TO THE PRESENT

*E*mma shook herself out of her memories and could hear Jeremy moving around in his room, getting ready for the day. She moved to the side of the bed and stood up. She immediately sat back down, feeling dizzy. *I got up too quickly, that's all*, she told herself.

She tried again and felt a sharp abdominal cramp that made her sit back down again. She took a moment and breathed deeply until the dizziness passed. She tried a third time and, when she did not feel any additional pain, she moved to the lavatory to wash her face. She put the experience out of her mind as she returned to her room to get ready for her day. Cole had contacted her last night and asked her to stop by to review a case with him.

She and Jeremy met in the hallway and descended the stairs. "I think we should get a carriage to the office, that way you have your bike after the meeting."

"I agree." They ate quickly and walked her bike to the street to hail a cab. When they arrived, handed off her bike to one of the Pinkerton staff. Jeremy went to his office and she went directly to Cole's office. She knocked and was called in.

As Emma entered, she was surprised to see a nun sitting by Cole. The woman wore a gray habit with a black hood. *I'll need my best manners for this meeting*, she thought.

When Cole saw her, he said, "Emma, hello. Please join us."

Emma walked over and sat in the chair opposite the couch. She looked over at Cole as he started the introductions. "Sister Catherine, this is Emma Evans, one of our detectives."

"It's very nice to meet you. We do need help with this matter," said Sister Catherine quietly.

"Sister, why don't you describe your concerns and the support needed?" Cole encouraged.

Emma pulled out her notebook.

"The concern involves the Sisters of Charity hospital. We believe someone on our staff is stealing our medication; specifically, our morphine and laudanum," said Sister Catherine, sounding disappointed.

Emma looked up from her notebook to ask, "Do you have a medicine control system in place?"

Sister Catherine answered, "We keep the drugs in a closet, and it's locked. There is a sign-out sheet, and we inventory weekly."

"Who has access to the drug closet?"

"All the doctors, nurses, and some aides have access to the key," she admitted.

"Who has actual custody of the key?" asked Emma.

"Our medical secretary keeps it."

"Where's it kept when he's off of work? I would assume you need access to the drugs twenty-four hours a day?"

She looked a bit embarrassed at this question. "It's kept in a drawer and people that need it, know where it is."

Emma felt a bit exasperated at that answer but kept her tone civil. "Do you have any suspicions?"

"I hope it's not one of our sisters. Honestly, though, given the system, it could be anyone," answered Sister Catherine. "We would like you to come in undercover and observe the activities going on at nighttime. The hospital should be on lockdown with only the Sisters and staff in place."

"We can't make any assumptions at this point. I can be there starting tomorrow evening. What type of job are you thinking of for me?" asked Emma.

"I was thinking of a volunteer; they assist the nurses," she suggested.

"That should work," said Cole. "It will be a physical job, but at night you'd be able to observe staff activities without much notice. Will you do it?"

"Yes, of course," Emma replied as she sat drumming her fingers on her lips, thinking ahead. "Is there a uniform I'll need to wear?"

"Yes, there is a uniform top, but you can wear clothes under it. I'll have that delivered to you," said Sister Catherine.

"Who will I report to?"

"Sister Mary Faith. She's the head nurse at night and runs the staff."

"Is there anything I should know about her?" asked Emma.

"She's very efficient at her job and is good with the patients. She won't know you are there for any other reason than volunteering," said Sister Catherine.

"Do you suspect her in this?"

"I hope not," the woman said.

Sister Catherine finished confirming the information with Emma and Cole before departing quietly.

Emma looked over at Cole consideringly and said, "Cole, this case seems simple, catch the person stealing the drugs, but I am wondering if there is more to it. What are the drugs being used for? It seems more than one person's addiction,"

Cole was stroking his goatee. "Yes, I think there is more to it."

"Do you think the sister knows?" she asked, bewildered.

"I don't think so but we will keep her informed," he said. "Any issues with starting tomorrow?"

"No, I'm between assignments right now. I can do it and I've never worked in a hospital before," Emma commented.

Cole nodded and said, "Keep in contact with me. Hopefully, this is a short-term job, a week at the most. Keep it as observational only and no interaction."

"Are you sure?" she teased.

"Only if necessary and in defense of life," he said seriously, knowing how things could change. "Take your knives with you."

"I'll start tomorrow night," she said as she closed her notebook and headed out, her head down.

Jeremy stepped into her path. "Hi, I thought you would stop by after your meeting."

"Oh hi, Jeremy, just thinking about the new case and I got distracted. It's always nice to see you," she said sincerely.

"I saw the new client. Very solemn."

"Yes, could be interesting, though," she said.

"Share the details at dinner tonight?" he asked.

"Out or at the boarding house?"

"Out. Let's have some quiet time. Alone," he suggested.

"Definitely." She kissed him sweetly and left to work some courier jobs that afternoon.

He watched her go, tapping the folder in his hand. He had just been notified that Zeke Jones had escaped from prison in Washington State. The information did not indicate he was on his way to Chicago, but he would have to put a protective order in for Clair and Emma. He planned to tell both as soon as he got an idea of Zeke's direction. Emma went about her day and stopped by the museum to see Tony. She carried her bike in and the security guards at the door took it for her.

One of them indicated, "Mr. Marella is in his office."

She thanked him and headed that way. As she reached to

knock on his door, it opened. She laughed when she came face to face with Tony.

"I didn't know you were stopping by," he said as he hugged her.

"Well, I couldn't let you head overseas without seeing you. When do you leave?" she asked, walking in.

"In a few days," he responded.

"Do you have time to review the trip with me?" she asked, interested where he would be going and what he would see.

"Of course," he said, pulling out his itinerary. He sat next to her on his office couch. "First, we take the La Bretagne and arrive in Havre before traveling by day train to Paris."

"Where will you stay in Paris?" she asked.

"The Saint Laurent. We have a suite reserved with multiple bedrooms. We'll need to store any artwork we purchase to be shipped home," he said.

"Will you mostly stay in Paris?"

"Yes. But there might be day trips to see various artists in other provinces."

"Will you get to see some sights?" she asked.

"Philip said there would be time to see some palaces and other historical locations."

Emma had a dreamy look in her eyes, imagining it all. "Oh, Tony, I can't wait to see Paris. Are you excited?"

"Yes, definitely, though there will be a lot of work, learning about the different art techniques and such. So much is going on in the art world, and Paris is the center of it all," Tony said.

"How long will you be gone?" she asked.

"More than a month," he responded.

"Wow! You will send me letters and let me know how things are going?"

"Of course. One day, you'll have to visit Paris with me," he said casually.

Emma smiled sincerely at the offer, thinking she would love

to go one day. They talked for more than an hour before she stood, patting her courier bag. "I still have some deliveries to make today."

"Will I see you before we head to New York?" asked Tony.

Regretfully, she shook her head. "I have a new case starting tomorrow night."

"I'll send you a note when we reach Paris," he offered.

"I'd love that! I'll miss you. Enjoy yourself and see everything," she said as she stood and gave him a long hug.

"I'll miss you," he said. She didn't see him wipe at his eyes as she got organized to leave.

Later that night at dinner, Jeremy was asking questions about Tony's trip. "A month? Will the museum here be closed all that time?"

"It'll stay open. They have a business manager for these situations where Philip or Tony aren't available," said Emma.

Jeremy admitted to himself that he was using Tony to delay any communication about Zeke. He would wait to tell her until he knew for sure there was a worry. The conversation turned to her new case. As she described it to him, he was frowning.

"The case seems a bit light."

Emma nodded and said, "I agree. I'm going to approach this as more observation and less action. This could be resolved in one night if a staff member is involved."

"True. Would you like me to meet you to walk home after your shift?" Jeremy knew Zeke wasn't in the area yet, but he did like spending as much time as possible with her.

"That would be nice," she commented, knowing she wouldn't be seeing him at night.

When she and Jeremy arrived home, she found her uniform shirt and confirmation of a time to start work from Sister Catherine. She and Jeremy took advantage of their last night together.

CHAPTER 30

The next morning, she heard Jeremy wake and leave the room quietly, letting her sleep. He knew she needed to rest as long as possible. She didn't want to be too tired on her first night at the hospital.

Much later, she climbed out of bed, dressed, and made her way downstairs for breakfast. *Well,* she thought, looking at the time, *it's after 2pm. It's more like a late lunch and I'm starving.* She opened the door to the kitchen and saw Tim and Dora sitting at the table.

They looked up and Dora said, "We didn't know if we would see you before this evening."

"I slept all I could. I hope I'm able to make it the entire night," Emma said as she yawned.

"Tell us more about the case," encouraged Tim.

"There isn't a lot to share right now. The first night is for observing more than anything. I report at 6pm and should be off around 4am," Emma said yawning as she sat down.

"Will you need to wear a disguise?" Dora asked, handing her a sandwich and an apple.

"No, I can be just myself," she said as she started to eat.

She read and relaxed the last part of the day, getting dressed at 5pm.

"Emma," called Dora, "your meal and snacks are in the kitchen."

Emma went to the kitchen and got her food. "I'm headed to the hospital," she called back.

It was 6pm when she arrived. Even though she wasn't undercover, she didn't want to call attention to herself, so she walked rather than rode her bike over. She had on her white uniform top, a black blouse, and a black skirt underneath it. She also wore a jacket over the top. She saw a Sister at the reception desk and approached her.

As she approached, the Sister said in a commanding voice, "Well, what are you here for? Speak up."

The tone caused Emma to fall silent a moment. She finally said, "I'm here about the volunteer position. Sister Catherine told me I could start my temporary job here tonight."

The sister frowned at her and checked her book. "Yes, I see here you're expected. They're letting girls do this work now?"

Because it didn't seem like a question, Emma waited for her instructions.

"You may go up to the second floor. Sister Mary is in charge there. Get with her and find out what your duties will entail."

Emma nodded and placed her hat back on her head. She made her way up the stairs. A woman was cleaning the floors. As she walked past, Emma sent her a quick smile and got one in return.

She exited the stairs into a long hallway and followed it down to the nurses' station. Several Sisters were working at the desk. As Emma approached, one stood and asked quietly, "Yes?"

"I was told to report to Sister Mary about a temporary job as a volunteer. Sister Catherine set it up," Emma explained.

"I'm Sister Mary," she said. "You may put your things in there." She indicated the small room used for breaks. "I'm glad you have your hair tied up. There will be physical labor, changing beds, and preparing for the morning. Taking water or other needs to patients. You must not take food or water to a patient without asking. At night, when a patient can't sleep, we like to keep an eye on them. Can you read?"

"Yes, I can read," commented Emma.

The sister paused a moment in her directions and sent her an appraising look. "You may read to them if they would like you to. If you have any books, you can bring in, we would appreciate it. Now, let's go through the ward. The patients are kept in one large room. Children and adults are kept together in the same ward."

There was some moaning and crying as they entered. Emma looked around. There was so much to take in. The large ward was filled with so many beds. Sister Mary explained her job duties and sent her on her way.

She spent the first few hours of her shift helping distribute food to the various patients. She moved bedpans and brought blankets. Nurses distributed medication and changed bandages.

It was much later in the night when the ward settled down. She sat with several children, talking to them quietly and telling them silly stories. A Sister came up to her and told her to take a break. She nodded and winced as she stood. The pain was brief and stopped as soon as she started moving.

She made her way into the break area for orderlies. They were sitting talking together. She took her seat and ate her snack of German pancakes and fruit.

Emma finished her snack and sat back in the soft chair, listening to the orderlies talking about their weekend plans. She stood, put away her lunch pail, and left the area. Looking around, she pulled out the map Sister Catherine had sent over with her uniform and made her way around the floor.

She reviewed the areas listed: the main ward, offices, nurses' station, and finally the long hallway to the supply closet. After ensuring she was alone, she nonchalantly tried the lock, which appeared intact. *Well, that's good,* she thought. Quickly, she pulled a pin out of her hair and kneeled to pick the lock. As the tumblers clicked, she turned the knob and entered the small room.

She pulled the door shut behind her and secured the lock. The small room didn't have any lights, she reached into her pocket and pulled out a small portable gas lamp. Once lit it, she held up the light to see the drugs lined up in vials and bottles. Labels identified each one. She shook her head. *The first thing I'm going to recommend is a stronger lock.* As she looked around the small room, she noticed the closet was just big enough to have several shelves on her left. There was also a table with some storage underneath. Suddenly, the sound of shuffling steps and a rattle of keys sounded. She dove under the table, shoving blankets in front of her.

It was one of the Sisters. She watched the Sister gather supplies, checking off things from a piece of paper as she gathered items from the shelves. Emma stayed where she was until she exited. *They a list of approved people allowed to enter the room,* thought Emma. Emma came out from under the table and checked what the Sister had removed. The gaps showed at least 4 containers of laudanum and 4 containers of morphine had been taken. It seemed a lot, but it might just be for patients that evening. She extinguished the light and opened the door slowly, glancing around to make sure no one saw her. When it was safe to exit, she headed back to the ward. *Where is the sister I saw in the closet?* The wards were quiet and she walked around and identified each one. *She wasn't there!* She made a note to get detailed information on each staff member. This case might take longer than she'd expected.

She finished up and was walking home when Jeremy approached her. She stopped and gave him a slight smile. "Hey, thanks for coming to meet me."

"Tired?" he asked.

"Yes. Long night."

He took her arm, and they made their way home. He gave her a minute, then asked, "Did you find anything out?"

"Well, one thing is for sure, we need to add them to our charity list. They're working with so little money and doing so much." She went on to describe things she had seen.

He looked over expectantly, but she still hadn't mentioned the case. "Will you be back tomorrow night?"

"Yes, I'll have to be. The only person I saw getting drugs was one of the Sisters, or I think it was a Sister. I documented what she took to compare with Sister Catherine tomorrow."

"You mean today," he teased. He got a small, tired smile in response. He asked, "You think she might not be a Sister?"

"I'm unsure. I didn't get a good look, as I was under a table," she stated wryly. "I don't think she was one of the sisters working that night."

"Were you able to follow her?" he asked.

"No, I thought she'd be in the ward, so I didn't. I'll keep a closer eye on her tomorrow night. Can you give Cole an update for me?" she asked with a yawn

"Yes, of course. Is there anything else?" Jeremy asked, knowing Cole would like the information.

"Yes, Sister Catherine needs to confirm the inventory. Here are the amounts of medications I saw removed," she said as she tore the page out of her notebook and handed it to him.

As he took the note, he pulled her in closer for a long kiss. "Want to head home?" he asked, looking deep into her eyes.

She knew that look. "Definitely." They made their way to the boarding house.

CHAPTER 31

*E*mma slept hard that day and returned to the hospital in the evening. She thought about the Sister from the night before and pulled out her notebook. *What was different about that Sister?* she asked herself, evaluating her notes *She was not wearing an apron over her dress. The Sisters I have been working with wear these routinely to protect their habits. I had not seen her previously, either in the ward or at the nurses' station. A count was needed of all of the sisters on duty at night. Was it an imposter?*

She started gathering names as soon as she arrived. She found that the Sister at the desk was very friendly and talkative, offering nearly all the information Emma needed. On her break, she studied the list and made notes about each Sister. *2nd floor: Sister Mary, the talkative Sister, has delicate features and is slight of stature, appears to be in her late 20s or early 30s; Sister Magdalene is just the opposite, tall and commanding, appears to be about 40; Sister Anne is very quiet and average, appears to be in her 50s; Sister Maura is a hard worker and very pretty, the youngest in her early 20s and a novice Sister.*

What surprised her was that they were women like her aunts or friends. They talked, laughed, and occasionally argued with each other. These women were not subjugated. They were smart and seemed very happy with their lives. She had wondered about that. *Were they forced to be in the Church or was it a decision they made on their own?* These women showed her that it had been a higher calling.

She closed her notebook and returned to following the Sister's orders. She started with delivering water and other items, reading books she had brought in, and comforting as best she could.

CHAPTER 32

The next few days were routine, with no more unexplained visits to the drug closet. One particular evening was very quiet when she had finished checking on patients. Emma was making her way to the break room when she saw the strange "Sister". She ducked into a side room, watching, positive she was an imposter.

The other Sisters moved with a certain grace. This "Sister" was doing a quick step to the closet. She wouldn't find any changes to the locks. Emma had asked that the closet locks and process remain the same, so no one would suspect they were investigating the matter. As she opened the closet, Emma noticed she didn't stop to get the keys from the drawer. *Hmm,* she thought, *she has her own keys. It does lessen the chance someone from the hospital isn't involved. The keys are easily accessible, and she could have made a clay impression of the key. That would have allowed her to make a copy and not have to chance using the one kept in the drawer.*

Emma stayed where she was and let the "Sister" get the drugs she was after. She wondered about the quantities being taken, thinking to herself, *She's smart and must have been running this scam for a while. She probably got away with more over the long term than she would have with a one-time theft.*

The "Sister" also seemed to know the other Sister's schedules of when they would be out of the area. Emma waited in hiding, as the "Sister" made her way to the back staircase. Emma took off her shoes to follow her silently. She hung back and let her exit the building. She could see through the windows that the "Sister" went to the right.

Emma slipped off her white uniform top and threw it behind her in the stairwell. It would help her blend into the shadows as she trailed behind her. She kept following until she saw her enter an apartment building. Before the door shut the "Sister" glanced behind her. Emma ducked into an alley to avoid being seen.

After waiting a few minutes, Emma approached the building. The door creaked as she pushed it open slowly. There was no one in the area, she stepped in, listening for the sound of steps on the floors above. She looked up and could see the habit through the rails on the third floor. The sounds of feet kept moving to the next floor. She heard a banging and a door open and slam closed. *Fourth floor*, she thought.

She approached the floor and stayed on the stairs. From that vantage point, she could see each of the doors. *Which door?* The question was answered when a man stepped out one and Emma got a good look inside. The sister was there, she had pulled off the hood and her blond hair stood in stark contrast to the habit.

What now? She was unsure how to approach this. *Barge in, wait for her to exit, or go for help.*

Emma stayed put, slipping on her boots as she continued to watch the door. She was trying to get comfortable by leaning against the wall when the door opened abruptly; she barely had time to get out of the way of a man descending the stairs.

He had a small child with him, who couldn't have been more than five. The boy had red hair and a slight body. Emma looked at the boy carefully, he was walking sluggishly and appeared to be drugged.

The "Sister" stuck her head out the doorway and yelled, "Get him moving! They're waiting for him!"

"Yeah, yeah," he called back. "I'm on the way." He pushed the boy roughly down the stairs. "Get a move on."

Where are they taking the child in the middle of the night? She asked herself. Emma watched and worried. The child took precedence over the drug theft. She followed the man and the sluggish boy, deliberating what to do. She had to make sure she wasn't interfering in a family matter. She could hear him muttering, "I want my mama."

She listened intently. *He's Irish.* The accent was a familiar one, she had heard she'd heard while delivering to Chicago's Little Hell. She thought about the conversation between the man and the "Sister"; they weren't Irish. She stayed at a safe distance and watched as the man pulled the boy by his small arm into the street. Her decision was made for her when he raised a hand and slapped the child hard across the face.

She pulled her clutch knife and rushed them. *I really should have put together a plan,* she thought. Executing a flying kick, she planted her pointed boots into the man's soft stomach. He went down hard, the breath taken from him. She had the knife to his throat before he could recover. "I'm taking the boy and you'll forget you saw me."

He was panting, staring at her with wide eyes. She let the knife tip his skin to show him she meant business. The blood dribbled down to his shirt as he stuttered, "I won't say anything."

"If I hear you do, I'll come after you. Do you understand?"

"But—" he started

"Yes?" she interrupted, showing him her bloody knife.

"Nothing, nothing at all." He put his hand up to his neck and pulled it back covered in blood. "What did you do to me?"

"I'll do much worse if you come after us," she threatened.

She knelt by the boy. He had laid down on the ground when she attacked. While she checked him, she kept a wary eye on the man. She said loudly, "You need to go now." When he didn't move, she yelled, "I said *now!*"

He did as he was told and ran off thinking, *When I tell this story later, I'm going to say it was two large men.* He believed her when she said she would find him. He ran; he would hide out and not report in until later.

Emma watched him run off and then reached over to pick up the now passed-out little boy. She hugged him close as she knelt on the ground and thought about what to do next. The best thing she could do was to take him to the hospital.

She stood up with him in her arms. The streets were quiet as she made her way back to the hospital.

When she arrived, Sister Mary confronted her. "Just where have you. . ." She then realized she was carrying a child. Her demeanor changed immediately to one of concern. "What's wrong with him? Where did you find him?"

Emma spoke in a low voice, saying, "Sister Mary, we need to keep this quiet."

She frowned but did lower her voice. "We have a private room we can use, this way." She motioned for Emma to follow her to the room.

Seeing Emma look around with a frown on her face, Sister Mary commented, "The other Sisters are making rounds. We have some time."

Emma hugged the boy close, wanting to protect him. "Put him down please," requested Sister Mary. Gripping him tighter she didn't want to relinquish him, but Sister Mary needed to examine him. Emma laid him down on the bed and brushed his dark red hair off his head.

"What happened?" Sister Mary asked quietly.

"I think he was kidnapped from his parents," she said quietly back.

"How did you get him?" Sister Mary asked.

Emma kept looking at the boy and didn't say anything.

Sister Mary looked resigned. "Okay, keep your secrets." She looked him over and said, "He's bruised but nothing appears to be broken. He should be all right once he sleeps off the drugs he was given."

"Can you tell what they gave him?" she asked worriedly.

"It appears to be laudanum. He'll have to sleep the medication off. He'll also need to stay here, under observation, until he wakes up," she said firmly.

"Yes, I agree," said Emma, as she pondered what to do next. She came to a decision and asked, "Can you watch him while I get some help to manage this situation?"

Sister Mary looked again at her and said wryly, "Not a normal volunteer, are you?"

"No, not really," Emma said as she headed to the door. She turned back to Sister Mary and said, "I'll be back soon. Please, stay with him. Someone dangerous might be looking for him." She didn't wait for Sister Mary's answer as she turned and left the room.

She headed out, ran down the stairs, and didn't stop until she reached the boarding house. Letting herself in, she went up the stairs to her room. There was no hesitation as she crossed over to the connecting door.

"Jeremy, wake up," she said and jostled him.

"Emma, are you home already?" he asked, yawning. "Did I forget to get you?"

"No, Dear-One, I need some help. I need you to go get Cole and wake Tim and Dora to meet at the hospital. Oh, and tell Cole to bring Sister Catherine."

That woke him abruptly. "What's happened?" he asked, catching her hand as she turned to go.

"There's a child in danger," she said simply. "Please, get everyone there. I don't want to be away from him for long."

"All right," he said, already up and pulling on his pants. She headed back out through her connecting door, secure in the knowledge he would get everyone together.

She ran back to the hospital, hoping the child was going to be okay. She thought about his accent and hoped Tim might have an idea of where to find his family. He was on her mind as she reached the second floor. She glanced at her watch and saw it was 4am. *It should be quiet for a while longer.* She could see two Sisters sitting at the nurses' station.

Sister Agnes frowned and said, "Where have you been?"

"Something came up," replied Emma in a firm voice and looked her in the eyes.

"Well, if you want to volunteer here, this has to be. . ." Before she could finish, Sister Mary stepped out of the private room where the child was located.

"Emma, please come here." She didn't look at the other Sisters and closed the door after Emma entered.

"He's sleeping peacefully," she said as Emma immediately went to the bed and took his hand.

"He does seem better," she said in a relieved voice, looking over her shoulder at the Sister.

"Yes, he's been calm."

"Was he given too many drugs?" she asked worriedly.

"I think he was given too much for his size, but I believe he'll be able to sleep it off. What are we going to do now? "Sister Mary asked, clearly worried.

"I have my team coming," Emma assured her.

"You have a team? You're definitely not just a volunteer. How is it you have a team that could address this?" she asked.

"Well, the truth is," Emma started and was stopped with a knock on the door. Sister Mary opened the door and found Sister Agnes there.

"Sister, there are a lot of people here who want to see our volunteer. What should I tell them?" asked Sister Agnes, clearly bewildered.

Sister Mary came to a decision. "Show them to the meeting room and I'll need you to come in and sit with this child." When Sister Agnes started to interrupt, she stopped her by saying, "No questions, please."

Emma stepped out of the room. Cole was waiting there. "I have one of my men here," he nodded to a Pinkerton detective, "to watch the room while we talk."

Emma smiled, grateful for the forethought. He offered her his elbow and they walked together to the meeting room.

Emma and Cole entered the room and she saw that her team had assembled with little information provided. It brought tears to her eyes, but she quickly wiped them away.

Cole directed, "Emma, fill us in on what's happening."

Emma started, "As you know my current case involves tracking the morphine and laudanum losses at the hospital. I was able to determine that the thief was a Sister." She noticed Sister Catherine frowning and reassured her, "Not to worry, Sister Catherine. She was an imposter. She wore a similar habit to yours but was not wearing an apron. I followed her out and stayed a good distance back. I followed them into an apartment building. I waited in a stairwell, still planning only to observe, but then a man exited the apartment with a small boy. He was pulling him by the arm and pushing him downstairs." She finished up with, "I believe the child had been kidnapped."

"What led you to that conclusion?" asked Jeremy.

"I did hesitate, at first, but I kept observing them. The man and the child didn't have the same accent. Also, the boy kept asking for his mama."

"What made you decide to take the child into custody?" asked Dora hesitantly.

"When the man started hitting the boy," she said and shrugged. "I just had to stop it. So, I intervened."

Jeremy held his tongue on that one, knowing he would get the whole story later.

"How is the child now?" asked Cole.

Sister Mary spoke up and gave his status. Sister Catherine looked on in approval.

"Tim." Emma looked at him thoughtfully. "I believe the child is one of the kids living in the Hell's Irish sections."

Tim nodded. "Very probably. I can ask around and find out if a small child is missing. Do we know his name?"

"Not until tomorrow; he needs to get some rest tonight. The earliest he'll be able to answer questions will be in the morning," stated Sister Mary.

"Will he be safe here?" asked Dora, looking at Tim. "Should we move him to the boarding house?"

Sister Catherine spoke up, "Before any decisions are made on moving him, I would like to keep him here until he wakes. If at that time he responds well, I see no issue with him being moved."

Cole looked over at Sister Catherine and said, "Sisters, thank you for your support. Could you give us some time alone?"

"Yes, of course," Sister Catherine said as she and Sister Mary quietly exited the room. Jeremy closed the door behind them and took his seat.

"Emma," Jeremy asked, "what do you think is happening here? What's the big picture on this?"

"I believe I may have stumbled onto a kidnapping ring," she answered simply.

"For what purpose?" asked Dora, perplexed why children, especially poor children, would be kidnapped. "There would be no money in taking them."

Jeremy answered, "I think I can answer that. We're hearing

more cases like this throughout the country. They're using them for pickpocketing and prostitution rings."

Dora had such a soft heart and started to cry softly. Tim pulled her in close. She looked up with tears streaming down her face and asked, "Can we see him?"

Emma said, "Yes, of course. Dora and Tim, I wanted you so you could be here for him until we find his parents."

"Of course, poor little boy. We'll go over now," said Dora. Tim guided her from the room.

Emma, Jeremy, and Cole were the only ones left. Cole asked, "Emma, do you have any idea where they might be keeping the kids?"

"No, I meant to follow the man to the location, but when the abuse started, I felt I had to intervene. I'm sorry if I did so at the wrong time and prevented the larger case from being solved."

Cole said immediately, "No, you did the right thing. I'll have some detectives cover their movements."

Jeremy asked, suddenly worried, "What about the man you took the boy from? Will he tell them about you?"

She smiled rather evilly. "No, I think we can rely on his vanity for that. I don't think he'll say someone like me beat him up and took the boy."

"No, I wouldn't think so," murmured Cole, wondering how she'd managed it. He would have to ask Jeremy for details later.

Jeremy took the conversation from there, saying, "We can have men in place, watching the path to the apartment, and when the false Sister comes back for more drugs, we follow her to the final location. Hopefully, we'll find any kids who may have also been taken."

"Cole, we had planned to add new locks and security measures to the management of the drug closet. Do we add the security to the closet as we had planned?" Emma asked.

Cole thought a moment and said, "Let's call Sister Catherine back in."

Jeremy did so. Sister Catherine entered the room gracefully and stood in front of Cole.

"You asked to see me?"

"We would like to be able to keep the current security measures in place so we can track the drugs back to the kids."

"Do you think she'll be back?" Sister Catherine asked, suddenly worried about her staff.

"We do, but she's never approached anyone here. They should just go about their normal schedules. Once she has the drugs, we'll have her tailed."

When she looked doubtful, Emma said softly, "We'd like your help with this Sister."

Sister Catherine nodded and said, "If it will help get children home, we'll do what we can to help."

Cole said, "Jeremy and Emma will take the lead on this and keep me informed on the progress." He wiped a tired hand on his neck. "I'm heading home; this early hour is wearing." He exited the room with Sister Catherine.

Jeremy and Emma stayed in the room, sitting quietly for a moment before Jeremy said, "I'll have men stationed covertly to watch for the 'Sister.'"

Emma confirmed, "I'll continue to work here as a volunteer."

"You've been here when she's come in. What are you thinking about how often she appears? Do we wait for a night or have everyone set up just in case?"

"I've been thinking about that. She's pretty routine with her times," she said, looking at her notes from Sister Catherine on dates when shortages were noticed. "If she follows the schedule, it won't be for another three nights."

Jeremy thought about what she had said and responded, "I'll get the men in place tonight. That way, in case their schedule changes, we'll be ready."

"Let's go check on the boy," Emma suggested.

They made their way down and found Dora and Tim sitting

with him. He was sleeping soundly. "Dora, Tim, you can head home now," Emma said softly.

Tim looked at Dora and back at Emma, saying, "We want to stay with him until he wakes up."

"That could be a long while," cautioned the nurse, sitting next to him. "I don't expect he'll wake until well into tomorrow."

Jeremy took in the room and said, "I'll have a Pinkerton detective, in plain clothes, sit with him and that will allow you both to get some rest."

Tim squeezed Dora's hand and said, "That sounds like a good idea. Let's head home and we can come back refreshed tomorrow."

Dora looked hesitant but nodded. "We can wait for your detective, Jeremy."

"Cole has already notified them, and he should be here soon."

They heard a knock on the door; Dora looked worried. Jeremy went to the door, opened it a crack, and saw it was his detective.

"Come in," Jeremy opened the door to let him in. He started giving introductions, "This is Detective Kilroy. He'll be here through tomorrow." Jeremy introduced him to each person in the room.

Kilroy nodded his head and said quietly, "I won't let anything happen to the boy."

Jeremy said to him, "Come with me, and I will introduce you to the other Sisters working tonight."

When everyone felt the security was in place and that the boy was well protected, they headed home. It was after Emma's shift and she accompanied them home for some sleep.

CHAPTER 33

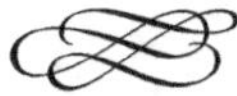

She and Jeremy got back into bed at 5am and slept until 10. They heard a knock on the door and a voice said, "Emma, we're going to the hospital soon. If you're coming with us, you need to come down now."

Jeremy said in a low voice to Emma, "Have you had enough rest?" He was concerned because she would have to go back that evening.

Emma yawned broadly. "I'm tired, but I would like to be there when the boy wakes up."

"So, we go?" he asked, sitting up in the bed.

"We go," she confirmed.

Jeremy retired to his room to get ready for the day. Emma did the same. They met outside their rooms on the staircase to head down to the kitchen.

Dora was there and had breakfast ready for them. She saw Emma and said, "I'm sorry I woke you."

Emma hastened to assure her, "No, no, I want to go with you. It's okay, I'll get a few hours' sleep this afternoon."

They ate their breakfast and headed down to the hospital together. They made their way up the second floor, passing people on the stairs. Emma looked around, thinking, *It's so different in the daytime. I wonder what kind of security is in place during the day? I'll have to follow up on that with Sister Catherine.*

They exited into the hallway and Emma noticed the day Sisters were in place. She would have to get their names. Sister Catherine was already there waiting for them outside the boy's door.

She smiled as they approached and, before they could ask, she said, "He's fine and he's awake. Follow me, please."

Tim and Dora had wide smiles on their faces as they approached the door. What they found when they entered was an animated little boy. His face was flushed almost the color of his bright red hair.

Doesn't even look like the same boy, Emma thought to herself. *The drugs really changed his personality.*

Jeremy looked at Detective Kilroy and inclined his head for him to follow and give them a debriefing. Emma motioned to Tim and Dora that she would be following behind Jeremy.

On his way out, Kilroy said to Tim and Dora, "Oh, his name is Patrick. His mom calls him Pat."

Dora nodded, not taking her eyes off of Patrick. They wanted to get him moved to the boarding house to keep him safe. They also wanted to find out more about his parents so he could go home.

Emma motioned to Sister Catherine. "Could you let Tim and Dora know if Patrick is okay to go home with them?"

Sister Catherine acknowledged the question with a nod of her head, knowing he would be safer away from the hospital. "I'll let them know now."

"Sister," Emma reached out a hand toward her, "thank you so much for helping Patrick."

Sister Catherine took her hand and said, "We're here for him as long as he needs us." She gave Emma's hand a brief squeeze before walking toward Patrick's door. She knocked and Tim immediately answered.

"Could I speak with you and Dora for a moment?" Sister Catherine inquired.

Tim nodded and called back to Dora, who joined them out in the hallway.

"Would you accompany me to my office?" Sister Catherine asked.

"Of course." Tim waved to Kilroy to come back into the room. Jeremy and Kilroy had completed their meeting and were waiting in the hallway. "We need to meet with Sister Catherine," said Tim.

Kilroy nodded and returned to his post.

Tim and Dora followed Sister Catherine to her office. Tim inquired as the door closed, "Were there any problems after we left last night?"

Sister Catherine started. "No, completely quiet. I wanted to speak with you about Patrick." Dora sucked in her breath, afraid of what might be coming next. "He seems in perfect health. There appeared to be no effects from the drugs he was given."

Dora released the breath she was holding, crossed herself, and sent a silent prayer in thanks. Tim reached out his hand to her.

Dora took it and said hopefully, "Does that mean we can take him to the boarding house?"

She smiled. "It does mean he can be moved."

Dora said, with tears in her eyes, "Thank you so much. We'll work hard to locate his parents."

"I have faith in you both and pray for the safe return of his family." With that, she stood and showed them to the door. They headed back to Patrick's room. Emma and Jeremy were waiting outside for them.

Dora rushed up and said, "Emma, Sister Catherine says we can take Patrick to the boarding house."

"Good," she said, relieved. "It will be easier to protect him there."

Jeremy said, "I'll arrange the transport. We should be ready to go in about an hour."

"I'll stay here and help with the move when you are ready," said Tim. He looked at Dora and said, "We need to tell Patrick what is happening so he won't be scared."

"Yes, all of us together," said Dora.

As they entered the room, they saw Patrick talking with a Sister. "Dora! Tim! You're back!"

Dora smiled brightly, covering up her sadness. "Patrick, yes, we're back and we would like to talk to you about something." He looked curious and waited for her to continue. "We would like you to come stay with me, Tim, Jeremy, and Emma. We have a house where we all live together."

"But what about Mom and Dad? Will they come there also?" he asked, puzzled.

Dora clarified her statement. "We would like you to stay with us until we can locate your mom and dad. Would you like that?"

"I would love that! Can we go now?" he asked excitedly.

They laughed at his exuberance, but under the surface, they were sad he wasn't coming with them for happier reasons.

Jeremy stuck his head in the door and said, "We're ready."

"Okay then." Emma looked at Dora and Tim and asked, "Can you get Patrick dressed?"

"I think we can handle that," said Tim, grabbing Patrick's pants and tossing them at the laughing boy.

"Okay, we'll be in the hall waiting for you," Emma said as she exited. She wanted a final meeting with Sister Catherine, to confirm she would be back that night.

When everyone was ready, they exited the room and the group headed out. They had arranged for two cabs to be waiting outside for them. On the landing, Dora knelt in front of Patrick and said, "Patrick, we need to be as silent as a mouse. Can you do that for me?"

He seemed to understand that he needed to listen and follow their direction. He nodded and took her hand. Kilroy and Jeremy checked the alley before allowing them to exit the building. Once it was confirmed to be clear, they covered Patrick with a blanket and placed him on the floor of the carriage. Jeremy had arranged for Pinkerton detectives to be the drivers, in case of trouble.

Arriving home, they moved Patrick quietly into the house. Emma was very grateful they no longer had boarders who were not team members. Dora had cautioned the team that they must keep quiet about Patrick living there.

The minute Patrick was in the house and the blanket was removed, he wanted to see everything. Dora could tell they weren't going to get much information at that time and said, "Let's have lunch first, and then we'll sit and talk with him." She thought of something and asked Emma in a low voice, "Emma, do you have any of our old toys?"

Emma thought for a moment and whispered, "I have some blocks and a dancing man toy."

"Bring them down and we can talk with him in the library after lunch," Dora said.

Tim, Emma, Dora, Jeremy, and Patrick sat down for lunch. Once they finished, they moved to the library to speak with Patrick. Dora planned to take the lead in the questioning; she sat on the floor with the toys and said, "Patrick, I have some toys here if you would like to sit down and play with me."

He had seen the toys and hoped they were for him to play with. He nodded eagerly and sat on the floor with her, picking up the blocks.

As he played, Dora asked, "Patrick, do you know your last name?"

"Blake," he said as he stacked the blocks.

"Do you know your mom and dad's first names?"

"Da's is the same as mine," he said proudly, tilting his head up. "He is senior, and I am junior."

"Wonderful. Patrick. Can you tell us when you last saw your parents?" Dora asked casually as she added blocks to his building.

He didn't answer. Instead, he picked up the dancing man and tried to operate it. Emma knelt next to him and showed him how to make it dance. It made him smile, and they let him play with it for a moment.

Dora tried again. "Patrick, can you remember when you last saw your parents?"

This time, he answered. "We were at the fair. They had ponies and fun games."

Emma jotted down the information. She edged closer to Tim and asked, "Is that enough for you to look into his background?"

Tim said in a low voice only she could hear, "Yes, I'll ask around this afternoon."

"Quietly," she cautioned in a low voice.

"Yes, of course," he said, watching Dora with Patrick.

Dora wasn't finished with her questions. "Patrick, one more thing. Does your Da work?"

"He sells fruit," he said proudly. "He gets all the fruit we want to eat. "

Tim waved to Emma and Jeremy to step into the foyer. "I'll head there now."

"Tim, do you need someone with you?" asked Jeremy.

"It couldn't hurt, but you'll need to change," Tim commented, looking at Jeremy's nice suit.

Jeremy looked down and smiled. "I think I have some things I can wear. Meet you downstairs in five?" He went quickly upstairs and changed into an older set of clothes and went back down to meet Tim.

Before Jeremy left, he turned to Emma and reminded her, "You need to get some rest."

"I will," she promised.

She headed upstairs as soon as they left.

Dora spent the afternoon with Patrick, playing and showing him how to make pastry.

CHAPTER 34

Jeremy and Tim took the wagon to the outskirts of the Hells. Tim directed, "We'll walk from there."

Tim saw a boy he knew hanging out nearby and called, "Hey, John."

"Hey, Tim. What's up?" John asked as he walked over.

"Can you watch the wagon and horse for me?"

"What's in it for me?" he asked, knowing Tim.

"How about this much?" he asked and counted out 50 cents. The boy's eyes went wide, and he tried to be nonchalant, saying, "I can only be here for a little while."

"Okay, we'll be back." They headed down the main road, where most of the vendors had set up booths to sell their goods. These included fruit, vegetables, meat, and other types of items. The smells and the people's accents made them pause occasionally to take it all in.

"Where are we headed?" asked Jeremy.

"I know one of the fruit vendors who might know Patrick's parents."

They continued further down the street, avoiding pickpockets and many offers from vendors. When they reached the booth Tim had been looking for, he called out, "Sean!"

The man heard his name and looked their way. He came over when he saw who it was. "Tim! So good to see you. Got any pies with you?"

"Not today," Tim said regretfully. "Jeremy, this is Sean O'Connell. Sean, we're looking for someone, actually a family. The name is Patrick Blake. I don't know his wife's name, but they have a five-year-old son."

Sean heard the request and replied in a very quiet voice, "Yes, I know where you can locate them." He looked over his shoulder and asked loudly, "Hey, Tom, could you watch my stand?"

"Sure, don't be long," Tom commented as he walked over from the stand next store.

"Come with me," said Sean. They accompanied him into an alley over a few blocks and into a business. Tim and Jeremy realized where they were; it was a mortuary parlor.

"What happened?" asked Tim quietly.

"Little Patrick went missing. Patrick senior and Adeline, that was the mama's name, went to find him," said Sean.

"When was this?" asked Jeremy.

"A few days ago. Their bodies were found yesterday morning, just tossed in a ditch. Sadly, they had no money and will have to be buried in potter's field."

Tim muttered, "I think I can manage the funeral cost."

"Make that both of us," said Jeremy.

Sean's eyes teared up, and he was not embarrassed to let them fall. Once he got his emotions under control, Jeremy asked, "Does Patrick have any other family here?"

"No, they were first-generation from Ireland. Most of their family died in the potato famine. I understood there were no other relatives. Were you able to find little Patrick?" he said, hope in his voice.

"Yes, but don't mention that to anyone. We're trying to figure out who took him," requested Jeremy. He continued, "Do you know if any other children have gone missing?"

Sean sat down heavily on a chair, saying in a weary voice, "I don't know how many, but yes, we have children missing. People are scared to go to the police, and they are keeping their children close." He looked over at Tim and asked, "Is there something you can do?"

"There might be. Where were the kids taken from?" asked Jeremy.

"We aren't sure. They just didn't come home from school," Sean said. He gripped his knees and stood. "I need to get back."

Jeremy broke the silence on the way home. "Can you get us a list of the children?"

"Yes, I can put it together now—if you have time," Sean said.

"We do." Jeremy and Tim said at the same time. He nodded and they followed him back to his stand.

Tim took out a piece of paper and a pencil and said, "I am ready."

Sean listed the names that he had heard. They thanked him and went to retrieve their wagon.

"So many," said Tim, shaking his head.

"There are at least 20 names here and he said he wasn't sure he had all of them. I need to see Cole about what we learned. Keep the information about other kidnappings quiet for now. We need to form a plan."

"I will. Can I share the information about the parents with Dora and Patrick?" asked Tim.

Jeremy sighed. "Yes. What about Patrick? Who will he end up with?"

"I think Dora will have an idea on that," he commented, certain she was already falling for the boy.

Jeremy nodded and said simply, "I'm glad."

They made their way back to the wagon and thanked John

for watching it. Tim dropped Jeremy off at the Pinkerton office to review the current status of the case with Cole. He then went home, in a deliberately slow manner, thinking how to tell Dora about Patrick's parents. He entered the boarding house via the kitchen. He saw Dora wasn't there and when Amy saw him, she said, "She's in the dining room."

"Thanks, Amy," he said and headed there. Dora looked toward the door as he entered and started to go to him. The expression on his face caused her to sink back into her seat. "Where's Patrick?" Tim asked.

"Papa took him downstairs to show him some experiments," Dora said quietly, searching his face for information.

"Has Emma left yet?" he asked, delaying the inevitable conversation.

"Yes," she said slowly, "she left about thirty minutes ago. I did get her to eat and to promise to rest if there's time." She couldn't wait any longer and said pleadingly, "Tim, tell me!"

"Let's go into the sitting room," he suggested. She nodded and followed. She sat down and watched as he sank heavily onto the couch and put his face in his hands. He finally lifted his head and gazed at her, saying simply, "Dead."

"Dead?" she asked incredulously.

"Yes. Patrick's parents tried to find him on their own and were killed. Their bodies were tossed in a ditch," he said, his voice turning hard.

Dora was thinking ahead. "Is Emma in danger?"

"No, she has what Patrick's parents didn't—a team behind her, who won't let anything happen to her."

"What will happen now?" Dora asked.

"We found out other children are missing. It might all be connected with the drugs and the hospital. Jeremy said they would continue to the investigation."

"You say, children? So, it's bigger than just Patrick?" she asked.

"Yes, Sean provided a list of at least twenty who have disappeared."

"So many, will they find them all?" "Even if we find where they are holding them, they all might not be there."

"No. That many children would be hard to manage."

"They may have moved them already."

Dora didn't cry this time; she knew she needed to be strong. "Did you find out if Patrick has family he can go to?"

"There's no one. No family either here or in the old country."

At that moment, Patrick raced in and jumped into Tim's lap. He was such a lovely child.

"What about us, Tim?" asked Dora, watching him pull Patrick close to his chest. Patrick giggled and struggled to get out of the hold.

"I would love that," he said and reached out a hand toward hers. She took it and they sat wondering if this was their new family. They hadn't expected Patrick to need them as parents; they only wanted to care for a lost child. Tim cleared his throat and took Patrick off of his lap so he and Dora could talk to him.

Dora started, "Patrick."

"Yes, Dora?"

"Do you know what heaven is?"

Patrick suddenly smiled and said, "Yes, my grandma and grandda are in heaven. God watches out for them."

Dora forced the tears back and Tim cleared his throat. "Patrick, you know I went to look for your parents today? We told you that earlier?"

"Yes," Patrick said, going very still. Children always seemed to have an awareness of sad events.

"We spoke to your neighbors and friends. Do you know Sean? He works next to your Da's booth and sells fruit?"

Patrick didn't say anything; he just waited with wide eyes.

Dora said softly, "Patrick, today we learned your parents have gone to heaven to be with your grandparents."

"Why would they go? Was I bad? I didn't mean to be taken," he said plaintively, wiping tears from his eyes with his sleeves.

Tim hastily assured him, "No, Patrick, that was bad people doing bad things."

Patrick sat down on the floor, picking up loose blocks. He finally looked up at Dora and said in a heartbreaking voice, "I want my mama."

He started to cry, and Dora gathered him up with her on the couch. Tim moved closer and they sat there together for a long while. They would give Patrick time to adjust to the news before suggesting he stay with them permanently.

CHAPTER 35

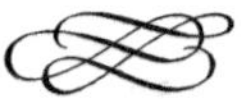

Jeremy strode up to the Pinkertons offices, saying over his shoulder to the staff, "Be prepared for a meeting in a few minutes," and entered Cole's office.

"Hey, Pops," he said as he sat in the guest chair in front of the desk.

Cole started, "The boy's parents?"

Jeremy sat forward, a frown darkening his face, and said, "Dead. Probably killed by the same group we're trying to locate."

Cole pushed back his chair. "Horrible. Do you think there are other children involved?"

"Yes, we got a list of kids who have gone missing." He handed it to Cole. "We have to stop them."

"Agreed," Cole said firmly.

"Are the men in place for tonight?"

"Yes. We want to keep a low profile. We don't want to spook them," directed Cole.

"Do you think she will try again so soon?" asked Jeremy.

"I think she will. They had a child get away and the medicine was probably for that child. They'll have to make up for losing him," Cole said, understanding the children were part of a plan in a very ugly business.

"I'll notify Emma about our plans and what we found out," Jeremy said, standing. "I told the men to meet in the conference room for an update."

"Good, let's head in now," Cole said as he accompanied Jeremy out.

Jeremy was thinking about the meeting as he headed back to the boarding house. He found out that Emma had already gone to the hospital and headed there to inform her about what was going to happen that evening.

As he entered, he went directly to the second floor. The Sisters saw him approaching and motioned him toward the patient ward. He walked to the large room looking around, finally spotting her sitting next to an elderly lady holding her hand and reading to her. They both seemed to be enjoying the company.

He walked up quietly and tapped her on the shoulder.

She looked up with a smile on her face. "Jeremy, hi. This is Martha."

He took Martha's fragile hand in his and leaned over to say, "It's very nice to meet you."

Martha was an elderly woman with white hair and a pale complexion. She blushed when the good-looking gentleman paid attention to her. "Can I steal her away from you?" Jeremy asked kindly.

"You may, young man," she said and looked over at Emma. "Come back to see me?"

"I will," Emma promised, leaning down to kiss her cheek. She got up and followed Jeremy out of the ward and into the hallway. "Visiting?" she inquired.

"Yes and no." He briefed her on Patrick's parents. "We think the 'Sister' will be back tonight."

"Yes," she said, trying not to think about Patrick's loss; she followed his train of thought. "If this does involve a certain number of children, she will be short, with the loss of Patrick. That means an additional kidnapping and more drugs to keep them subdued."

"What time did you see her access the closet?" Jeremy asked.

"3:30am. I expect she'll follow the same schedule since she's gotten away with it up until now."

"Okay, so we wait," he agreed.

She nodded.

"I'll be outside watching, and we'll tail her," he suggested.

Emma was drumming her fingers on her lips and asked, "What if you miss her coming in?" A thought came to her, and she pointed to the window facing the road. "I know! I can use my portable gas light to signal you from that window there. When she's headed down."

"Good idea," he said. "I'll be close and will keep an eye on it." They parted ways with a soft kiss.

The evening went along quietly with Emma completing her rounds and helping the Sisters. She looked at her watch and realized it was nearly 3am; she hurried to finish wrapping bandages and put them into the cupboard. Rushed footsteps sounded, giving her just enough time to crawl under the nurses' station. Emma had made sure all of the Sisters stayed in the ward during the hour she thought she might arrive. She didn't want them in harm's way. The door closed, and she lit her lamp quickly and went to the window.

A creak could be heard as the door opened, she extinguished the light and dove back under the nurses' station. Staying still she waited for the door to the stairway to open and close. She stuck her head out and looked tentatively around. Once she confirmed the 'Sister' had left, she quickly went to the ward door and waved at Sister Mary.

She approached Emma and said, "Yes?"

"She was here. I'm going to follow her," Emma said quickly.

Sister Mary nodded and said quietly, "Careful."

"I will be," she said and headed down the stairs. She caught a glimpse of Jeremy's team tailing the "Sister" and stayed back, letting them take the lead. She caught up with them as they surrounded the apartment building, waiting for someone to exit.

They waited 20-30 minutes and, this time, two men in working-class clothing exited the apartment building. They had another child with them—a little girl. She was noticeably drugged and one of the men carried her loosely on his shoulder.

Jeremy had cautioned everyone to remain unemotional and follow the men and child to the drop-off location. They walked a few blocks and climbed into a waiting carriage. Jeremy had planned for this contingency and had transportation nearby. His men followed on foot to get the direction the men were headed in.

Jeremy waved for Emma to join him and the two detectives. When she got in the carriage, he commented, "The others will follow."

They were able to catch up to the two men and kept the carriage within view as they made their way toward a warehouse at the dock. The carriage pulled over, they moved past and pulled out of site into an alley. They approached the warehouse, Jeremy had the men divided in half to enter from the front and the back. "We need to approach this silently and do not draw your guns unless there is no other choice," he directed.

Emma had her large knife out and followed the direction of the agents entering the front of the building. Their group made their way through the mostly empty space. As they approached the back, they saw a room with a single door. Jeremy signaled the team to hold back and waved at Emma to approach. She glanced in the room through the window in the door. Ducking down after a long glance, she signaled to Jeremy, holding up four fingers, and mouthed, "Four men and the kids are there."

Jeremy got the message and signaled the men to hit the door hard with guns drawn. The men knew there were children in the room, and they were instructed not to fire unless fired upon.

It was a mad rush, the men inside, not expecting the ambush, were easily subdued. As they were taken into custody, another man walked in casually from the back, wiping his hands. When he realized what was happening, he grabbed the nearest child to shield himself and started yelling, "You're going to let me out of here or I'll kill her!"

All of the agents had their guns directed at the man, but they didn't want to hurt the child.

Jeremy glanced around, saw Emma, and motioned to her. The man holding the child would expect a gun but not a knife. She gripped it in her hand and waited until he was looking at the guns. He was continuing to talk, demanding to be allowed to go.

Emma took the opportunity to throw her knife. She had a clear path to his right shoulder. As soon as the knife hit, he dropped the child and an agent rushed to grab her before she hit the floor.

As he collapsed to the floor, gripping his shoulder, Emma walked over, put her boot on his neck, and pressed down as she reached for her knife. She pulled it out and wiped it on the man's shirt, saying laconically. "Well, Harry, we meet again."

He looked at her in surprise. "You again!"

"You think I wouldn't know you? You're the same as you were before, a coward. You have a thing for kids, don't you?" She pressed harder on his neck with her boot and said in a low voice, "You don't involve children. Ever. Do you understand?" She leaned down while examining her blade, thinking she would have no problem plunging it into his chest and ending him.

Jeremy saw the emotions across her face and took charge. "Nick, take him."

"Sure, take the scumbag away," Emma said. Jeremy sent two of his guys to get Cole to provide transport wagons for the criminals and the children.

"Jeremy, we need to get them out of here fast," she said, referring to the children.

"What do you suggest?" he asked, looking at them lined up on the floor in two rows of 15 total.

"Let me check each one first," Emma said.

She had learned how to take pulse rates at the hospital. She checked each, trying to not look too closely at them. Emotions need to be removed from the situation until they had them in a safe location.

Emma called to Jeremy as she finished with the last child. "They are breathing. If we each take a child, we should be able to get them out of here and to the hospital."

They had the fifteen men they needed. Each took a child and exited the building. Cole had sent wagons over immediately and asked that they meet a few streets over, going through the alleys.

They made their way to the waiting wagons, each agent staying with their assigned child. The trip to the hospital was handled quietly. Emma went up and notified the Sisters that they would need temporary space for the children. The Sisters used a portion of the ward not occupied by patients and started making pallets on the floor for them.

The Pinkertons moved the kids upstairs and helped roll out blankets for each child. It was a very crowded space, but it was warm.

Sister Catherine had been notified and arrived to help. She just shook her head when she saw them. "I'm relieved we found them before further harm could come to them. "

The nurse was checking pulse and heartbeats. "God was with you," she said, crossing herself.

Jeremy wanted to get to the apartment to see if Cole needed help and said to Emma, "Can you keep an eye on the situation? We'll leave guards here."

"Yes, I'll be here," she said, wanting to stay with the children.

"Thank you," Jeremy said before leaving.

Sister Catherine came over to stand next to her. Emma looked over at her and gently teased, "I guess we need to discuss increasing the security on your drug closet now."

"Yes, but if she hadn't stolen from our less than secure drug closet, we wouldn't have had you here and these children may not have been saved," Sister Catherine said, looking at the bright side of things.

"Yes," agreed Emma.

"Prayers were answered with your intervention tonight."

Jeremy had rushed out to see if any help was needed for the takedown at the apartment building. He got to the location as they were bringing out a very angry woman. She was still wearing the habit but had taken off the coif. While Cole lead her out, she didn't look defeated; she still looked defiant. Cole was aware she thought she had won and said to Jeremy so she could hear, "Did you get them?"

"Yes, we have them all and the crew is in custody. Oh, and surprisingly, Harry Simpson was involved in this," commented Jeremy.

That caused a reaction from her. She opened and closed her mouth, the false bravado visibly sliding away.

"You're going away for a long time," said Cole, pushing her forward.

She dug her heels in and said, "What if I can give you someone else?"

Cole stopped pushing and looked at her consideringly. "We will listen, but because you involved children, there will be no special deals." He handed her off to a police officer to place into the wagon.

As they watched her go, Cole asked, "How are the children?"

"Sister Catherine seems to think they will just sleep it off. I left the men there to guard them. Do you think they will come for them again?" asked Jeremy.

Cole was contemplative about that. "I wouldn't think so. This type of operation only works if no one suspects it's happening. They will probably disappear for now."

"Will she give us a name?" Jeremy asked curiously.

A shot rang out and, as Cole and Jeremy dove for cover behind the carriage, they saw the 'Sister' go down. Cole waved at his men to investigate where the shot came from. They watched and all stayed quiet. They made their way to where she lay on the ground. She had a hole in her head that exited out the other side." I guess they didn't want her to talk," said Cole wryly.

"Doesn't look like we will get much information out of her," responded Jeremy in a similar tone. "What about Harry? Do you think we will get a name out of him?"

"He probably only knows her name and not the mastermind. I'll be surprised if we find out anything more from tonight's activities," said Cole.

CHAPTER 36

POLICE STATION

The police chief walked in, immaculate as always, and said, "Well, what do we have here?" Cole listed the information they had, the arrest they had made, and where the body was located. "Any idea who the woman was?" he asked his assistant.

"Several of the people we got from the warehouse have said Beatrice Purvis," he replied.

The police chief asked Jeremy, "The kids?"

"They're okay, but we'll need help locating their families."

"Of course. I'll send some officers over," said the police chief.

They continued discussing how they might get the kids home when a delivery boy came into the station stating, "Note for Jeremy Tilden."

Jeremy took the note, opened it, and read. He suddenly started laughing and folded the paper up before saying, "Emma has an idea that could help identify the kids in a faster manner. She would like to use Jake to take pictures of them and put their names on them to make the identification easier. She recommends setting this up for early afternoon tomorrow when the kids are expected to be awake"

"Jake Cooper is our forensic photographer," reminded the police chief's assistant Jim. "He's very good at his job."

"Yes, he's also a team member of Emma's and lives at their boarding house," commented Jeremy.

"Interesting," said the police chief, thinking of the young man who kept to himself. He nodded decisively and said, "That is a good idea. Jim, send a note over to Jake to work with Jeremy on the pictures." Jim was taking notes and nodded.

CHAPTER 37

HOSPITAL

Jeremy came back to the hospital to sit with Emma. The kids were on pallets and a guardian sat next to each. He murmured, "The police chief likes your idea of utilizing Jake."

"Good," she said quietly. She asked, feeling too tired to go herself, "Would you mind contacting Tim to let him know about our plans and Jake's involvement?"

"I will." He kissed her head and went to find Tim at the boarding house. It was about an hour later when she felt him return to her side.

"What did Tim say?" she asked, dropping her head on his shoulder, fatigue making her voice lower.

"He agreed to make sure Jake was on board in the morning," he said. "Try to get some rest. I will watch." She was so tired, she didn't argue.

It was a long night sitting with the kids and everyone was very tired, but no one wanted to leave until the first child woke up. The morning was slow in coming but when the first child awoke, the entire ward became invigorated.

CHAPTER 38

BOARDING HOUSE

Tim waited until early morning to have a conversation with Jake about their plans for identifying the kids.

Jake wasn't sure overall. "But I'm supposed to be at work."

Tim had dealt with Jake on many occasions and said in a reasonable voice, "Jake, listen to me. The police chief wants you to take the kid's pictures as part of your job. You saw the note."

Jake was unconvinced. "This isn't part of my normal duties. I'm not sure."

"Jake, I promise that, as soon as we get the pictures developed, you can go to your work and print them."

He seemed reluctant but finally agreed to take his camera and accompany Tim to the hospital.

They found Emma still there. Tim saw her wince as she stood.

"Emma, we can handle things from here; you should go home and get some rest."

She waited a moment until the pain subsided. "I'm okay. I was just sitting funny," she insisted. "Though I could use some sleep," she admitted.

"Is Jeremy still here?" asked Tim.

She shook her head and said, "He wanted to see if Harry had told the police any additional information last night."

Tim nodded. "We'll get the pictures and names of the kids so we can meet with the community leaders."

He started to turn back to Jake when Emma said in a low voice, "Tim, I need to speak with you."

Before he walked with her, he said, "Jake, I'll be right back. Wait for me here." Jake nodded, not looking up from his equipment. Tim glanced around and said, "Over here." They retreated to a small alcove where they could have some privacy.

Emma started, "The police investigating the warehouse came by this morning; they found some kids who didn't survive. They must have been experimenting with how much of the laudanum and morphine to give them."

Tim froze at the news; he didn't move until Emma called his name, concerned.

He shook his head and said, "I need just a moment." He gathered himself and wiped his eyes as he tried to be unemotional. "I think we need to have pictures of them also."

"Yes. Jake should be okay with those. Taking pictures of the dead is part of his normal job."

"I'll get him started. We'll get both sets of prints completed," said Tim.

*E*mma felt another pain in her abdomen as she headed home. She stopped and put her head down, the dizziness became overwhelming. She sat on the sidewalk and waited until the dizziness had gone away. *Did I strain something when I lifted the children?* She pulled herself up and forced herself to her home. She slowly made her way home and entered the front door.

Dora was waiting for her in the dining room. When she saw her, she said, "Come in here, you need to eat."

"Yes," Emma said, her voice strained. She noticed Patrick playing nearby. "Dora, can you have Amy watch him for a moment? I need to talk to you."

Dora could tell Emma was serious and did as she asked. "Amy, could you come get Patrick?" She looked at Patrick and asked, "Would you like to help Amy ice a cake?"

He nodded eagerly and when Amy came out, he rushed to grab her hand and headed into the kitchen.

"He seems to be doing pretty well," commented Emma, watching him leave the room.

"Yes, I think it affects him mostly at night—nightmares, crying," said Dora.

"That sounds familiar," said Emma.

"Yes," agreed Dora. "I hope we can be here for him like you and Papa were for me. Let's move into the sitting room."

They walked arm and arm into the room. Emma sat down on the couch and let her head fall back.

Dora waited as patiently as possible and finally said, "Emma, tell me."

Emma sat for a moment, staring off into space, then stated abruptly, "Dora, they killed five of the kids. We think they were experimenting on the number of drugs to keep them quiet."

Dora covered her mouth, tears streaming down her face. Emma just felt too tired to cry. Dora came over and sat next to her. She pulled herself together and said, "You need to eat and go to bed."

"But—"

"No! We have plenty of people working on this, and I don't think working yourself to exhaustion will help anyone."

"Yes, Mom," she teased.

"Can you make it upstairs by yourself?"

"Yes," she said, though she felt another twinge of pain.

"Are you okay?" Dora asked, concerned with the pain Emma appeared to be in.

"Yes, I just lifted too much today." She headed upstairs, washed up, and changed into her nightclothes. As she was climbing into bed, Dora brought a tray up to her.

She helped settle it on Emma and said that she had prepared her favorite things: chicken soup and fresh bread. Dora sat quietly as she finished her meal.

She took the tray and said, "Get some rest."

Emma settled down to sleep. Just before she nodded off, she heard the side door open and the bookcase shift away. A cold body slid in next to her. They didn't talk; they just slept.

CHAPTER 40

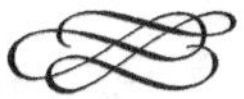

BACK AT THE HOSPITAL

Tim and Jake worked with each child to get their names and pictures. The older children helped supply names for kids who were either too scared or too young to answer.

When they had finished, Tim addressed the group. "Listen, we'll be developing the pictures today and meeting with your parents to have you picked up. Until then, the Sisters and these gentlemen will continue to watch you."

Jake and Tim took the camera to the police station to develop the pictures.

Jake worked through the afternoon to get the film developed and Tim worked as his assistant. The time was fast approaching for a meeting with the parents.

Cole and Jeremy picked up Tim to go to the meeting. They had told the families of the missing children to be there at 8:30pm. It was very crowded when they entered, and the masses surged toward them. Everyone seemed to be demanding, "Did you find them? Where are they?"

"Let's quiet down!" A local policeman from the area stepped between the crowd and Tim, saying, "If you sit, we can begin."

Some looked like they wanted to argue, but they took their seats and waited.

The officer introduced Tim, Cole, and Jeremy to the group. Tim stepped up to the podium and said bluntly, "We have found some of the kidnapped children."

That statement caused the group to start speaking all at once. Tim responded by holding up his hands and saying, "Please, be patient. We need to tell you how we're handling this."

"How long will we have to wait?" shouted one of the parents, desperation evident in his voice.

"Just overnight. We'll have the pictures and names all organized by that time." People were murmuring when the mention of pictures came up. "We need you to keep quiet for now, until we can get you the pictures for you to identify your child," Tim continued.

"Why can't we go identify the kids in person?" one woman asked, bewildered at their methods.

"We don't think we got everyone involved in this, and we want to make sure kids get back to their actual parents. What we would like from you are your first and last names. For the children, that should include names, descriptions, and ages."

They agreed to provide the needed information and kept the news about the dead children quiet. The families started to line up to provide the information.

The man who had asked the earlier question asked, "You are sure we'll see the pictures in the morning?"

"We're working on them now. We'll all meet here tomorrow at 10am," Tim confirmed to the group. Most nodded and agreed to be there to view the pictures.

As they were leaving, a woman came up, crying heavily. "My Shannon, have you seen him?"

A man rushed up to take her in his arms. "Doireann, let them get the pictures to us. We'll see them tomorrow." He tried to take her away.

"Are they safe where they are?" she asked, not willing to move.

Cole confirmed softly, "We have protection in place for the children."

"Thank you," she murmured. She visibly calmed down and allowed herself to be led away.

As they were headed home in the wagon, Cole said, "That went well, or as well as it could have."

Tim said, "Now, we wait for Jake to complete the pictures."

That evening, Emma returned to the hospital and started reading to the children. She noticed her audience included some of the more mobile adults as well.

After she completed her story, Emma was giving out crackers to the children when the familiar pain on her right side flared up again. Only, this time, it seemed to be spreading to her lower back and belly. The pain became so intense, she doubled over. When it passed, she stood and took two steps before falling to the floor. She didn't hear the children calling for help.

She didn't know how much time passed before she woke, but she realized she was in a bed. A doctor was leaning over her, pressing on her stomach, making her cry out in pain.

"What's happening?" she asked in a dazed voice, realizing she was laying on her back. She looked around and saw she was in one of the private rooms.

The doctor ignored her question and asked one of his own. "How long have you been having this pain?"

"Off and on for a few weeks," she admitted.

"Shut the door, please," the doctor requested, and a Sister assisting him immediately did so and returned to the bed.

"Emma, are you having amorous congress?" the doctor asked.

"Yes," she said, aware of what the term meant. She refused to show any embarrassment.

The sister's color deepened a bit, but she did not offer any judgment.

"I will need to check your breasts. Is that okay?" he asked.

"Yes," Emma said, trying not to be uncomfortable.

He then pressed on her breasts and noticed her moving restlessly. "Turn on your back, please." He moved his hands down to her lower back and belly. She yelped in pain. "When was your last menstrual cycle?" he asked, attentive to her pain.

"I'm late," she muttered. "I didn't think anything of it."

"How late?" he inquired intently.

"About four weeks, though I've had some abnormal menstruation-just off and on."

"Have your breasts been tender?" he asked, watching her response as he touched them.

"Yes," she admitted.

"Cramping?" he inquired.

"Some, but light," Emma said. She was usually the one asking the questions and had to know what he was thinking. "Doctor, what's your suspicion?"

He looked at her for a long moment and said, "Your symptoms are leading to a diagnosis of ectopic pregnancy." He watched her and she didn't react, waiting for more information. "Your symptoms include all three of the main signs: a missed period, vaginal bleeding, and belly pain."

"Well, I certainly have those symptoms," she gasped out as the pain returned and she bent over. She took a deep breath as it passed and asked, "What do we do now?"

"I have some good news on that. There has been a successful surgery for an ectopic pregnancy performed by Doctor Lawson Tait in 1883."

"Can you perform the surgery?" she asked.

"I can," he acknowledged. "I trained with Dr. Tait in England."

"Is it dangerous?"

"It can be, but the survival rate is quite high for this procedure."

"Please, go into detail," she requested, trying to breathe through the pain.

"I will remove the affected tube along with the embryo. You may not be able to have children, but the surgery could save your life," he said seriously. "This will need to be scheduled—" He cut off when she doubled up in pain again.

The door opened and Jeremy rushed in. "Emma, are you all right? What happened?" he asked, panicked. Emma was his rock.

She was in too much pain to answer. His eyes searched the room, looking for answers.

The doctor stepped closer to the bed. "Are you her friend?" he asked. His tone indicated he was asking if Jeremy and Emma were more than friends.

"Yes," answered Jeremy, aware there could be judgments about their arrangement. "What's wrong with her? Why is she in so much pain?"

"She has an ectopic pregnancy," he said.

"She's pregnant?" Jeremy asked, dazed.

"Not in the way you mean," commented the doctor.

"Can the baby survive, Doctor?" asked Jeremy. He wanted to have all of the facts.

"No, I'm afraid not. It's not where it should be and it could kill her," he said regretfully.

Watching her, Jeremy was concerned that she was almost doubled up in pain and couldn't talk. He said, "Doctor, she's getting worse. What can you do for her?"

"Right now, we need to start preparing her for surgery. We'll give you some privacy." He and the Sister left with that comment.

Jeremy could do nothing but sit with Emma and hold her hand as she continued to struggle with the pain. He had never felt so helpless in his life. The door opened with a slam and the Sisters rushed in to move her and her bed out to surgery.

Jeremy sat in his chair, watching them move her, unsure what to do next. He got up and walked dazedly into the hall. Dora and Tim rushed down the hallway toward him.

Dora reached him first. "Jeremy, what happened? Where's Emma? Sister Catherine notified us that she collapsed."

"They took her to surgery," he said in a hoarse voice.

When he realized Jeremy wasn't able to share what was happening, Tim said quietly, "Dora, I'll go get a Sister to talk to us." He strode away, leaving Dora to comfort Jeremy.

A few minutes later, Tim and a Sister walked up. She said, "If you will accompany me into Emma's room." They nodded and followed behind her. Jeremy went to the nearest chair and slumped down as the Sister quietly explained what had happened.

"Oh goodness," Dora said, going white. "Will she be okay?"

"I'm sorry, we don't know at this time. We're hopeful, and she has the best doctor for this type of surgery," said the Sister compassionately.

"They don't know if she'll be okay!" Dora cried and buried her face into Tim's chest. He could only hold her and worry.

The Sister understood they needed some time, but asked that they move to the waiting room. Cole and Ellis arrived together to join the family waiting for word on Emma.

Ellis went to Dora. "Dora, what's happened to Emma? Was she in an accident?"

Dora said, "Papa, let's go sit down for a moment." They went to a quiet corner of the waiting room and she started to explain what had happened.

Papa listened and tears started to flow down his cheeks. "Will she be okay?"

Dora tried to keep her tears back. "They don't know, Papa. We need to pray that Sister comes through this."

Papa wiped his face and said, "Emma has always enjoyed a challenge. She will come through this." He took Dora's hands and they prayed for Emma to come through the surgery.

The time seemed to drag. Cole tried to get Jeremy to eat something, but he just stared forward.

The doctor finally appeared hours later, tired, and pulled off his cap.

Jeremy stood and waited. He shook himself out of his haze. "Is she okay?"

"Yes."

"Oh, thank goodness," Dora said, grabbing Papa's hand. He squeezed it and waited for the doctor to continue.

"Unfortunately, we had to remove the tube where the embryo was located. It will have long-term effects on her fertility."

Jeremy didn't care about anything at that moment but Emma's health. "How is she?"

"She'll be tired, and it will take time for her to recover."

"How long will she need to be here?" asked Dora.

"Just a few days, if you can get her to stay in bed for at least three weeks at home."

Jeremy smiled wryly and said, "That will be the hard part." Everyone laughed.

They all waited until Emma was moved back to her room. Once they had her settled, the group moved quietly to her side, staying until here her eyelids fluttered.

Emma said as she awoke, still not able to focus. "Dora, are you here?"

"Yes, Sister, I'm here," Dora said, squeezing the hand she was holding.

She closed her eyes and said, "Papa, Jeremy?"

"We're all here, little girl," Papa replied.

"Good," and she went back to sleep.

Emma slept through the next few days. Jeremy sat at her bedside the entire time. He didn't want to budge from that spot.

Papa and Dora took turns coming to visit, bringing food and drinks.

CHAPTER 42

On the third day since her surgery, Emma was fully awake and was asking to get up. The doctor came in and cautioned her to take it easy. "You don't want to ruin my good work, do you?" he teased.

"No," she said grumpily. "How long until I'm back on my feet?"

"You're healing well, but it will be three weeks before you'll be allowed up," he murmured as he checked her incision.

"Three weeks!" she exclaimed.

"Emma," Jeremy started, "you have to listen, or you could hurt yourself."

"Okay, but I can go home?" she wheedled.

"Yes, this evening if you like," stated the doctor.

"Really?" asked Emma.

"Yes, I'll leave directions for your care with the Sisters. However, if you don't follow my orders, you'll end up back here. Do we understand each other?" he asked, looking her in the eye.

"Yes, I understand. I'll do as I'm told," she said earnestly.

Jeremy muttered something under his breath and Emma shot him a look that said for him to be quiet.

"I'll leave you now," said the doctor as he exited the room. He believed her when she said she'd listen and take it easy at home.

Emma was being very quiet and drumming her fingers on her lips. Jeremy knew she was planning. He grabbed that hand and said, "Emma, you know you have to rest."

"That doesn't mean bed, though. I could work on projects," she said evenly.

"Yes, and I'll be there to keep you company," he said firmly.

"Hmm." She started to think about the case. "Jeremy, I've been so out of it. Could you tell me about the children? What's happened?" she asked.

He started explaining. "We weren't able to get any further information from Harry other than to confirm Beatrice was his main contact."

"So, a dead end?"

"Yes, unfortunately," he said.

"What about the kids?"

"Jake got the pictures ready and we were able to identify the parents. We had some happy reunions."

"What about..." She trailed off.

Jeremy knew what she was asking. "The dead children?"

"Yes," she said steadily.

"We were able to narrow down who they were and identify them by clothing and hair. Those meetings were not fun," he admitted. "Cole and Tim did most of the communication."

Emma asked tentatively, "I understand you've been here with me all this time?"

"Where else would I be?" he asked, looking at her unwaveringly.

"Nowhere else," she acknowledged quietly. "Jeremy, let's go home."

"Let me get a Sister and make sure we don't do anything to hurt you."

He left the room and returned with Sister Anne. The

instructions were simple: rest for at least three weeks and then light walking.

"No bathing and no activities of a physical nature," the Sister said, turning a bit red.

Jeremy and Emma understood, and both said, "Yes, Sister Anne."

"I'll bring you some water and help you wash up before you leave," she said and exited to retrieve a washbasin and towels. She came back in as Jeremy was helping Emma sit on the side of the bed.

As they washed her, Emma pushed her hair back and said, "Ugh, I'm going to have to wash my hair."

"Just no full baths until the doctor releases you officially," Sister Anne reminded her.

Emma nodded.

"We can wash your hair at home. Maybe you can sit in front of the fire to dry it," he said, tempting her.

"That sounds like a plan," she said, wanting to feel clean again.

Sister Anne left to allow Emma some privacy to dress. Jeremy helped her pull on her skirt and top. She watched him struggle with her boots and said, "Could be worse. I could've had knives that popped out," she teased, referencing a previous case where the villain had knives as weapons in his shoes.

"Yes, well, this was hard enough," he said as he gave the boots a final tug.

A knock sounded at the door. "Come in," said Emma.

The doctor walked in with a smile on his face and said, "You look anxious to leave."

"Yes. I'm ready," Emma commented.

"We've had some problems keeping your visitors low. It will be way quieter for us with you gone," he joked.

Emma smiled and said, "I agree."

Jeremy stood and bent down to pick her up.

"Jeremy, I'm too heavy," she protested.

He just gave her a look; she saw it and stopped arguing. He carried her out of the room.

Papa met them at her hospital door saying, "Ready to go home, little girl?"

"Yes, Papa," she said, looking around. "Are Dora and Tim here also?"

"No. They're at home waiting for you. We didn't want to give the Sisters more people to deal with," he said softly. "Let's get you home."

They exited the hospital and Emma saw a carriage had been arranged to pick them up. Papa climbed in the conveyance and Jeremy handed her to him. As Jeremy climbed in, Papa carefully moved her to Jeremy's lap and put her legs over his.

Papa gave instructions to the driver, "Please, pull off carefully. We'll be taking it slow."

The driver nodded and started them off at a slow, steady pace. As they arrived home, Emma was again handed down to Jeremy. They climbed the stoop to the boarding house and saw Tim and Dora waiting in the foyer as they entered.

Dora rushed forward, kissed her on the cheek, and said, "You're finally home." She could tell how tired the short trip had made her and said, "Jeremy, take her upstairs. She'll need to rest."

"But—" Emma tried to protest.

"No. You're under my watch now." She saw Emma's face drop and said consolingly, "If you're good, I may let you sit downstairs with me later."

"You need to listen, little girl," said Papa.

Emma realized she was too fatigued to fight and acquiesced. Jeremy was worried; he had never seen Emma this tired.

"It's okay," mouthed Dora when she saw his expression.

He nodded and noticed Emma drifting off.

"Okay, let's get her upstairs," said Dora. Jeremy followed her up with a now sleeping Emma and laid her carefully on the bed. They removed her boots and loosened her collar. She didn't stir as they pulled her blanket over her.

They exited the room quietly. Dora was concerned about Jeremy; he had been at the hospital constantly since Emma had been ill.

"Jeremy, are you all right?" Dora inquired

"Yes. I think I'm just really tired also," he said, pushing a hand through his curly hair.

"Why don't you get a nap. too? I'll wake you both later," suggested Dora.

"You know, that's a good idea." He nodded, going into his room.

Dora smiled and watched him go into his room. Tim came up behind Dora, wrapping his arms around her waist, and asked quietly, "Are you going to tell her?"

Dora frowned at the question. "I'm not sure. I don't want to hurt her."

"I'm sure she will be happy for us," he tried to reassure her.

"Let's give it some time," she suggested.

"Not too much," Tim laughed and rubbed her slightly protruding tummy, "or the news will be obvious."

CHAPTER 43

Jeremy locked his bedroom door and walked through the secret door into Emma's room. He locked her door, as well, before slipping into the bed.

"Hmmm," she murmured as he embraced her. "So nice to finally be back here again."

"Yes," he agreed, quietly allowing himself to drift off to sleep. That was the last word spoken until they heard a knock on the door.

"Emma, are you ready for something to eat?" Dora asked through the door.

Emma said loudly, "Yes, I'm hungry. Will you ask Jeremy if he'll join me?"

Jeremy unlocked Emma's door and slipped through the secret door to his room. Dora was aware they were together but went along with their ruse to protect their privacy. She knocked on his door and said, "Jeremy, Emma would like to eat with you in her room. I'll bring up some food in a few moments."

"Thanks, Dora. I'm up," he called.

He changed his shirt and went to the washroom before

going to Emma's door. As he reached it, he knocked softly. "Come in," Emma called. Jeremy entered and saw she was sitting up and trying to move to the bedside.

Jeremy rushed over. "Emma, you still need to take it easy."

"I will," she promised, knowing she had to follow the doctor's orders to get well. "Can you help me to the washroom?"

"Oh! Sure. Let me help you," he said as he lifted her and carried her there. He waited patiently and carried her back to her room when she finished.

"Dora's bringing your tray up here. You don't need to get up," said Jeremy.

"Could you ask her if I can go downstairs? I promise to take it easy."

He thought for a moment and said, "I think I can arrange something," He bent down and scooped her back up. "I'll set up two chairs, one for your bottom and one for your feet." He juggled her to grab a pillow and placed it on her stomach.

They made their way downstairs to the dining room. Papa was with Patrick at the table, playing with his blocks. When he saw them, Papa immediately jumped up and pulled out a chair for her.

"Grab a second chair for her feet," Jeremy directed. "Emma, hand Ellis the pillow."

Once she was arranged, Jeremy went to the kitchen to tell Dora they had moved to the dining room.

Emma looked over at Patrick and said, "Patrick, how are you?"

He turned his big brown eyes on her. "You disappeared. You weren't here."

Emma felt so sad for the little boy who had lost so much. She held out her hands to him, saying, "I didn't go away on purpose. I got sick. I'm back now. I just have to take it easy."

"Did they hurt you, too?" Patrick asked in a low voice.

"Oh, baby, no," she said and held open her arms. He walked

over to lay his head on her chest. "I was sick before that, but I didn't know it. I was lucky to be at the hospital when it got worse." She asked teasingly, "So, are you living here now?"

"Yes, Dora and Tim asked if I could be their little boy now," he said, quietly looking at her.

"And what did you say?" she asked, knowing his answer.

"I said yes. Tim and Dora are my new mommy and daddy now," he said proudly.

Dora and Tim stepped into the room and heard the last statement. Dora buried her head in Tim's shoulder.

Tim stroked her hair and said, "Patrick, since you've finished your lunch, Amy said she'd love to play ball with you outside."

"Really?" He took off running, shouting, "Amy!"

They heard Amy reply and the back door open and then slam shut.

The group in the dining room smiled. "Patrick seems to be settling in," commented Emma. She was happy he had a family.

The conversation moved to the topic of children. "The funeral planning is still ongoing for the kids," Tim said

"Who's paying for them?" asked Emma.

"I'm unsure," admitted Tim.

There was a knock on the door as Dora headed toward the kitchen. She glanced toward Papa and said, "Papa, could you get the door while I make Emma's plate?"

"Yes, of course," he said, putting down his paper.

They heard a female voice and Papa saying, "Clair, welcome. Come in."

"How is Emma?" she asked, her voice tinged with concern.

"She's doing well. She's in the dining room getting some lunch. Won't you join us?"

"Please," she responded.

She entered and immediately to Emma's side. "Emma, I was so worried about you. I tried to come to the hospital to see you, but they limited your visitors."

Emma smiled broadly. "Clair, I'm glad to see you. I'm feeling well. Now, I just have to rest." Emma saw Jeremy nodding out of the corner of her eye. She focused back on Clair, saying, "We were just talking about the children's funerals and the cost to the parents. I'd like us to review taking care of that. They've already been through so much."

Tim added, "I'll have to check with the families, but that area is very poor and I doubt most have the money to pay for proper funerals."

Clare was aware of the children being kidnapped and knew some had died. She pulled out her notebook to take notes. "Do we know the family names?"

"We can get them. Cole has a list of everyone," Tim stated.

Jeremy was grateful Tim had been helping Cole and said, "Thanks so much for your assistance, Tim."

"We're family," he said. "You do for family."

Emma warmed at this comment. She teared up and tried to cover it with a statement to Clair. "Claire, I'd like you to speak with them. Find out about each child and what they would like." She looked around at the group and said, "I assume my board members would approve this?"

"We'll have to make it official," said Clair, "but we can move forward and get all the details. I'll have a formal vote sent out to everyone."

"Wonderful," said Emma, relieved to be able to help those families who experienced loss.

"Would you like something to eat?" Dora asked Clair.

"That would be nice," she responded.

They all settled into lunch. After they ate, Tim said to Clair, "If you would like to come with me, we can go get the details from Cole."

"I would appreciate that," she said. "As soon as we finish?"

"Yes, we can do that," Tim confirmed.

Dora said, "Clair, you and Thomas need to come by this weekend for dinner. It's been a little while."

"That would be lovely," she said and looked toward Emma, "if you're up for company?"

"I will be," she said.

Tim had gotten his jacket and asked Clair, "Ready?"

She held up a hand. "Tim, just a moment. Dora, could I have a word with you?"

Dora immediately nodded and asked, "Kitchen?"

"Yes." She stood and turned to Tim, saying, "I'll be ready in just a moment."

Emma frowned as she watched them leave the room. *What's going on here?* she thought.

Jeremy said to Tim, "I think I'll come with you and check-in at the office. I have a few cases that might need my attention. If you're okay with that," he said to Emma.

She smiled. "I'm fine now that I'm home. You do what you need to do."

Dora and Clair came back out quickly. Dora's cheeks were red, and Clair was smiling. She bent over and kissed Emma on the cheek. "I'm very happy you're home."

"Me, too. Let us know if you need any help with the details for the funerals. I could help from here."

Clair looked at Jeremy in askance. "As long as she takes it easy," he cautioned.

The afternoon wore down slowly. Emma worked on her lace designs after being moved by Papa into the sitting room.

Mark and his parents joined her there before dinner. She briefed them on what was happening with the children. "It is so terrible," said George.

"Yes," Emma agreed.

He looked at Elizabeth and back to Emma before saying, "Have you looked at who else might be involved in the kidnappings?"

"Do you mean other than the people we caught?" asked Emma.

"Yes, I think that the investigation should also include the people who targeted them."

"Who would that be?" asked Emma.

"You would be looking for people that are already in the kid's lives," said George.

"Why makes you say that?" asked Emma curiously.

Elizabeth responded. "Kids wouldn't normally go with someone they don't trust. Well, the older ones anyway"

Emma thought about that.

CHAPTER 44

PINKERTON OFFICE

"How is Emma?" asked one of the detectives sitting in the outer offices as Jeremy, Clair, and Tim entered.

"She's home and being forced to take it easy," Jeremy commented.

"Not easy for her."

Jeremy smiled. "No, definitely not."

Cole heard his voice and stuck out his head. "Jeremy, come see me."

When he saw Clair and Tim had accompanied him, he stepped out into the hallway. "Welcome, what can I do for you?"

"We'd like to have a list of the children who died so we can inquire about helping with the arrangements," said Clair.

"That's wonderful. Allen," he called, "can you assist Clair and Tim?"

Allen came up and said, "Why don't we meet in here?" He escorted them into the conference room to help them with the information request.

Cole and Jeremy watched them follow Allen down the hallway. Cole looked at Jeremy and said in a serious tone, "Jeremy, come into my office."

"On my way," Jeremy said. He knew that tone.

"How's Emma?" Cole asked as he entered.

"She's good. We both finally got some rest today. It was good to be home," he said.

"Are you okay?" his father asked, knowing the stress Jeremy had been under.

"I am now. I was so scared," he admitted. "I thought I was going to lose her. She was in so much pain. She is better now and will be herself soon."

"I'm happy to hear the charity will be helping the families."

"Yes, the money will be helpful."

"Sit, please," Cole said, indicating the couch.

Cole sat down next to him. He looked very serious and said, "We finally think we found him."

"Where?" asked Jeremy, knowing who he was referencing.

"We know Zeke was in prison in Washington State. He was transferred there after New York and was tried for an outstanding warrant. He escaped and we have had word he has been spotted in Montana and Wyoming."

"Heading east," Jeremy said, thinking. "Do we know his final destination?"

"I think here," Cole said, sounding resigned.

"Is he after Emma? Or Clair?"

"We can't know for certain."

"I'd like to go after him," stated Jeremy in a tone that didn't invite argument.

"Let's work on finding him first," Cole suggested.

They made a plan to find Zeke.

CHAPTER 45

BOARDING HOUSE

*P*apa had moved Emma back to her bed. "Thank you, Papa."

"Anything for you, little girl. Get some rest," Papa murmured. He stood looking at Emma and started to cry.

"Papa? Why are you crying?" Emma asked.

"Oh, my little girl. I was so afraid I was going to lose you."

"I'm fine now. You won't lose me," she said.

Papa wiped his face and hugged her. He caressed the side of her face, smiled, and exited the room, leaving Dora and Emma together.

Dora fussed with Emma's blanket and averted her eyes.

"Dora?" Emma inquired quietly.

"Yes," Dora said absently.

"Are you avoiding being alone with me?" she asked, watching Dora's reaction closely.

"No, of course not," Dora said as she kept her eyes averted.

"I think you are," Emma said and started to get out of bed.

"No, don't get up on your own," Dora said, reaching for her.

As she got close, Emma grabbed her by the arms and said triumphantly, "Got you."

"Fell for that, didn't I?" Dora asked, knowing it was impossible to keep anything from her.

"Yes," Something occurred to Emma. "Dora, are you disappointed in me for having this happen outside of marriage?" she asked referring to the pregnancy.

"What? No!" She looked her in the eyes and assured her, "Never."

"Then what's wrong?" Emma asked, bewildered. Before Dora could answer, Emma took a long look at her, noticing things she hadn't before. Her rounder face, fuller hips, shiny hair, and lastly, her breasts. "Dora, you're having a baby!"

"Yes," she admitted, turning red.

"Why didn't you tell me?" Emma asked. Something else occurred to her. "Clair knew, didn't she?"

"Yes, she figured it out also. I didn't tell you initially because you were involved in the case. Then you had your procedure…I just couldn't tell you, knowing you might not ever be able to have children." She felt so miserable knowing she would have something Emma could not.

"Dora, I mean it when I say I don't want kids. I don't want that, but that doesn't mean I won't be a good aunt to your baby." She reached out and said, "May I?"

"Of course, I felt a little something earlier today," she said as she lifted her shirt to show a small rounding of her belly.

Emma reached over and felt the firm skin. "What does it feel like?"

"Tiny butterflies," she said placing her hand over Emma's.

Emma asked, "Wow. How do you feel?"

"Good. Scared. This is something Tim and I have wanted for so long," she admitted.

Emma grabbed Dora's hands and said, "Please don't keep anything from me."

"I won't," she promised. "Tim is so happy. He already wants to start decorating the nursery."

"I'll make you a cover for the bed with a lace trim," she promised.

"That would be lovely." Dora hugged her suddenly and said, "I'm so glad I can share this with you."

"Have you told Patrick?" asked Emma, knowing Dora was protective of him.

"We told him he was going to have a little sister or brother. He was happy," Dora said softly.

Emma was thinking aloud, when she said, "I would guess she has seen the symptoms in her girls." Clair had run a bordello and pregnancy would have been a normal occurrence.

"Did she say what they did in those cases? Did they keep their babies?" asked Dora curiously.

" I've heard about the ways women can get rid of the baby," commented Emma.

"Get rid of?" Dora asked, not understanding.

Emma explained that herbalists or apothecaries carry the herbs that seemed to encourage miscarriages, such as tansy and pennyroyal. The herbs would be made into a tea or infusion and taken by the patient in the hopes of encouraging uterine contractions.

"How do you know about this?" Dora asked, astonished at the information.

"Clair shared it with me when I was thinking about being with Jeremy," she explained.

"I don't understand it. A baby is. . ." she said, holding her stomach protectively.

"A miracle," she said with a smile.

"Yes."

They talked into the next hour about baby names.

CHAPTER 46

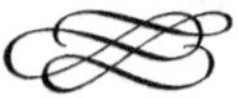

As Emma convalesced at home, she spent time thinking about the children and what George and Elizabeth had said the day before. She made a list of who could be around kids: parents, teachers, preachers, and older sibling's friends.

My team, she thought, *we need to bring them in and talk about this. We also need to have George and Elizabeth there. They can share their reasoning for this theory.*

Emma hadn't been allowed to walk yet, so she called loudly, "Dora!"

Dora walked out of the kitchen, wiping her hands on her apron as she made her way into the sitting room, asking, "Emma, do you need something?"

"Yes, sit here with me for a moment. I want to ask you something," Emma said, patting the seat beside her. Dora sat and waited for her to continue. "The case we are working on, with the children. . ." Dora nodded. "Cole has Pinkertons working on leads for the case, based on the fact Harry was involved. They're also trying to check out the background of the 'Sister,' but I think those leads aren't going to get us to the main person involved."

"What are you thinking?" Dora asked curiously.

"I'm thinking about a conversation I had with George and Elizabeth," she said and went on to describe the new theory.

Dora said thoughtfully, "You know, they're right. Kids are rather insulated from most adults."

"I was thinking of calling a team meeting after dinner, and including George and Elizabeth," said Emma, continuing to make notes.

"Yes," agreed Dora. "If we can help find out who did this to Patrick's parents and those poor children, it is the right thing to do."

Later that evening, Tim, Dora, Jeremy, Cole, Jake, Emma, Elizabeth, and George were sitting at the kitchen table. Emma started, "I invited Elizabeth and George because they might have some insight into our current case." She looked over at Cole and asked, "Could you update us on the current status?"

Cole nodded. "We looked into the Harry connection first. He was a visible connection between the child murder found by Mr. Marella and the dead children now. We questioned him and he only admitted to involvement once the kids were delivered. He was also in charge of administering the drugs; he's confessed to experimenting on the amounts. He will hang for those murders."

He paused, as he needed to clear the emotion out of his voice. He started again, "He said he reported to the 'Sister' and her name is Beatrice Purvis. She was the only one who knew who their contact was in this area."

Emma asked, "Has anyone interviewed the children to find out if they are aware of who initially took them?"

Cole answered, "We did interview them before sending them home from the hospital. They weren't able to communicate much. Their memories were affected by the drugs."

Dora's thoughts were about the children's well-being. "That is a blessing."

Jeremy looked at Emma and said, "You mentioned a new theory?"

"George," prompted Emma, "could you explain to the group what you were saying about who might be taking the kids?"

George sat up straighter and said, "Elizabeth and I work with children in our jobs as teachers, we have a special bond with them. They see us every day and know their parents trust us. We believe the people behind this might have thought of the same thing."

Jeremy was pondering that and said, "So, teachers, preachers, parents."

Emma was checking off her list and added, "Also older sibling's friends."

Dora said, "We don't want to forget about community people, people they see every day: grocers, store owners, ones who tend to have a lot of kid traffic."

Cole was taking notes. "That does help with direction. I can have people watch the more open places: grocers and stores with kids." He looked up and said to the group, "Does anyone know the priest or preachers in that area?"

Tim suggested, "Father Cavanaugh, our parish priest, he could help with that and any rumors."

Elizabeth spoke up, "George and I have an idea about the school."

The group looked on expectantly as she continued, "We've talked about teaching at the school there. They need teachers and we could be used to keep an eye on what might be happening."

Dora asked surprised, "Would that mean you'd move?"

"We'd hoped to stay, but we would need transportation to and from the school each day. We'd need help on that."

Tim raised a hand. "We can help with that, we have several couriers who could take you in the wagons and bring you back."

Cole asked, "How hard would it be to move over to the school?"

George looked at Elizabeth and said, "We've already inquired, and they said we can start as soon as we can get released here. We expect to be able to move over next week." Their jobs here hadn't been made permanent yet and there was some flexibility.

Jeremy frowned. "My only concern is your safety. We'll want you to observe and report anything you see."

Cole cautioned, "This may be long-term. We may have driven them underground."

"We're okay with that. We plan on staying permanently. We feel this is where we're supposed to be teaching," said George.

"Okay then, we'll get everyone in place. If something is needed to be reported, send a note to the Pinkerton's office. We'll have a weekly group meeting to discuss updates," stated Emma.

CHAPTER 47

The next day, Cole and Jeremy had the teams set up to watch the stores. "I thought we'd have fewer kids to worry about on the streets," he said, watching the children play and run around.

"You have to remember these are working families and they do the best they can. There isn't always money for people to watch them. They do seem to be hanging around in groups and not individually," said Cole thoughtfully.

That week went by quickly, and they were soon sitting down for their first group meeting at the boarding house. Emma looked toward Cole and Jeremy and asked, "Anything to report?"

"There are more kids out than I would have thought, but they seem to have group leaders. I haven't seen any of the owners approaching them, except to have them leave if they get too rowdy. We'll keep watching," he promised.

"Tim?" Emma continued around the table.

"Father Cavanaugh said there are several churches in that area—Catholic and Protestant. He knows both men. The priest is quite old and may not have the mobility required. The Protestant preacher has been on a missionary trip for the last few weeks."

"What about their replacements?" asked Emma.

"The Protestant church is just meeting for prayers as a community, so I think we can discount them. The priest does have a younger replacement, but he only started about a year ago."

Emma mulled that over, *The first child abduction I was involved in was six years ago. If this is part of that original case, it would involve someone who lived in the area at the time.*

"George, Elizabeth?" Emma inquired.

George looked at Elizabeth and she started. "We're just getting to know everyone. Most are married men or unmarried women."

"What about single men?" Jeremy asked.

"There are a few," she admitted.

"Are they close to the kids?" asked Tim.

"Two of them work on special programs helping them after school. Albert Chastain and Lee Jones," George said.

Jeremy said, "I can find out from the parents if any of the children taken were in these programs."

Emma closed her notebook and said, "Good work. This will take time."

Cole said, "We need to be aware that, if the person is still here, they might try again. We know that the money involved would be hard to turn down."

"Yes," they all agreed.

Elizabeth spent the next week paying particular attention to the two after-school groups she'd mentioned to the team. She went to the schoolroom where the students would be that afternoon, pretending to look through her papers. She noticed Albert preparing drinks for his group; it seemed to be some type of punch.

"What do you have there?" she asked curiously from the doorway.

"Just a little punch to help the kids make it through an extra hour of teaching," he said, giving her a sideways glance.

"Oh," she said trying to be nonchalant. She had seen him make these drinks before and knew the kids would grab the cups quickly as they entered. She excused herself to go find George.

She found him and said in a low voice, "George, I'm going to stay around a bit today to grade some papers. Could you let Lester know?" Lester was their driver to and from school each day.

"Sure, I'll wait," he said, reading the stress in her eyes.

"Okay, I'll meet you." She quickly went back to Albert's room and stayed in the hallway watching the kids enter. Her tally was twelve of various ages. They seemed to be settling into their lessons and she went down to get the papers she needed to grade. As she returned she sat in her chair, positioned near the room. She glanced in the windows and the first thing she did was count the children. *Eleven. Weren't there twelve earlier?* She frowned.

She waited for the program to be completed for the day and, as the children left, she said to a tall boy, "Are you all here? Did someone leave early?"

He shook his head. "Maya was a bit sick, so she laid down in the large closet." He didn't say more and just walked away.

She continued to watch the room and saw Albert locking up and turning off the lights to his room. She had to act; she couldn't wait for help, so she stuck her foot out and tripped him as he exited. He fell face-first on the floor and looked at her accusingly. "You tripped me!"

George was just coming around the corner, saw Albert on the floor, and asked, "What happened?"

"I fell," he said, still looking angrily at Elizabeth.

"George, I think we need something out of his school closet," she said.

George took the hint and said, "Albert, can you open your closet for us? We need to borrow a book from you."

"What book?" he asked belligerently.

"Does it matter? Why don't you open the closet for us?" George asked, stepping toward a still sitting Albert. "Why don't I help you up?" As Albert put out his hand, George grabbed it firmly and pulled him up and toward him. "Now, that closet."

Albert nodded and turned toward it, seeing George was serious.

"I think one of the girls in his class is missing," Elizabeth murmured as they followed.

Albert opened the closet and Elizabeth went in.

She came out and said, "She isn't there."

Lester walked into the classroom and asked, "Ready to go?"

"Not yet. Could you go get Cole and Jeremy for us? Tell them we need help," George requested.

Lester got serious quickly and said, "Yes, on my way." They could hear his steps as he ran down the hallway.

As they watched him leave, they noticed Albert trying to sneak away. Elizabeth looked him in the eye and asked, "Albert, where is Maya? I heard she got sick."

He looked a little evasive but muttered, "She didn't feel well so I sent her to the nurse."

Elizabeth said, "Hold him." George took him by the arms and restrained him while she ran to the nurse's office. She saw her leaving and yelled, "Wait!" The nurse looked wide-eyed at her office, then at Elizabeth, and started running toward the exit.

Elizabeth didn't go after her; she was more concerned about Maya. She tried the door to the office and found it locked. There was a small window on the door; she broke it and managed to get the door open. She glanced around and was about to leave when she heard a small moan. "Maya!" she said dropping down to look under the desk. The girl was there. Elizabeth crawled under and wrapped her arms around her and pulled her out. Holding her close, she rushed back to the room with Maya in her arms and said, "The nurse is gone."

"Thank god she didn't take Maya," George said fervently.

"Yes," she said, holding her tightly. "She ran out the back when I was coming up."

"Well, we have him," George said, nodding at Albert. "We'll wait for Cole and Jeremy."

Albert slumped to the floor, knowing he was left with all the blame.

CHAPTER 48

Cole, Jeremy, and several Pinkerton detectives arrived. Cole and Jeremy immediately wanted to question Albert. He sat straining at his bonds and sweating profusely. Elizabeth and George had briefed them on his and the nurse's activities.

"Lester, could you take Elizabeth and George to the principal's office and see if we can contact Maya's parents?" Cole asked.

Lester nodded. Elizabeth continued to cradle Maya as she and George followed him to the office.

Jeremy bent down and got face-to-face with Albert. "Come on, you know you want to tell us what's happening here."

"No, I don't want to talk," he muttered, looking away.

Jeremy came at him harder. "So, you like to hurt children?"

"No, no, of course not. I'm a teacher," he stuttered.

"What was in that punch, Albert?" Cole asked quietly.

"Nothing."

"Want to try that answer again?" Cole asked, his voice low and dangerous.

He looked mutinous but saw Jeremy was carrying a gun. "I won't go down for her."

"Her?" asked Jeremy.

"Yes, Christy Black. She's the nurse here. This was all her idea," he said.

Principal Harrison stood at the door and said, "She's a traveling nurse, going to schools here and on the east coast."

"Allowing her to set up networks to remove multiple children," commented Jeremy.

"Yes," Albert admitted.

"Why did you do it?" asked the principal, not understanding.

"Money. There's always a need to have more," he said quietly.

"But they were children!" the Principal said.

Albert looked down, knowing it was over for him.

Cole looked at the principal and said, "We need the records for where she lives in the area and what other schools she works for."

He nodded and said, "I'll get the information immediately."

CHAPTER 49

BOARDING HOUSE THAT EVENING

Cole and Jeremy brought a chalkboard to the boarding house to demonstrate the extent of the missing children case. The team was in the sitting room, watching Jeremy document the nurse's schools. "We have information showing she was working at four schools in Chicago and six in New York State. We also have her in Boston and other cities up the east coast."

Jeremy drew out the information, showing she had access to kids all over.

"Have you contacted the schools in those areas to ask about any missing children?" asked Emma.

"Yes," he said. "I got the telegrams off and hope to hear something soon. I also gave them warnings about the nurse."

Cole added, "I've notified the Pinkerton offices to send detectives to the schools to see if they can find her. I also mentioned the punch and to apprehend anyone serving it to children."

"So, what happens now?" asked Tim.

"We wait. We can't get to the areas to help, so we have to check our schools here," said Cole.

"Frustrating," said Emma.

"Yes, but we have to trust they're doing everything they can," said Jeremy.

CHAPTER 50

NEW YORK STATE

"They know who she is?" the older man asked quietly.

"They do," the younger man answered in the same tone.

"You took care of Beatrice?" he asked.

"Yes. We had a man in the area, and he prevented any information exchange."

"Should we worry about the people they have in custody?"

"No, they only knew Beatrice and no one else. We're well insulated," he said calmly.

"Good," said the older man. He looked thoughtful and said, "It's time to shut this operation down. Can you take care of it?"

"Yes."

"Make sure she's found quickly. It needs to be a statement."

"Of course."

"Terrible business. I never should have allowed it to happen," the older man said regretfully.

"It was very profitable," the other man murmured.

"Yes, but hugely emotional. It could have taken us down. This should remove all connection to us."

"I'll take care of it now."

He waved him off and said, "We'll talk later."

"Yes, sir," the man said as he stepped back and pulled the cell door closed with a loud clank.

John Hardin sat thinking about how his operations were running very smoothly from prison. He mulled over how the current enterprise had ended. *Emma, we will meet again.*

CHAPTER 51

PINKERTON OFFICE

$\mathcal{A}$ telegram was brought in.

Cole read it and then looked at Jeremy. "Miss O'Brien has been found."

Jeremy smiled and asked, "Good. When can we get her here for an interview and trial?"

"Never, I'm afraid," Col said without expression.

"Why not?"

"She's dead. She was found in a very public place, outside of town hall in New York City. She was tied up and shot in the head. Someone wanted an example made of her. I'm assuming this was a statement they're done with this business."

Jeremy frowned. "Do we believe it?"

"I'm sure it will stop for a while. It would seem rather risky at this time."

"Do we have the numbers of kids taken from each location?" asked Jeremy.

"Each precinct is working on that now. We should have the final numbers soon."

"Is there a chance to find them?"

"There will be raids on bordellos that have underage children, but they could be anywhere," Cole said regretfully.

CHAPTER 52

The funerals were set for that day. In all, five children died. The families decided to have the services together. Emma and Jeremy were in her room at the boarding house, discussing the event.

"Emma, it will be a long day," he started.

The event would be long, but Emma did not want to be kept home. "I think—"

"Emma, if you would let me finish," he interrupted, arching an eyebrow at her. "I would agree it's time and you should be there. You weren't able to save those five, but fifteen went home to their parents."

She took a deep breath, admitting, "It is going to be a long day."

"Yes," he said as he helped her get dressed. Their clothing was sober, a stark contrast to the sunny day.

Tim, Jeremy, Cole, Dora, and Emma moved to the carriages. Patrick would remain with Papa for the day. Patrick had attended his parent's funeral and they wanted to protect him from more sadness.

When they got to the church, they saw Thomas, Clair, and

her assistant Sam. Clair walked over, saying quietly, "Everything is arranged. I have places reserved for you all." She'd had the charity set up and paid for all the children to have services and be buried.

As she walked them in, Emma asked, "Why are we going toward the front? That is for the families of the deceased."

Clair stopped and turned back to their group. "The families requested it."

Emma nodded, not knowing what to say, and continued to follow her up the aisle. *There are so many people. Children's funerals are always crowded*, she thought. Her condition had prevented her from meeting with the families, so she didn't know they were eager to be introduced.

As she approached the front, she noticed several women nodding toward her. They broke away from their group and started toward them.

"Miss Evans?" one asked tentatively.

"Yes. Call me Emma, please," Emma asked, unsure how they would react to her. She was the one who had found the location of the children, both dead and alive. *Do they hate me?* she wondered. She waited for someone to talk.

The other ladies gestured at one to start. "Emma, we wanted to thank you for bringing our children home." Emma didn't realize she was crying until Jeremy handed her a tissue. She smiled at him gratefully.

Jeremy was watching her and saw her energy dwindling. She was white as a ghost. He leaned over and said, "We need to sit you down." He turned to address the others. "Ladies, she shouldn't be standing too long."

"Yes, of course. We would like a chance to speak with you later," the leader of their small group requested.

Clair interceded and said, "There'll be time after. We'll have a wake, with food for everyone. I've arranged a hall."

The women nodded and returned to their families.

Jeremy and Emma made their way to their seats. Thomas nodded toward Clair as he sat with Emma and the family. Clair and her assistant Sam approached the priest to discuss any last-minute issues.

Emma looked around and noticed that a large number of Sisters from the hospital were present. She saw Sisters Catherine, Ann, Mary, and others. Catching Sister Catherine's eye, she nodded toward her. Sister Catherine acknowledged her, nodding in return.

Emma turned back to the front of the church. Flowers overflowed atop the church altar. The priest stood in front of the pulpit to read the Gospel. It was a traditional service—prayers were said; families cried.

When it drew to a close, the fathers of the dead children stood. The priest had agreed to let them make a statement, and their speaker stepped forward. "We want to thank you for being here for us and our families today. We have lost something that can't be replaced. We love and will always miss Christopher, Michael, Cindy, Evelyn, and Katherine." His voice broke and he stopped a moment; he took a deep breath to clear his voice and continued. "We can't stop blaming ourselves for not being able to protect our children. We are at this lovely service today because of the charity. We've also been informed that they want to set up a location for children who are home alone. Mrs. Callahan, could you come up?"

"Yes, thank you," Clair said graciously. "We want to make a safe place for the kids to be kids. We are looking for a location in your areas where they can get to safely after school. My assistant, Sam Peterson, will start having community meetings to discuss the progress."

At that final statement, the fathers and men in the audience surrounded the caskets and raised them on their shoulders. The small size of the caskets affected everyone. All movement was done in silence.

They were moved to waiting wagons and would be transported to the local cemetery. They'd chosen a close one so the families could walk.

"Will you be able to make the walk?" a concerned Jeremy asked Emma.

"I can take her to the hall," volunteered Sam. "I need to check on the arrangements."

"We'll both go and meet everyone else there," suggested Jeremy.

"Yes, let's do that," she said and followed him to the carriage.

The hall was both sober and beautiful. Food was provided on side tables and arriving families talked together quietly. The services were completed and the mourners arrived at the hall. The mothers of the lost children wanted to have some time with Emma, and she followed them to a side room. They allowed her to sit down and one of the ladies started. "We appreciate you finding our children so they could be buried properly."

"I'm just sorry we weren't able to save all of them," Emma said helplessly.

"No! You're not responsible for that. Other people are. Without you, we would never have known what happened to them."

They were all crying at that point. Several of the men came in and one spoke up. "Okay now, let's break this up. We're sure Emma is getting very tired."

Emma realized she was tired, but not exhausted. *I'm better*, she thought. She returned to the hall and Jeremy. He raised his eyebrow at her and she said, "Later."

When they were heading home, alone in their carriage, she told him what the ladies had wanted.

"They are amazing people," Jeremy commented

"Yes, I think they have to be," she said. She looked over and stated, "Jeremy, I am getting better. I can feel it."

He smiled and said, "We could start with a short walk this evening and build up your energy each day."

She smiled, happy as always that they were on the same page.

On the way back from their walk that evening, she saw a courier ahead of them near the boarding house. They followed him up the stoop and got to him before he could knock.

"I can take that," stated Emma.

"Do you live here?" the courier asked.

"Yes, who's the telegram for?" she asked.

He looked down and read, "Emma Evans."

"Well, that's me," she said with a smile.

He had her sign for it and went on to his other deliveries.

"Who's it from?" asked Jeremy, always curious about a telegram.

"Tony," she said simply as she opened it.

"Oh, the world traveler," he said lightly. "What does he say?"

"Oh no!"

"What is it? "

"The museum curator, Philip Johnson, has gone missing. Tony's requesting my help."

"Help where? Overseas?" Jeremy asked incredulously.

"Yes," she said, tapping the letter on her hand. "I could go by boat and be there in a few weeks."

"Be where?" Jeremy asked, bewildered.

"Paris. It shouldn't be a problem, and it would give me time to rest and walk before I get there," she said, planning.

Jeremy thought at first to say it was too soon, but then he thought of Zeke. The latest intel continued to indicate he was heading straight for them. *This might not be a bad idea. It would get Emma out of the way,* he thought. "I think that sounds like a plan. Tony could use a friend there," he said positively.

She frowned. "Jeremy, aren't you angry about this?" She had expected a very different response.

"You going to Paris? No," he answered firmly.

"By myself? To see Tony." She didn't know why she kept questioning if he had no objections.

"Well, you are not one-hundred percent yet. Do you need someone to accompany you?" he asked, thinking.

"I don't think so, but couldn't you make time to come with me?" she asked hesitantly. It would be a long separation.

"I have several cases at critical points. I have to be here for them," he explained.

There's something more, thought Emma, but she couldn't read his face. "Okay, I'll send a telegram to Tony and tell him I'll be going over to see him." She wanted to be excited, but she was unsure why Jeremy was acting this way. She looked at him thoughtfully and wondered if she was worried about nothing.

"I'll go with you to send it."

As they made their way to the telegraph office, Emma was still contemplative. She thought to herself, *I need to refocus. I'm going to Paris to help Tony.*

CHAPTER 53

The next morning, she took a carriage to the office to get tickets for the ship. She would be going to Havre, France—a port city—and catching a day train to Paris. The initial trip would be about six days on the La Bretagne if there were no delays. They got Emma reserved in 1st class. That would allow her some privacy on the trip.

As she was making her travel plans, she worried about leaving Dora.

"Emma," assured Dora, "my doctor said I'm doing well and have a long way to go before the baby is born. I'm not due until well after your return."

"You're sure?" Emma asked. "I can have a Pinkerton detective go over for me."

"Emma, it's Paris. You've always dreamed of traveling, and you know you wouldn't want anyone else to help Tony," she said, understanding Emma still cared deeply for him. She looked at Emma consideringly and said, "You'll need clothes for the trip, and fast."

"Yes, the seamstress we work with might be able to make me some travel clothes. We can go see her today." They both went that afternoon. Luckily, there was an order almost completed, then canceled. The clothes were fitted to Emma and promised to be delivered in the next few days.

She confirmed her ticket and arrival data via telegram to Tony, remembering their conversation before he'd left. He had been so excited about learning more about the masters in Paris. His eyes had lit up as he talked about what he and Philip would see. Tony had raved about the main innovation of the era—the collapsible tin paint tube, invented in 1841 by American painter John Rand. This revolutionized the color palette and technique of Plein Air oil painting by offering a range of pre-mixed colors in a convenient, portable medium. This was a major factor in the emergence of Impressionism. He couldn't wait to see the paintings in person.

CHAPTER 54

*J*eremy planned to accompany her on the train to New York and drop her off at the ship. He was withholding the information about Zeke until the last possible moment.

Everything came together quickly, and they left a few days later on the train to New York. Their time together was very pleasant, except for Jeremy's continued concern about her reaction to his deception.

They switched trains and moved into a carriage for the final leg of the trip. They went directly to the ship; it would be leaving that evening.

As they pulled up, Jeremy removed her luggage and waved over a porter to move it onto the ship. They followed him on board and found her cabin assignment. The porter stowed her bags while Jeremy and Emma stood at the rail to say goodbye. Jeremy looked pained when he said, "Emma, I have to tell you something."

She frowned; he sounded upset. "What is it Jeremy?" she asked, concerned.

He pulled her close, laying his head on her shoulder. "I really want to go with you."

"You still can. I have a private cabin. Would you like me to change the arrangements?" she asked and tried to step back to see if she could do so.

He pulled her back and looked her in the eyes. "No, you don't know what is going on. Zeke Jones escaped from prison and has been tracked heading toward Chicago."

"Zeke," she echoed, going white.

Jeremy replied, "Yes. We found out he had escaped a little while ago, and we've been getting reports he's been seen traveling East."

"Going after me and Clair," she said, finishing his statement. "I need to stay and help catch him," she said, trying to move toward the gangway to disembark.

Jeremy pulled her to a stop. "No, Emma, you're going to stay on this boat and stay safe."

Emma thought of Tony and asked, "Is Tony's telegram a lie?"

"No," he insisted. "I love you so much and, just this once, I want to be the one to protect you. Can you let me do that, please?"

Tears filled her eyes. "If you get him—"

"When," he interrupted.

"When you get him, can you make sure we don't have to deal with him again?"

He got her silent message and promised, "I'll make sure." He wanted off the topic. He didn't want their last moments together to be about Zeke. "Will Tony meet you in Havre? Or in Paris?"

Emma let him change the topic and responded with, "He said he would be in Havre, and we'll take the train to Paris together. He can brief me on the details before we arrive."

A loud voice sounded, calling for visitors to leave the ship. Jeremy looked like he didn't want to leave her.

"Get some rest, please. Send me a telegram when you arrive in Paris," he requested.

"I will," she said softly. "When I return, we will be together again." Her cheeks flushed.

"I look forward to that," said Jeremy, enjoying her embarrassment.

They called a second time for visitors to leave the ship. "I have to go."

She grabbed him and kissed him hard, then broke away to say, "Jeremy, I love you. Be safe."

"I love you, I have to go now."

She walked him to the gangplank, and they kissed softly. She watched him walk down and then waved as they got underway. She waited until she couldn't see him anymore and headed to her cabin to rest before dinner.

As she entered her cabin, she looked around and was surprised at how nice it was. The floors were darkly stained wood with rugs throughout. She had a sitting room and a small bedroom.

She turned and locked her door before going to the bed to lie down.

CHAPTER 55

She slept hard and woke in time for dinner. The ship had sent an itinerary to the rooms dictating the time and location. She would need to get dressed and go straight down. Since it was the first night, the itinerary also indicated that the dress for dinner would be casual. Her outfit of choice was a black skirt and a red blouse. Carefully making her way down, she passed many couples on the walk down and nodded politely. The dinner line was short as she waited to be seated by the host.

"Your name?" he inquired

"Emma Evans," she supplied.

He looked down at his book and looked back up to say, "Yes, we have you sitting with a group. Is that okay?" he asked politely.

"That would be nice." She followed him to the assigned table. It was a large room with burgundy carpet and white tablecloths covering round tables. The chairs were painted a gold color and seemed to sparkle in the evening light. They reached the table and the host pulled out her chair. Her gaze fell on those she would be spending the next six days with. They were a friendly bunch and were already talking animatedly about their destination.

An older woman across from her was saying to the group, "Paris, can you imagine? I understand many artists are working there now."

"And the food is supposed to be wonderful," responded a young woman next to Emma.

"Yes, but can you speak French?" asked the older woman.

"I hadn't thought of that, but I'm sure they speak English," the younger woman responded.

I wouldn't be so sure of that, Emma thought. As soon as Papa learned Emma would be going to France, he'd had a specialist come to the house and practice pronunciations with her. Her advice had been to keep as quiet as possible and try to speak French, never to assume they spoke English. *Thank goodness Tony took French lessons for months to prepare for his trip*, she thought to herself.

The older gentleman opposite Emma suggested introductions. *Hmm*, she thought, *this will allow me to put my observational skills to work. I'll need to document who's at the table. There are eight people in all.*

"Young lady, would you like to start?" he asked, indicating Emma.

"Yes. I'm Emma Evans, and I'm on my way to meet a friend and see Paris." She kept her information simple. No need to share why she was going there.

"Are you traveling alone?" asked the older gentleman's wife.

"I am," Emma responded.

"Aren't you nervous?" she asked.

"No, not really. My friend will meet me when we dock," she said casually.

"Well, just let us know if you need anything," her husband responded.

"I will, thank you," said Emma sincerely.

The older gentleman continued with the introductions and looked at the couple sitting on Emma's left. "Would you like to introduce yourselves?"

"Yes," the gentleman answered for them. "We are Scott and Meghan Bauer, and we're on our honeymoon."

"Congratulations," said the group.

Emma watched them closely; something about them made her uneasy. She noticed Scott spoke for both of them and Meghan kept her eyes down. Emma noted the rings Meghan wore. Evidently, she'd married into money.

The couple on Emma's right was next. They were an older couple, probably in their mid-fifties. "We are Richard and Susan Billings, and we're traveling after selling our business to our son and his wife. We are also celebrating our thirtieth anniversary."

"Congratulations," said the group.

The gentleman seated next to her was next. "I'm Walter Garber. I'm not married and I'm on my way to Paris on business." Emma noted his age to be about thirty. "And," he teased, winking at the two ladies who had spoken earlier about the French language, "you should practice your French. The trip will be more entertaining for you. I can help you if you would like."

The older gentleman who had started the introductions went next. "We are Lloyd and Merry Jackson. Merry has always wanted to see Paris, and I just couldn't say no. So, we're off on an adventure."

Emma noticed Merry seemed to have tremors in her hands, and she kept them hidden in her lap when she wasn't using them. *Would medical issues be another reason for the trip?* she wondered.

Dinner was then served. The main course was Beef Wellington with carrots and peas. During dinner, there were conversations with Walter on his business. The group wanted him to give them details about what they might see in Paris

Walter continued to talk at length about castles and other lovely architecture. Emma was fascinated and she could tell her fellow tablemates were also.

The one outlier was Meghan. She seemed distracted. She didn't say a word and let her husband continue talking for her. Emma wanted to speak with Meghan and mention she had options if she needed them.

When Meghan got up to look at the dessert display, Emma followed and said in a low voice, "If you need help or want to talk, I can assist you."

Meghan replied in a low voice, "I can meet you after midnight. Scott is normally passed out drunk by then, and I should be able to sneak out. Meet by the railing by the lifeboats?"

"I will meet you," Emma promised and moved away. Emma noted Scott watching, but he didn't seem concerned.

CHAPTER 56

*L*ater that night, Emma left her cabin and made her way to the prearranged meeting location. Nearing the lifeboats, an argument made her pause. It was Meghan and Scott.

She continued toward them and saw they were struggling with one another. *What is going on? Is she ...* Before she could finish the thought, Scott went over the side of and of the ship! Emma ran to the railing to see if she could see him. She noticed immediately that Meghan was not looking and had not called for help. Emma started to yell when she heard someone else call out, "Man overboard!!" The boat started slowing as the search teams were sent out.

Meghan's mood was oddly calm. She didn't cry or even seem upset as she stood with Emma. That all changed when the captain strode up to them.

She immediately started crying. "My husband fell overboard! He was trying to push me off and he fell instead. I don't know why he would want to kill me! Emma saw him attack me!"

Emma watched her, not knowing what to believe. Something about the struggle she witnessed was bothering her but she was unsure what it was.

The captain said, "We can get into that later, the rescue is our priority currently."

The crew sent out boats all night and into the next day. Scott's body was not found. An emergency station had been set up within a conference room, near the captain's cabin. Meghan and Emma waited there as the search took place. When it was called off, Meghan was notified and promptly fainted. They transferred her to the doctor's office and Emma accompanied her.

Meghan came to as the doctor was examining her. Emma stayed to help her take off her shirt and skirt, revealing bruises on her forearms and the front of her legs. Emma noticed there was no bruising on her back or areas that would be unreachable by Meghan herself.

Emma had worked helping women who were actual victims of physical abuse and knew what self-inflicted wounds looked like. They weren't as deep as wounds inflicted by assault, due to the difference in the force applied, and were often found on forearms or legs, less vital areas of the body.

She might be faking it, though she couldn't be for certain that she did this to herself, Emma thought. *Her husband had been insensitive and selfish. Was he also a wifebeater?* She helped Meghan dress and sit up. The captain joined them and immediately Meghan's behavior changed. She ran to him and her body shook as she cried in his arms.

Meghan could turn the grieving wife display on and off at will. The captain was solicitous, patting her on the back and saying, "Madam, I'm so sorry, but we must keep our schedule. We've put out notices to passing ships to watch for him." He seemed at a loss as to how to comfort her.

Emma took that moment to step in and say, "Captain, I'll take care of her."

He looked at Emma gratefully and said, "Miss Evans, we appreciate your help in this matter."

"I'll accompany her back to her cabin," Emma said, offering Meghan a hand up.

When they reached her cabin, Meghan turned to her. "I'm just so tired. I would like to rest now."

Emma wanted to get into the cabin to look around and said, "Why don't I come in for a bit. We can talk?"

"NO!" Meghan shouted. She realized how shrill she sounded and said in a calmer voice, "No, I really want some time alone."

Emma looked at her and thought, *There's no place for her to run, and I can confide in the captain concerning what I believe happened.* She said out loud, "If you need to talk, just have a note sent to my cabin."

"I will," she said softly. "Thanks for trying to help me."

Emma frowned, and finally said, "Okay then, get some rest and I'll see you in the morning." The door closed and stood in the hallway for a long time. She was suspicious and felt they needed to look at the wife's role in this event. The captain needed to know of her suspicions. She headed toward his cabin. A ship's officer was stationed outside of his door and she asked as she approached, "Does he have time for me?"

"Just a moment," he said. He knocked on the door and stepped into the cabin.

He stepped back out and said, "You may enter."

The officer pushed the door opened and she stepped in. The captain was there sitting in a heavy brown chair. He stood, walked to her, and said, "Yes, Miss Evans? Is Mrs. Bauer okay?"

"Yes, I believe so," she said.

"Would you like to sit down?" the captain asked.

Emma nodded and took a seat on his couch. She stated, "Captain, we haven't had a chance to talk since I boarded your ship."

He looked at her consideringly and replied, "No, I've been busy."

She smiled at that and said, "Yes, well, I'm an investigator. I work investigative jobs for my business and the Pinkerton Detective Agency."

The captain knew the Pinkerton name well. "Isn't that unusual for a woman?"

She thought, *One day, I hope that won't be a question when I talk about my investigative work.* Out loud, she answered, "Yes, it is."

"Does this have something to do with Mrs. Bauer?"

Emma figured being blunt was the best option for the disclosure of this information and started, "I believe Mrs. Bauer has murdered her husband."

He frowned and sat forward in his chair. "I think you'll need to explain yourself. As I understand it *you* saw Scott try to force *her* from the ship."

"I did see them grappling with one another," she confirmed. *I need to think about what I saw.*

The captain continued, "And from interviews with fellow passengers, we determined he was abusive and controlling. Out doctor said there was evidence of abuse in the form of numerous bruises."

Emma pulled out her notebook and opened to the page where she had documented the bruises. "I believe those bruises might be self-inflicted."

"Explain yourself," he commanded.

She showed him the notebook and explained the injury locations and intensity. "It's very unusual that a beating would only occur in areas she could reach."

"Hmm," he said, reviewing the notes.

"Also," she continued, "what we saw was merely the appearance of abuse. For instance, he answered for her, and she was very quiet and didn't say anything. I believe that was also an act."

"Why would she do it?" he asked, at a loss.

"I believe the motive might be money. Her husband appeared to be quite prosperous," she stated matter-of-factly.

"But she appears so young. . ."

"Yes," Emma commented.

"We won't have access to background information until we reach France."

"I'll have to get her to talk to me," she said.

"I don't think it would hurt anything, and if nothing comes of it, we don't disclose the investigation," stated the captain, unsure what to believe.

"Agreed."

She made her way back to her cabin to get some rest. She slowly undressed, missing Jeremy. As she lay down, she thought about her plans to investigate Meghan. Her thoughts went back to what she witnessed before Scott went overboard. Something clicked and she smiled. *I've got you! Meghan believes she has me fooled, that I think she's the victim. I need her to keep talking to me to keep up that façade. I have four more days to figure out how to get her to admit she killed Scott.*

She fell asleep pondering the case.

CHAPTER 57

DAY 3 OF 7 ON THE LA BRETAGNE

The next morning at breakfast, Emma saw Meghan sitting alone at their group table. She made her way forward, saying casually as she sat down, "Good morning, Meghan. I hope you're doing better this morning." She watched her closely and didn't notice any evidence that she had been crying.

Meghan looked her in the eye and said, "I'm fine."

"Have you heard anything more about Scott?" she asked.

"No, the captain said was presumed dead and that he would notify the authorities once we reach Havre."

"I'm so sorry," said Emma, reaching out. Meghan looked at Emma's hand but moved hers to her lap to avoid the touch.

"You saw what kind of person he was, what he did to me," she said accusingly.

"Your bruises? Yes, I saw them. Are you saying when he fell overboard, did you plan it as punishment?" Emma asked innocently.

"No, what I am saying is he was going to hurt me again, and we fought. He tried to push me overboard. You saw!" she said with a frown.

"Yes, I saw something," Emma said cryptically. She continued, "You had mentioned that he normally was asleep from heavy drinking at that time." She made a mental note to find out if he'd had drinks at dinner or in his cabin.

"I thought he was passed out, but he must have followed me when I went to meet you last night," she explained.

"Hmm," Emma murmured.

Meghan fell silent and began eating again. Emma waved to the waiter and ordered breakfast. As they ate, the quiet settled around them.

Meghan finished her meal, folded her napkin, and said abruptly, "I'm going to the upper decks for some sun."

I'll use this time to check out her story. Emma nodded to Meghan. "I'm going to get my book from my cabin, and I'll join you in a little while."

Meghan looked so relieved that she wouldn't insist on joining her, Emma had to hide a smile. She watched her leave and was thinking about what she'd said about Scott's drinking. She asked the waiter, "Can I speak to the main steward?"

He inclined his head and said, "Yes, madam." He walked over to the main desk and spoke in low tones to the man there, gesturing to Emma.

The man walked over and inquired, "Madam, you asked to see me?"

"Could I inquire about the alcohol set up for the cabins?"

"Yes, these are set up at the guest's request. Would you like us to have something delivered to your cabin?"

"What? Oh no." She laughed. "But thank you."

"If you will excuse me." He bowed slightly and turned to leave.

Emma sat by herself, thinking over her next steps when her other tablemates arrived. They started to eat while discussing the day ahead when Emma asked Walter casually, "Did you happen to notice if Scott drank a lot last night?"

He sat back and considered her question. "No, in fact, he didn't drink at all. He said his stomach was not doing well and the alcohol would just cause him more problems."

As the group moved on to other topics, Emma considered his answer. *I need to get into Meghan's cabin*, she thought.

She excused herself, saying she wanted to lie down for a while. She was heading toward her cabin when she noticed Meghan's door ajar and the maid service rack in the hallway. She quickly stuck her head into the space and, when she did not see the maid inside, hurriedly went inside, searching for the alcohol setup. She found it almost immediately on the table beside the dresser.

She examined each bottle. They appeared to be untouched. She looked around the rest of the cabin quickly and opened the closet. It seemed to only have Meghan's clothes inside. *She certainly didn't waste time*, thought Emma.

She exited the cabin without being seen and headed to her room thinking to herself, *What do we know?*

She went over the facts so far. *Scott didn't drink in public, and the alcohol in the cabin was unopened, despite Meghan saying he'd indulged. Most likely, no additional alcohol had been ordered for their room, though that needed to be confirmed with the ship's bar. The bruising on her body appeared to be self-inflicted. Scott was wealthy, and they had been married for just a short time.*

Emma drummed her fingers on her lip, thinking, *Is it possible she's done this before? I need more background on her to figure that out. She does seem rather practiced at this type of deception.*

She documented her studies in her notebook; only four days left (including today) to figure this out. She headed to her cabin to get some more rest, wanting to be as healthy as possible for Paris.

After her nap, Emma went back to Meghan's cabin to walk her to down to dinner. She knocked, hearing a scrambling from within as she pressed her ear to the door. *There was someone else in that cabin.*

"Who is it?" Meghan called.

Emma didn't have time to think about it when the door opened suddenly. "Is everything okay? Did you have company?"

Meghan frowned severely. She didn't like being questioned. "No, I was just reading and was startled."

"Oh," Emma said, putting on a concerned tone, "I thought I heard someone else's voice in your cabin."

"No," Meghan said forcefully, "you would be wrong. Let's get going." She grabbed Emma's arm and pulled her away from the cabin.

Emma let herself be yanked down the hall, thinking, *This is getting interesting. Who's involved in this? Another passenger? Someone working on the ship?* She would watch tonight and see if anyone got special attention from Meghan or, alternatively, who is she pointedly ignoring.

As they made their way to dinner, Meghan commented she was worried but still had hope Scott was alive. Emma nodded and said she hoped so as well. "Where did you and Scott meet?"

"Could we not talk about that? It just upsets me," Meghan said shortly.

"You brought him up. I thought I'd inquire, in case you wanted to talk about him," she said reasonably.

"Well, I don't!" she nearly screamed.

Emma dropped the topic and they didn't say anything further until they arrived at the dining room. They sat with the group, filling out the last seats at the table. They had removed Scott's chair so it wouldn't be obvious someone was missing. Everyone was initially quiet when the ladies sat down.

Their companions seemed to be waiting for someone else to start the conversation. Mr. Jackson, who had introduced everyone the night before, took over and said to Meghan, "My dear, we are so sorry about your husband."

Meghan was clear-eyed as she said, "Thank you for that, but let's not talk about it. It upsets me."

"Of course, my dear, of course," he said consolingly.

Everyone started to talk, trying to fill the quiet by sharing stories of their day. Emma listened and participated in the conversation, all the while observing Meghan's behavior. She seemed to be specifically avoiding Walter. He also seemed to be animated with everyone but her. He was even working on the other lady's French accents.

Emma waited until dinner was being served before asking him a question. "Walter, how many times have you been to France?"

"Oh, many," he said.

"What business do you have there that takes you so often?" she asked curiously.

He waved his hand vaguely. "Oh, buying and selling."

"Buying and selling what?" she pressed.

"This and that," he said, clearly wanting her to accept his answer and end the conversation.

Emma let it go and continued to watch everyone at the table, conscious that time was running out to solve this mystery.

She followed Walter to his cabin after dinner, hanging back at a distance. She paused around a corner, waiting to see if Meghan would turn up. A lady with a shawl covering her face eventually appeared and knocked softly on the door.

Got you, thought Emma, ready to step out and surprise them. She hesitated a moment to see how Walter would react to the woman. As he opened his door, he saw who it was, and a wide smile spread over his face. The woman's shawl slipped and Emma ducked back in surprise. It was not Meghan, but Susan Billings!

She pulled herself further away and thought, *I'll have to rethink my list of suspects. Who do I still have on the list? I need to head to Meghan's cabin NOW!*

She hurried there and stayed around a corner to ensure she was not seen. Meghan's door opened and the captain stepped out, holding her hands. Emma narrowed her eyes. Was the captain involved in this? She watched their body language. *No, not him. He's there to reassure her, but not in a romantic way.*

She watched him leave and waited to see what would happen next. She thought about her list of suspects, *It's not Walter or the captain. Who else is there?*

Just as she was ready to head back to her cabin for some much-needed rest, a cabin steward knocked on Meghan's door. She heard him inquire, "Miss, would you like some additional towels?" Emma yawned, not expecting much. A surprising thing happened next; Meghan placed her arms around him and pulled him into her cabin.

Emma smiled. The steward. The same man who had "looked" for Scott when he went overboard. *I'll bet that, even if he had seen him, he wouldn't have said so. Now, I have the who, what, and why.*

She closed her notebook and thought, *It's time to meet with the captain. Not much can happen tonight. I'll tell him my findings tomorrow.* She headed to her cabin to sleep.

CHAPTER 58

DAY 4 OF 7 LA BRETAGNE

*E*mma dressed and went to the captain's cabin before breakfast. The officer saw Emma approach and asked, "Would you like to see the Captain?"

"Yes, if he has time," she responded. "Wait a moment," he said and went in to check. He returned a moment later, saying, "You may go in."

The captain was donning his jacket as she entered. He looked over at her and said, "Miss Evans, please come in. Have you completed your investigation?" he asked and smiled at her, not expecting much.

"I would not say completed but captain, I have some things to share," she confirmed. She detailed the information she had found. "I never saw Scott drink, so I checked with our meal steward and he confirmed Scott did not order any drinks. The only drinks in their cabin were unopened. I also checked with the bartender and no additional drinks were ordered for the cabin. That, along with the self-inflicted injuries, leads me to believe she planned this. I didn't mention it before, but she set me up to witness their struggle; we had planned to meet there at midnight."

"Why were you meeting with her at that late hour?" he inquired.

"I work with a group of people who help women at risk," she explained.

"So, you believed she was at risk," he stated.

"I did initially," she admitted, "but I believe I was used to be a witness to prove she was the one being attacked."

"Are you sure about this?" he asked, with a frown.

"When looked closer I saw discrepancies in her story. Captain, I think your issue here is how could a woman do this. Don't underestimate us; women can be the bad guys. I want to show you something. Could you stand here with me?"

He looked like he might say no, but he complied.

She started, "Okay, if Scott was trying to throw Meghan overboard, I think his arm placement would have been different than what I observed when I came onto the deck."

"How so?" the captain asked, curious where this demonstration was headed.

"Watch," she said as she grabbed him by the shoulder; his response was to grip her back. "Look down at the hand placement."

He did so. "My hands are under yours."

"Yes. But, when I saw them, I expected that his hands would be higher if he was trying to push her overboard; however, hers were higher. It's also possible she drugged him to make him easier to manipulate."

"So, you think she drugged him and pushed him overboard. But why?" he asked.

"There's one more fact I have to share. I was observing her cabin last night and saw one of the stewards join her."

"What's unusual about that? The stewards work in the cabins at all hours. Maybe he was just there to do his job," he said. He was, understandably, being protective of his staff.

"This steward was kissing Meghan, and she gave an enthusiastic response before pulling him into her cabin. I also heard a man and a woman's voice in her cabin that morning," she explained.

Shaking his head in disbelief, he said, "So, you think she did all of this to get with a steward she just met?"

"I think it's more than that. I think they planned this together, and I believe they murdered her husband," she stated firmly. "Do you have any background on this steward? Where did he come on board? Is he one of your regular crew? Do you have access to that information?"

"My dear, I am the captain," he said, straightening his white jacket. "It's my ship and all of the information is mine."

She saw his serious expression and reacted in kind saying, "Of course."

"Come with me."

As they exited the cabin, he told the officer where they were going and ordered him to stay put. They made their way downstairs to the administration office. He produced a key, opened the door, and turned back to her saying, "They won't be in until after 9am."

He immediately went to the drawers containing the personnel information. He pulled the steward's employee file, saying, "Hmm, he is a first-time crew member."

"Do you normally have new employees working alone?" she asked, surprised.

"No, normally customer service is crucial, and a new member would shadow another member on their first trip," he explained.

"How are members hired?"

"We have a pool of available people. If someone wanted to become a member, we take recommendations from another crew member."

"Is there someone listed for him?"

"Yes," he said quietly. "My main steward who is in charge of this area. It appears they have the same last name."

"Brothers?"

"Yes. It would have been easy for him to slip in unnoticed. A boat this size, I wouldn't have noticed a difference in staffing at this level."

"No, of course not," she said, understanding the complexities of his job.

"We're still more than three days out. Do we confront them now?" he asked earnestly.

"No, I would wait until the morning we arrive at the port. Make them believe their plans are coming to fruition," she suggested.

"I like the idea, but that is my busy time."

"Yes, but I think we'll have a worse time trying to figure out how to keep them under control if we take them into custody now."

"Yes, I think we can make that work. What do you suggest?" he asked.

She went over her plans.

CHAPTER 59

DAY 5 AND 6 OF 7 LA BRETAGNE

These two days went by quietly.

Meghan thought she had gotten away with her plan and had dropped the sad act altogether. She seemed to be enjoying herself. Emma stopped asking questions and Meghan was even friendlier to her.

CHAPTER 60

DAY 7 FINAL DAY ON THE LA BRETAGNE

The morning the ship was to dock, Emma had access to the dining room. She had requested that the captain bring his senior crew members and the brother of the steward there. The steward under surveillance was harder to locate because it appeared he'd begun sleeping in Meghan's cabin.

The captain accompanied Emma to Meghan's cabin and knocked briskly on the door. From the noise, it was obvious there were two people in there. Meghan finally answered, pulling her robe tight around her, and said, "Captain, this is such a nice surprise."

"Mrs. Bauer, we request your presence in the dining room," he commanded.

"Oh, okay. I need to dress. I'll meet you there," she said.

"I think not," he said, his tone stern.

She frowned, not understanding.

The captain continued, "I'll wait until you dress and escort you."

She noticed another officer was with him. After a minute, she nodded and started to close the door when the captain put his hand on it to stop her.

"And tell Steward Beardsley we'll be expecting him as well."

Meghan's mouth opened and closed several times. She tried to act like she didn't know what he was talking about when a voice sounded behind her.

"Yes, sir, I will be there."

Meghan's expression changed, her mouth tuned downward and her eyes closed. Emma had seen that look before; she knew she was caught.

The captain allowed her to shut the door and get dressed. There was nowhere for the two to go.

Things were very quiet within the cabin, and they wasted no time getting dressed and exiting. The officer went to stand by the steward, and the captain accompanied Meghan. She saw Emma watching and said, "I knew you were trouble."

"Not the first time I've heard that," commented Emma. She motioned to another senior crew member to enter the cabin and search it as they made their way to the dining room.

The ship had docked early, and the gangway was lowered. The captain's assistant had gone for the police. As they entered the dining room, they found the French police waiting.

Meghan seemed to shrink when she saw them. They put her and Steward Beardsley in chairs at the center of the room.

The captain stood in front of them and said, "We have some things to talk about." He looked over at Emma and said, "Miss Evans?"

Emma was talking to the person who had just searched Meghan's cabin. She thanked him and turned to the captain.

"Yes, I'll take it from here."

As she stepped forward, she pulled out her notebook and started going over her observations. "You're having an affair with Steward Beardsley. When you left your cabin just now, we were able to search it. As I understand it, Scott didn't have any alcohol on the ship. Comments from other passengers indicated he had said he couldn't drink due to a stomach condition. We found this in your cabin, hidden in your closet," she said, holding up a vial. "I will confirm with the doctor, but I expect you used this to make your husband appear drunk. I would assume you haven't had a chance to get rid of it."

"No one would leave me alone," Meghan said bitterly, knowing she was caught. "What made you suspect me?" she asked, curious.

"It was when I saw you struggle with your husband," Emma explained.

She looked confused at that statement. "Why's that?"

"It looked like he was struggling to get away from you, not you away from him."

The steward's brother, Charlie Beardsley was brought into the room, accompanied by another of the ship's officers. His brother, Nathanial, hung his head, not saying anything. Charlie immediately confronted him. "You just had to be with her, didn't you? You said this was all planned, and we wouldn't lose anything."

Nathanial grimaced. His brother was acting like all of this was his fault! He lashed out recklessly, "It worked great last time!"

"Nathanial! Shut up!" Meghan whispered fiercely.

Emma glanced between them. "So, there are other people involved in your scheme? I'm sure the French police can work that out."

The captain waved to the officers. "Take them away." He looked at Emma and said, "Emma, thank you. They would have gotten away with it had you not been here."

Emma smiled and said, "Thank you. Hopefully, they will also find out who else was involved in this. If you will take custody of this vial, I believe they will tell you it is what I suspect." She handed it to him.

"I'll send this and the details of which ships the Beardsley's have worked on and information about Mrs. Bauer, too. We have your hotel information in Paris if there are any further questions. You had best get moving, Emma. We've arrived at your destination," he said as he smiled broadly.

"Yes, you're right. I'll go get my bags now," she said, anticipating seeing Tony.

She had a porter carry her bags and they made it just in time to exit the ship ahead of the police escorting Meghan, Charlie, and Nathanial.

Tony stood at the bottom of the gangplank, watching her descend. He frowned, concerned when he saw the police. "Emma, is everything okay?"

"Oh, this isn't about me." She nodded toward Meghan, Charlie, and Nathanial, who were being led off in handcuffs.

"Did another adventure come your way on the ship?" he asked knowingly.

She smiled. "It is nice to see you, Tony."

He smiled back, looking strained, and said, "Emma, thank you so much for helping me locate Philip."

"Should we be going?" They were being jostled by passengers trying to leave the ship.

"Yes, sorry. I'm distracted. I have a carriage to take us to the train station. Come with me," he requested.

"My bags?" she asked. indicating the porter.

"Yes, please, follow us," Tony directed, his hands shaking as he indicated where the steward should go.

Tony was more rattled than she had ever seen him. They would have to talk on the train.

They made their way to the carriage, and Emma started noticing the voices around them. *Lovely language,* she thought.

CHAPTER 61

NEW YORK

*J*eremy climbed into his carriage after dropping Emma off. He looked around the area and thought, *New York isn't someplace I want to be without Emma. She'll be gone for at least a month if the case goes well. I'm going to miss her.*

He shook himself out of the melancholy settling over him and pulled his paperwork from his pocket. He glanced at it and then looked at the driver and said, "Please take me to the local telegraph office, located on Market Street."

"Yes, sir," the driver said and clicked at the horses to move on. When he pulled in front of the telegraph office, he looked back and said, "Sir, should I wait for you?"

"Yes, please," said Jeremy absently as he exited. He walked into the office and said, "I should have a telegram to pick up?"

The operator checked the stack in front of him and looked up at Jeremy. "Your name, please."

Jeremy looked him in the eye and said in a clear voice, "Jeremy Tilden."

He looked through his files. "Yes, this is it here." He reached out to hand the telegram to Jeremy.

Jeremy accepted the message and stepped back from the desk to read it. *Zeke found, but not apprehended. He appears to still be on a trajectory to Chicago. Witnesses in several states have said he was on his way to finish a personal vendetta.*

Jeremy thought about that information. Zeke was originally placed in the McNeal Island prison in Washington state. The penitentiary system had taken over the running of the prison in 1875. It was surrounded by Puget Sound. *He took a long, cold swim,* thought Jeremy. *It couldn't have been pleasant. He must be desperate to go through this much trouble to wreak his vengeance on Emma and possibly Clair. I'm very glad we kept it quiet that Emma has left the country.*

He started tapping the telegram against his hand. He nodded and thought decisively, *Time to head home and wait for him.*

He asked the driver to take him to the rail station. He was going to head home on the next available train. He arrived at the New Jersey rail station in time to take the day train to Buffalo. Once in Buffalo, there was a wait until that evening. As he boarded, he felt some frustration at not being able to arrive sooner. The only good thing was that Zeke was experiencing the same travel limitations and he had a greater distance to go.

CHAPTER 62

*J*eremy spent the next week on the train thinking about the best way to handle Zeke's return to Chicago. They would need to get the word out to the bakery staff that, if anyone asked, Emma was working the morning shift. They would put extra men at the bakery and Clair's house for protection. Cole was already guarding Clair at the charity but not at her house. They had time to get everyone in place before Zeke arrived.

There was also the boarding house to think about. They would need men there as well. Tim would be called upon to make sure Dora never went out alone. *And I can't forget about Amy,* he reminded himself.

What's the best way to let people know to be on the lookout for Zeke? he asked himself and remembered Dora's accounting books. She often drew pictures of her desserts and he had also seen a sketchpad around the house with family members drawn in coal and pencil.

That's what we need. A drawing of Zeke that we can distribute; Clair would be the best to help describe him, he thought to himself.

"Finally," he said as the train pulled into the Chicago station.

He exited and looked around. Jeremy spotted Cole waiting in a nearby carriage and waved.

Cole said, "In my boy, we have a lot to discuss."

"Yes," said Jeremy and he climbed on board. "Do we have any idea if he's closer now?"

"We've sent men along the route to Washington, but he must be taking alternate transportation. That will allow us more time to plan."

"I was thinking, no one should be told Emma's out of town. We should ask the bakery personnel to tell anyone inquiring that she still works there."

"Good idea, misdirect," commented Cole.

"I was also thinking of Dora. I believe she could provide a drawing based on an interview with Clair. That way, if Zeke does show up, people will know to avoid him."

"We've gotten word that he's already beaten up several ladies in bordellos on his way here," said Cole

"Okay, so we have Clair and Thomas distribute the drawing to those businesses. We'll make sure places where Emma has worked will have copies of the drawing and are notified to be extra cautious."

"Would you like to go home first?"

"No, I like the idea of seeing Clair as soon as possible," said Jeremy, wanting to put their plans into action.

"Good idea." Cole gave the charity address to the driver. They felt a tug as they started moving.

CHAPTER 63

Clair heard a light knock on her door and when it opened, she saw it was her assistant, Sam.

"Cole and Jeremy are here to see you."

"Show them in, please," she said, closing the books she was working on. She stayed at her desk and waited for them to enter. *I wonder what this is about?* she thought, watching the door.

Cole entered first, followed closely by Jeremy. They greeted her warmly.

Jeremy leaned over to kiss her on the cheek. "Clair, it's so good to see you. I appreciate you making time for us today."

"Anything for you, you know that. Would you like to move over here?" she said, indicating her couch surrounded by heavy chairs. Once they sat, she looked over and said, "Jeremy, it is good to see you back." She glanced at Cole and asked, "Is this about the charity?"

He didn't answer. Instead, he nudged Jeremy. "Jeremy, why don't you start?"

Clair's mind raced and, suddenly concerned, she asked, "Have you heard from Emma? Are there any problems with her health or her trip?"

"I expect to hear soon. The ship should dock in a few days. You haven't mentioned her trip to anyone?" asked Jeremy

"No, I kept it quiet, as you asked," she confirmed.

Jeremy was glad Emma was away from this. *Now, how to protect Clair?*

"Clair," he began, "We came here to share something serious with you. Zeke Jones has escaped." He hesitated when she let out a small scream, then continued. "We're getting intel that he might be on his way here."

She stood, needing to walk. "Do you think he is after me?"

"And Emma," confirmed Cole. "We need to get organized for him. We have time to put things into place before he arrives."

Clair asked him curiously, "Did you tell Emma about Zeke?"

He grimaced, saying, "I did."

"Was she upset to not be in on the action?" she asked, knowing how Emma felt about him.

"I think so, but honestly, she seemed more concerned that no one gets hurt." He smiled crookedly. "And she said to take care of him this time."

Cole smiled coldly and said, "Oh, we will take care of him."

"Yes," agreed Clair with a similar expression.

"Can you accompany us to the boarding house? I have an idea of where we can start," requested Jeremy.

She nodded and said, "Yes, of course." She called out, "Sam, please come in."

Sam did so and she said in a businesslike tone, "I'll be closing the office for today. I have personal business to attend to."

"Yes, of course. I'll continue to work and lock up at the normal time," Sam said, taking notes.

"Thank you," she said gratefully as she gathered her things. Sam brought her coat and assisted her in putting it on.

They made their way downstairs to the waiting carriage and headed to the boarding house. They arrived and climbed the stoop; Jeremy opened the door and held it for Clair. As they entered, he heard humming coming from the dining room. He spotted Dora working on her books at the table.

"Jeremy!" She jumped up as soon as she saw him. "I'm so glad to see you. Did Emma get off okay?"

"Yes, she should be there in a day or two," he confirmed.

"Funny. Just think, you can cross an ocean and it's the same timing as the trip from New York to Chicago," she said wonderingly.

"It is amazing," he agreed.

She noticed Clair and Cole behind him. "Oh, company! How is everyone? Would you like something to eat?"

"We're good," Jeremy answered for them. He looked around the dining room and nodded at her accounting books. "Dora, I noticed that you draw."

"Yes, documenting my desserts and for fun," she commented, wondering about this turn of conversation.

"Can I see your sketchbook?" he inquired.

"You're sure? It's just drawings I've done of the family," she said, confused.

"Please, it's important," he requested.

"I'll get it." Reading the seriousness in his expression, she went to the buffet and pulled it out, handing it to him for review.

He started flipping through the sketchbook and, after looking at each drawing carefully, he was sure it was the right decision. He looked up at Dora and said, "We'd like your help on a case."

"Shouldn't you be speaking with Emma?" she asked with a nervous laugh. She held her hand protectively on her stomach.

"No, you're the right person. Is Tim around?" Cole spoke up from behind Jeremy.

"He's in the kitchen," she said.

"I'll go get him," said Jeremy.

She frowned as she watched him go. He returned a

moment later with Tim walking behind him, frowning. Tim looked at the group and suggested, "Why don't we move to the study?"

Everyone nodded and followed him. As they entered the room, Tim pulled the doors shut to allow them more privacy.

"What is this about?" he asked.

"Zeke Jones is back," Jeremy answered bluntly.

Dora sucked in her breath and clutched Tim's hand. Tim's face went dark.

Dora thought about Emma and said, "Oh, Emma's leaving, that worked out well."

"It did actually. I waited to tell her until we were at the ship," he admitted.

"Was she angry?" asked Dora, worried about her sister.

"No," he said, "she understood, and she knows Tony needs help."

"Yes, that's true," she acknowledged.

Tim commented in a serious voice, ready to protect his family. "What is it you want Dora to do? Not fieldwork?"

"No." Jeremy smiled, understanding his concern. "We want her to sketch Zeke."

Cole looked over at Clair and said, "We brought you here to help us with the sketch. We would like to get a picture of Zeke plastered all over town. It'll help limit his movements if he makes it here."

Clair had gone pale, but she looked Cole and Jeremy in the eyes before saying resolutely, "I'll do anything to make sure he isn't free ever again."

"Dora, can you get your drawing pencils?" directed Jeremy.

Tim said, "I'll get them for you" and patted Dora's hand before he stood. He exited the study and closed the doors on his way out.

Clair took the opportunity to ask, "Dora, how're you feeling?"

"I'm good, though the morning comes up a bit faster than they used to."

"Crackers work," she commented. Jeremy missed the twinkle in her eye.

Dora saw it and said, "Clair, are you and Thomas?"

She blushed and nodded.

Jeremy noticed the nod and put things together. "Hey, what's this? Another baby?"

"Yes," she said, blushing again.

"Congratulations!" said Cole and Jeremy at the same time and laughed.

"Thomas must be overjoyed," said Dora.

"He is and he's trying to do everything for me," commented Clair.

"Tim is the same," she murmured as he approached. He not only brought her pencils; he also had her shawl.

"In case you get chilly," he said.

Clair laughed out loud. When Tim looked at her askance, she just smiled back.

Dora motioned to Tim and, when he bent down, she whispered in his ear. He turned to Clair with a wide smile. "Congratulations, Clair! You must send Thomas our congratulations as well."

Jeremy said, "Let's get started."

Dora opened her book and readied her pencils. "Clair, we'll work through this together. Let's start with the shape of his face; is it long and narrow, short, round?"

"Long and narrow," she said, trying to keep emotion out of her voice.

"His eyes, can you remember their shape?"

The only sound in the room was the scratching of the pencil.

"Yes," she said a bit shakily, "they're brown and the shape is. . ." She looked at Jeremy and Tim. "Smaller than Jeremy's eyes."

She watched Dora draw and commented, "No, there's a further distance between them."

Dora adjusted the eyes and asked, "Like that?"

"Better."

"How about his forehead—high or low?"

"High."

"His nose?"

"Straight and a bit turned in at the bottom."

Dora drew an exaggeration initially. It made them all laugh. She erased it and drew another. "Is that close?"

"A bit narrower here," she said, pointing to the bridge of his nose.

She corrected the drawing and asked, "What about ears?"

"Just regular, they didn't stick out much."

She added ears and Clair confirmed, "Yes, you're getting there."

"What about the hair?"

"Oh, that hair. He loved his hair. Thick black and he always wore it a bit longer than he should."

She added the hair. "Did he have bangs?"

"No, he took pride in it and had it combed back."

Dora took a moment to move the sketch pad toward her, completed the details, and asked the group, holding up the sketch for them to view. "Is this the man you remember?"

Clair went white. "Yes, you got him."

"Jeremy, Tim?" inquired Dora, turning it for them to view.

"He looks right to me," commented Tim.

Jeremy nodded.

"Okay, so how do we get this out for everyone to see?" Jeremy asked.

"Papa," suggested Dora. "He has a process to make copies."

Cole looked over at her and asked, "How does that work?"

At that precipitous moment, Papa opened the door and walked into the room. He answered their question himself.

"There is an ability to copy. I have the required hectograph, gelatin duplicator, or jellygraph. The printing process involves the transfer of an original, prepared with special inks, to a pan of gelatin."

"Papa, how did you know we needed you?" asked Dora, getting up to kiss him on the cheek.

"Cole mentioned I might need to come by," he said laconically.

"Did he tell you—" Dora started to ask tentatively.

"About Zeke?" he interrupted. "Yes. He knows if my girls are in danger, then I will be involved."

Jeremy handed him the paper to copy and Papa looked at it closely. "Good job, Dora. This looks just like him." He gestured to Cole and Jeremy. "The chemicals are in my lab. I have the setup down there."

"How long will the process take?" asked Jeremy, thinking ahead to distribution.

"If I get them started now, overnight to dry. We'll need paper to get us started."

"I can get that," indicated Tim.

"Okay, let's get going."

Tim got the paper to Papa, and they worked through the night, with Zeke's image spread all over the house to dry. Papa checked them and said they would be ready to go out the next afternoon.

Cole and Jeremy met early the next morning and discussed where the copies should be handed out. Thomas stopped by with information on the distribution. "Clair wanted me to give you a list of the houses he might frequent." He handed the list over to Cole.

"Hmm," said Cole, "good idea. We don't want anyone hurt in this. Thomas, thank Clair for us."

"We'll cover the bordellos, the bakery, the office, here at the boarding house, and next door. I'll also give these to our men on the streets," confirmed Jeremy.

They agreed and Papa, Cole, Jeremy, and Thomas headed out to distribute the copies. The more people who knew Zeke was in town and dangerous, the better. Tim wanted to help and started to leave with the group.

Papa stopped him. "Tim, I think it's best if you stay here."

He looked like he wanted to argue, then looked at his lovely Dora playing with Patrick. He realized his priority was there. "You're right, my place is here."

"Thomas, are the guards with Clair?" asked Cole.

"Yes, we also got two more for the charity."

"Good," Cole said.

They left taking different carriages to get the papers were distributed. Pinkerton agents were also placed in strategic locations around town.

CHAPTER 64

It would be another week before any information about Zeke started coming in. "We have a sighting," commented Jeremy, reviewing the note just delivered to their agency.

"Where?" Cole said, immediately standing and walking over to review the note.

"Where else? The Bordello on 5th," Jeremy commented.

"Is he still there?" asked Cole, ready to head over.

"No." He chuckled suddenly.

"Why is that funny? This man is dangerous."

"The lady he grabbed recognized him immediately and screamed. The others went on the attack. He barely made it out of there alive."

Cole laughed. "Did they say what direction he went in?"

"Just out. They managed to give him a limp and a black eye."

"Hmm, that also may make him more desperate to get to Emma and get out of town."

"I'm going to the bakery," Jeremy said, "to join the men there."

"Okay, keep me informed and I'll send over any information that comes in," Cole promised.

Jeremy headed over in a carriage and had them drop him off a few blocks away. He saw the Pinkerton men, some hanging out in the front of the bakery, others disguised as delivery drivers in the back.

Jeremy joined the men in the back. He pulled his hat down over his eyes and leaned again the wall, waiting. *So much of investigation is waiting*, he thought. He kept his head down but was watching the door closely. Several female bakers were exiting at the end of their day. He was worried; they appeared to be alone. He didn't have to wait long. Thomas ran out behind them saying, "Hey, wait for me. You promised I could see you both home."

They looked back and a small blonde said, "Oh, sorry, Thomas, we would like your company tonight." He stepped between them and they linked their hands into his elbows as they were leaving. Thomas saw Jeremy and walked past without any acknowledgment. He wouldn't give him away as undercover.

They were there through the evening until the last employees left for the day. As the final person cleared out, Jeremy told his men to get going and he started to make his way home. As he walked to the back gate of the bakery, he didn't feel the hit on the back of his head.

He woke up slowly and realized he was in a chair with someone tying his hands behind him. He was able to pretend to still be asleep as he flexed his arms to allow for a loose tie on the ropes. He continued to sit still, pretending to wake up at that moment.

He tried to figure out where he was without opening his eyes. *The room smells familiar.* He could smell baked goods. *The bakery. I didn't go far,* he mused. Pain radiated from his head and his arms were very sore. *He must have pulled me inside by my arms.* He let his eyes open slowly and saw Zeke pacing the office. He noticed Jeremy had woken up and was watching him.

"We got the nose right," Jeremy said, indicating the drawing Zeke held.

"This!" Zeke snapped, wadding up the paper and throwing it at Jeremy's face. "This is causing all of my problems! I can't go anywhere or do anything because of it."

"I did hear you went somewhere and. . . what was it?" he said consideringly. "That's right, you got beaten up by a bunch of women." He laughed.

Zeke looked like he would explode and used his arm to knock everything off the desk. The sounds were loud in the small office.

"Where is she?" he screamed.

"And who would that be?" Jeremy asked, taunting him.

Zeke's face went dark as he said in a low, menacing voice, "Where is she?"

"Far, far away from you."

Zeke used his fist on Jeremy's face in response. Jeremy let his head fall back, then he straightened and gave him a twisted smile. "We have you; you just don't know it yet."

"I have everything under control," Zeke said with false bravado.

"Why come back here?" Jeremy asked, keeping his voice light.

"To get her and that other one," Zeke answered.

"Other one?"

"The redheaded whore. She's going to get what she deserves, too," he threatened.

"Think so? I don't." Jeremy knew something Zeke did not. There were safety measures in place: all agents must check-in after leaving their final assignments for the day. He knew the

Pinkerton staff would notify Cole of his last location and check out the bakery first. With a head wound like this and Zeke being smaller than Jeremy, blood and drag marks were probably apparent in the dirt outside.

I would also assume, he thought, *the lock was broken when he entered the bakery. Just a matter of time now. The best thing I can do is keep Zeke talking.*

"Where to next after you take care of the two women?" he asked, not saying their names.

"I have plans," he said importantly.

"Plans?" he inquired.

"Yes, I have someone who'll help me. Someone important."

Jeremy nodded like he agreed. He heard something out in the bakery. The sound stopped their conversation.

Zeke said triumphantly, "They're early for the baking. Emma's always early. This will be easy."

"That's true," Jeremy said, going along with him. "She's always early to the bakery."

He listened and could hear a familiar female voice. Jeremy knew Zeke wouldn't know what Emma's voice sounded like. He said, "That does sound like her."

He didn't think he was putting anyone in danger. He knew that, at this hour, it was highly unlikely a bakery employee had entered the store. He suspected Cole was behind this visitor.

Zeke looked conflicted; he wanted to find out if it was Emma, but he didn't want additional people to monitor. He came to a decision and pulled out his gun, pointing it at Jeremy. "You, I will deal with you later." He opened the door slowly and looked out, listening.

"She's probably in front preparing the counters," Jeremy said innocently.

Zeke didn't think as he nodded and headed toward the front of the store.

Jeremy undid his hands and reached for the clutch pistol he kept in his boot. He was expecting that Cole had men scattered around the bakery, and he was right. As he made his way out of the office, Pinkerton men seemed to come from all sides. Zeke was not in the mood to go back to jail and started firing his pistol.

Jeremy realized he had the perfect shot, and he did not hesitate to take it. Zeke dropped to the floor, not moving.

He looked around and saw a woman standing nearby and said, "Savannah, I thought that was you. Were you in the bakery?"

"No," said Cole, coming up behind her, "not a chance. With her theatre training, I knew she could throw her voice. She never left my side at the door."

"Cole, if you don't mind, I'm going to head home for some rest. We, theater people, don't like to get up before noon," said Savannah, yawning broadly.

"Thanks for the help," said Cole.

"No problem," she said as she headed out.

"Dave," he called to a detective standing nearby. "Please escort Savannah home."

Dave nodded and followed her out.

Jeremy nudged Zeke with his foot; there was no movement. "No loss there," he said.

"No," Cole agreed. "Alan, let the police chief know we'll need help with cleanup. Also, before we move him, we need Jake to document the scene." He looked over at Jeremy and said, "You can head home and get some rest." He noticed the wound on his head. "Do you need to be checked out? The Sisters could probably do it for you."

Jeremy grimaced, touching the lump on the back of his head. "I might need to stop over there before I head home."

"Do you want me to send a carriage with you?"

"No, we're close by. I can walk," he said as he headed out into the night. Something was bugging him. *Zeke mentioned a benefactor, someone who had promised to help him. Is it someone we know?* He would have to think about it.

He made his way to the hospital and climbed the stairs. The Sisters remembered him and were immediately concerned with his appearance. Sister Mary said, "Sister Ann, please see to Jeremy. The rest of you, back to work." She motioned for the Sisters to disperse.

Sister Ann gathered up her medical tray and told him to sit down on a side chair by the nurses' station. "Jeremy, what happened?"

"Head got hit with something hard," he said simply.

"Let me take a look." She cleaned the wound, saying, "I don't think I'll need to put in any stitches. It looks worse than it is."

"Thanks, Sister, good to know," he said, grimacing as she finished and applied a bandage.

She was tidying up the bandages and replacing her equipment when she said, "You'll have a nice bump that you'll need to watch. Put cold compresses on it to help with the swelling."

"I will," he said as he pressed gently against the bandage.

"I do recommend that you have a ride home; you might still experience some dizziness. One of our volunteers can take you," she offered.

Jeremy realized how tired he was and said sincerely, "I would appreciate that."

"It shouldn't be a problem," she said. She called out, saying, "Dan, could you take Jeremy home?"

Jeremy told Dan the address and he said, "Sure, I know this neighborhood. I'll get the wagon ready to take you. Meet me downstairs?"

Jeremy nodded. They only had to wait a moment for the wagon to pull up in front of the hospital.

Jeremy looked at Sister Ann and said, "Thanks for helping me."

She reminded him, "Be sure to rest tonight and tomorrow."

"I will. Thank you again." He climbed into the wagon and thought to himself, *I'll go to the charity in the morning and confirm that Zeke is no longer a threat. We owe it to Clair and Thomas to let them know they're safe.*

CHAPTER 65

The trip home was uneventful. Jeremy climbed into his bed and slept hard. When he woke the next morning, he had a small headache, but it wasn't something that would stop him from spreading the good news that Zeke Jones was no longer a threat.

He headed downstairs and went straight to the kitchen, where he found Dora and Amy preparing breakfast.

Dora saw his bandage and immediately said, "Jeremy, what happened? Were you attacked?"

"Oh this," he commented, reaching up to touch it. "It's nothing." Before she could ask more questions, he said, "Dora, can you call Tim in? I need to speak with you both."

"Of course." She looked at Amy and said, "I'll be right back."

When Dora left to get Tim, Amy asked, "Should I step out?" She knew some cases were private and didn't want to intrude.

"No," said Jeremy. "You can stay for this news." He looked around, saying, "Where's Patrick?" He knew how much the boy loved to be in the kitchen with Dora.

"He's with Ellis. I believe they're performing some experiments," Amy commented, going back to frying her sausages.

Tim came into the kitchen with Dora trailing behind him. He asked, concerned, "Is everything okay? Dora said you've been hurt?"

Jeremy smiled reassuringly and said, "I'm good. Please, sit down." He waited for them to sit and said, "We got him last night."

Dora immediately put her hands together to give thanks. "You have him in custody."

"Better than that. He's no longer a threat," Jeremy said.

Tim looked at him shrewdly and said, "He's dead." It was not a question, but a statement of fact.

"Yes," Jeremy said.

"Good," said Tim, with no remorse. He was glad the threat had been removed from their lives.

"What now?" Dora asked.

"First, I'm going to see Clair when she opens the charity and give her the good news. Later, I'll send a wire to the hotel Emma's staying at and give her all the details."

"Not before you eat and put some cool water on that cut," said Dora.

Jeremy smiled. It was nice to have family taking care of him. He ate breakfast and let Dora minister to the wound before heading over to see Clair.

As he arrived at the charity, he noticed something odd. The two bodyguards Clair had added were not in the outer office area. Odder still, the two secretaries normally in position were also missing.

Jeremy frowned, looking around. He noticed Sam's office was open, but he was not there. As he approached Clair's office, he heard arguing—Clair's voice was raised, and he could tell from the tone something was wrong.

He knocked, saying, "Clair, it's Jeremy. I have some news to share with you."

More arguing ensued. Clair opened the door and said in a

strained voice, "Would you like to come in?" Her eyes were bright with tears and very red.

He mouthed to her, "*It's okay.*"

Her eyes got wider and they darted to the right. She mouthed, "*Gun.*"

"Sam, where are you?" said Jeremy in a clear voice.

Sam stepped from behind the door, behind Clair, waving a gun. He grabbed her by the hair and pulled her back with him.

Jeremy started forward, but Sam had the gun steady on him.

"Don't hurt her," Jeremy said. He looked around and asked, "Where are the guards and secretaries?"

"I told the guards they were no longer needed," he sneered.

"And the secretaries?"

"I sent them on a fool's errand to review some property for Clair."

"Why the subterfuge? What are you trying to accomplish?"

Something occurred to him; Zeke had mentioned a benefactor, and Sam had access to the charity accounts.

Jeremy asked softly, "Sam, are you waiting for someone?"

"What do you mean?" he asked nervously, looking out the side window.

"Maybe Zeke?" He narrowed his eyes, ignoring Clair's start at the name.

"What, what are you talking about?" he sputtered.

Jeremy said, "Sam, I know you're working with Zeke."

Clair looked shocked. She had hired Sam and trusted him.

Sam groaned and asked. "Where is Zeke? We were supposed to meet here this morning, get the money from Clair, and then make our escape."

"Bad news on that front. We got him early this morning," Jeremy said with an evil grin.

"Where is he?" Sam was still thinking he could get him. "I'll trade this whore for him."

"Well, I can't say I know where he is right now, but tomorrow he'll be six feet under," commented Jeremy.

"That Emma bitch! I tried to get her for him, but you kept her too well protected."

"At the funeral, you tried to get her alone at the hall," Jeremy recalled.

"Yes, I thought I took care of her. He just couldn't leave her alone!" Sam finally realized what Jeremy had said. "You killed him! But we were going to leave together." He wiped his hand over his eyes, growing more desperate by the minute. He didn't understand what was happening.

Jeremy was waiting for that moment when he loosened his grip on Clair. He yelled, "Clair, get down!" She immediately dropped out of the way.

Jeremy leaped forward and latched onto Sam. They wrestled on the floor. Sam was reaching for the gun when he was stopped by Clair. She put her heel on his wrist and pressed down. He screamed as she kicked it away. Jeremy jumped up to grab the gun. He put Sam's gun in his pocket and pulled out his own, pointing it at Sam. "A few questions for you, Sam. Who was Zeke to you?"

Sam didn't answer, just kept screaming. Jeremy looked at Clair and said, "Hand me some rope."

She kept some in a drawer for packages that might need to be sent out. Jeremy immediately grabbed Sam's wrists and tied him tightly. When he tried to allow some room in the ropes, Jeremy put a knee in his back and pulled back hard, saying, "I know that trick."

"Jeremy, sit him down. I would like some questions answered," stated Clair.

Jeremy did as she asked and guided Sam to a chair facing them. He had finally stopped screaming and was just sitting there, looking into space when Clair stated, "What did you and Zeke want?"

"What? The money, of course. You're handing it out. You can hand us some."

"The discrepancies, that was you!" she accused.

"It was," he admitted. "I wanted to see how much I could take without you reporting it to the board."

She looked at Jeremy and said, "I had the accountants reviewing the losses and I was going to share it with the board at that time. I didn't have a chance to review with Emma before she left."

Jeremy nodded, unconcerned; he trusted Clair. Jeremy continued to watch Sam and wondered what he was missing. There was something about him, his mannerisms, and then he remembered the hair pulling.

Jeremy said smoothly, "Sam, are you related to Zeke?"

"What are you talking about?" Sam asked, not looking him in the eye.

That's it, thought Jeremy. "How did he find you?"

He looked defeated. "He didn't find me. He wasn't even looking. I found him. I knew I had to come from someone better than my mother. She was a whore like you," he said with disgust toward Clair.

"So, it's better to be related to a monster than a whore?" asked Clair, anger in her voice.

"We were going to have a good life, away from here. But he just had to settle the score with Emma. He just wouldn't let it go."

They heard someone enter from the outer office and a voice called, "Clair!"

"It's Thomas!" said Clair. "We're in here," she called out.

"Where is everyone?" he asked, staring at them in astonishment. What he saw was Sam tied up, Clair's hair down around her shoulders, and Jeremy with an injury.

Jeremy took over and said, "Thomas, could you get Cole and tell him we need a team here?"

"Yes, but I want to check on Clair first." He went over and kneeled in front of her. "Are you okay?"

She started to tear up and said, "I am now. Jeremy, can I go with Thomas?"

"Of course, you can," he replied.

On her way out, Clair looked at Sam and said, as a parting statement, "Why is your family always pulling hair?" She didn't wait for a response and headed out with Thomas.

Jeremy sat with a very quiet Sam, thinking about what his telegram to Emma would say.

CHAPTER 66

FRANCE

Emma was struggling to remember her French as a porter retrieved her luggage. She said hurriedly, "Merci."

"Di rein," he said and inclined his head as he picked up her bags.

Tony noticed and said, "You've studied."

"Not as much as you," she said with a grimace. "I have a few phrases and will be relying on you for the rest."

It was quiet between them, but it was not an uncomfortable silence as they followed the porter to the waiting carriage that would transport them to the train station. "We're just in time," said Tony, walking swiftly, carrying Emma's bags to the train. They made their way to their cabin and got settled just as it started to pull out.

As it picked up speed and moved them toward Paris, she looked at him and asked quietly, "Tony, what's happened?"

He shoved off his hat. As it fell to the seat beside him, he answered, "We were involved in reviewing special works of art to determine their age. Philip has been working on putting together books about painting authentication. He began talking to various artists about a catalogue raisonne, a book that would provide a reliable method to examine the age of paintings."

Tony continued, "We've been examining paintings and documenting the smell of oil in the paintings. They should have an oily smell for many years until the oil fully dries. If you're looking at investing in an oil painting more than a few years old, it shouldn't have this smell. Next, there was the evaluation of age, the cracking of the paint on canvas."

He realized he was sharing too much detail. He tried to be clearer. "We were working on reviewing the age of paintings. We'd been here a few weeks and I was seeing so many great artists."

"So far it sounds great. What happened?"

"We received an invitation from the Laurel Museum to authenticate an important exhibit. Philip was very excited that the curator, Monsieur Martin, had invited us because he had known him since the beginning of his career. He was instrumental in helping Philip learn about art," Tony explained.

"Did something go wrong during the authentication?" asked Emma, trying to put the facts together.

"No, just the opposite. We reviewed the collection in detail and met with each artist to confirm the authentication. The job was completed with positive results," said Tony.

"Why do you think that museum is involved in Philip's disappearance?" asked Emma.

"On the night he went missing, we received a note from Monsieur Martin. They had received a late shipment and wanted Philip to see it before it was displayed," he explained.

"Did he go alone?" she asked, taking notes.

"Yes, I was tired. We'd been working all day. He said he wouldn't be long, so I retired for the night. When I woke the next morning, he hadn't returned."

"What did you do first?"

"I waited and went to our first morning appointment without him."

"Was it at the same museum?"

"It was. I headed there after breakfast, thinking I might find a very tired Philip."

"What did you find?"

"They were closed."

"Closed?" she exclaimed.

"Yes, the day before they were fully operational, with a staff in place and art on the walls." He appeared to be at a loss as to what could have happened.

Very odd, thought Emma. She continued with her questions. "Did you try the door?"

"I did, and it was locked," he confirmed.

"Windows?" she asked.

"Galleries typically want more wall space, so no windows," he explained.

"Okay, let's stop by. I can get us in," she said in a firm voice.

Tony smiled. He was glad she had come to help him. "I thought you'd say that."

She smiled back. "Tony, it is good to see you."

He looked at her for a long time before replying quietly, "You, too."

That long moment made Emma want to talk about something else. She requested, "Tell me about Paris."

He happily started talking about the location that was fast becoming his favorite place. "Paris is a place of extremes. There's so much art that you just can't take it all in. The food is amazing, with pastries that make your mouth water. Then there's so much poverty and so many dirty areas. The children pickpockets are worse than in New York."

"It's disappointing to hear that. I'll have to get some information on charities in the area for Clair," she said, making a note to follow up. She looked over at him and said, "I can't wait to see it. Tell me about the art," she added, knowing he wanted to talk about it. "Who have you seen?"

"Claude Monet, Edgar Degas, Pierre Auguste Renoir, and others. They're doing something called Impressionism. This group chooses the depiction of modern life."

"Impressionism. Interesting term. Where did it come from?" Emma asked curiously.

"Claude Monet says it is the visual impression of the moment. Emma, when you look at it, how he uses color and light, you feel something go over you. It's an emotional connection."

"Wonderful! Who else have you seen?" she asked, wanting to hear more.

"Women painters. Mary Cassatt, she is an Impressionist also." Remembering something, he said, "Emma, do you recall the John Singer Sargent painting you saw at the museum back home?" When she frowned, uncertain, he reminded her with one word: "Venice."

She suddenly exclaimed, "Oh, my. I would love to see more of his paintings."

"There is a wonderful portrait of Madame Pierre Gautreau, known as Madame X, currently on display. We can go see that."

"Who else?" she asked, fascinated.

Tony continued on his favorite topic. "Paul Cézanne is very interesting. He seems to be turning away from Impressionism, more objects and landscapes, going to their geometric forms: the cube, cone, and cylinder."

"Are these works of art from Cézanne very expensive?"

"Right now, the art world isn't keeping up with all of the changes. We believe their future value will be very high." They continued talking about art until they reached Paris.

"I have arranged a carriage for us," he said as they exited the train.

"My bags?" inquired Emma. They had taken them off the train and had them sitting next to her.

"I have them being picked up," he said as they approached the hired carriage.

"Bonjour, nous aimerions aller au musée s'il vous plait," Tony greeted in flawless French, greeting the man and asking to be taken to the museum.

He helped Emma into the carriage, from where she took in the sights. "Tony, there is so much building going on. Papa would love it here."

"There is The Basilica of Sacré-Cœur on Montmartre, built-in neo-Byzantine style. It was begun in 1873, that we can see. It won't be completed for a while, but the architecture is amazing."

"That would be lovely," she said, peering at the buildings as they drove.

Tony commented, "Some interesting history about the neighborhood organization: a guy named Haussmann had a gigantic building project, and it may have caused some social dispersal. He relocated thousands of families and businesses and had their buildings demolished for the construction of the new boulevards. He was also blamed for reducing the amount of housing available for low-income families. In the old design, the higher level of apartment buildings was stratified to have higher classes and lower classes occupied lower floors. The new design didn't allow that, so many had to move to lower-income areas."

Emma thought about that as they neared the museum, located on the west side of Paris. There were new boulevards, stewards, water supplies, schools, and gardens. She marveled at the many stone buildings and wide streets.

They pulled up to the museum and Tony climbed down first, reaching up to help her down. "Merci et pouvez-vous revenir dans une heure," he offered to the driver, requesting him to return in an hour.

The driver nodded and clicked at his horse to move on. As they watched him leave, Tony commented, "We should start looking around."

She glanced at the front of the museum. It had the appearance of not being occupied. The door was braced, with a chain and lock attached. Looking around the sides, she saw that Tony was correct; there were no windows to peer into.

The front was too exposed. "We need to go around the back and away from any prying eyes."

He agreed and said, "Follow me."

He started around the building and she followed. They exited the alley into the back of the museum. Emma saw that it butted up against another structure with no windows. There was an element of privacy that would allow Emma to access the locks. At the back door was another heavy lock and chain. She knelt and pulled out her kit, placing the tools inside the lock. She quickly manipulated the tumblers until she heard it open. She smiled as she opened the lock and removed the chain, handing them to Tony. He carried them as he followed her inside.

Emma looked around the rooms and said, "Whatever happened here, they left in a hurry." Art had been removed from the walls; wires and hangers were still in place. Packing papers were strewn all over the floor. "Tony, have you been in all of the rooms of this building?"

"Yes," he said as he laid down the lock and chain. "The authentications we were invited to perform involved a large group of paintings that had been recovered from a theft."

A memory stirred. "I read about that. It made news back home. They recovered the paintings, but they didn't know who took them."

"Yes. Finding the collection stopped a massive manhunt."

"How long was the current exhibit supposed to be here?"

"I believe the agreement was a limited time."

"But not this limited." Emma started looking around. "Was Philip suspicious of anyone here?"

"I didn't think so, but now I'm not so sure. He did take notes while we were walking around," he said, thinking back.

"Hmm, do you know where his notes might be?" she asked, thinking they would help tell them what Philip was thinking.

"I'm not sure, but he would have kept them in his room. We can check when we go to the hotel," he suggested.

She continued with her questions. "How many times have you been to this museum?"

"More than a few," he admitted.

"What was going on during those visits?" she asked, trying to get a mental timeline together.

"Initially, we walked around and introductions were made," he said. "After that, we spent time evaluating each painting. It took a few days. Even after the authentications were complete, we would continue to come back here, just to see the Vermeer painting," he explained. "It was one of the older artworks that did not have the artist to authenticate it."

"Was there something odd about the picture? Something that Philip saw?"

"I didn't think so at that time, but now I'm wondering," he said consideringly.

"Think back to that night he went missing. Did you talk?"

"Yes, Philip was discussing how Paris had changed and that it was the center of the art world now. He also discussed how troublesome it was to authenticate art here, especially with the new artists. They were creating part of the problem with authenticating pictures."

"Why is that?"

"We've found that the new artist will sign their art, but some have also signed good copies. It just makes it harder to authenticate."

"The Vermeer wouldn't have that issue?" Emma looked at her notebook, circling Vermeer several times.

"That's right. An older painting, such as those by Vermeer, is much harder to duplicate. The one on display at the museum was *The Concert*. It was a depiction of a man and two women performing music."

"Tony, could they have taken the other paintings to cover up the Vermeer theft?"

"It's possible."

"Tell me about the initial theft. Was the art in this museum?"

"Yes. The entire exhibit was missing for more than a month. Once it was found, the artists came in and verified their work. We reconfirmed that during our authentication."

"Is it possible there were forgeries in the museum after your authentication?"

"I don't think so, but we kept coming back for something. Something was bothering Philip."

"You said he knew Monsieur Martin?"

"Yes, they've been communicating by mail for the last ten years."

"Do you happen to have any of the letters with you?"

"Not with me," he admitted, "but they might be at the hotel."

"Okay. Let's finish looking around here and we can head back to check that out."

They went through each room, searching for anything out of the ordinary. They found more debris and wires. As they completed the viewing rooms, she looked at Tony and said, "We need to check the storage rooms."

He nodded and indicated to the back with his hand. "They're this way."

As they entered the door at the back of the room, they found extra crates and little else. Tony noticed something and bent down to examine the floor. "Odd," he said as he brushed two fingers against the ground. "There's paint here, on the floor."

"It is a museum. Wouldn't they have paint around?" she reasoned.

"Not this museum. The exhibit should have only been the recovered paintings. None of those were freshly painted."

"Rub some on my page here," she said and handed him the notebook. The paint was still tacky and allowed him to smear a small segment in her notebook. He handed it back to her and she documented the paint in her notes.

"Do you think Philip thought there was a con going on?"

"He may have, but he didn't share it with me."

"You mentioned Monsieur Martin and Philip were friends. He would have trusted him. So, he would go if Monsieur Martin requested him in the evening or the middle of the night?"

"Yes, he would have gone with no hesitation."

"Okay, so our theory is that someone here has forged art and is possibly holding Monsieur Martin and Philip somewhere."

"Yes. I hope Philip's all right."

"I know how much he means to you. We'll stay until we find him," she promised.

"Thank you." Something was bothering him, and he asked, "Emma, can I see your notebook?"

"Of course," she said, handing it to him.

He studied the paint color and said slowly, "Emma this paint. . ."

"The blue?" she asked.

"Yes, it is very similar to the ultramarine used on the Vermeer."

"Similar? Not the same?" she asked.

"The paint used in the Vermeer was made from an expensive mineral blue pigment extracted from the semi-precious stone lapis lazuli, which was imported into Europe via Venice from Afghanistan. This is similar but not the same," explained Tony.

"So, that color could confirm the painting might be a forgery?" asked Emma.

"Yes, it could," Tony confirmed.

"What have you done to find Philip this week?"

"I talked to the agents de police and reported him missing. They said they would make a report, but it didn't sound like an emergency."

"That's when you notified me," she finished for him.

"You were the only one I could think of to help," he said a bit helplessly.

She reached over and touched his hand. "I'm glad you contacted me." She glanced around and said, "What's that on the ground?"

"Just a piece of paper. It probably came from the packing boxes," he said as he reached for it. As he straightened, he noticed she seemed a bit unsteady. Alarmed, he went to her and said, "Emma, are you okay?"

She stood still a moment to catch her breath, taking a deep breath. "I'm just getting fatigued."

"Are you all right?" he said, immediately concerned. She was always full of energy. "Was there an accident?"

"No accident. I'm fine," she assured him. "I just get tired sometimes."

"Okay, we can go," he said, looking at his watch. "The driver should be waiting."

He drew her hand into his elbow and guided her out. He stopped as they exited and put the chain and lock back on. They made their way to the front of the museum to meet their carriage. "Hôtel Saint Laurent s'il vous plait," Tony said to the driver as they climbed in.

Tony let Emma rest against him as they made their way to the hotel. He had to tell himself to give her some time to tell him why she was feeling weak. As they arrived at the hotel, he nudged a sleeping Emma. She woke with a start.

"It's okay, Emma. We're here," he said, gesturing at the hotel.

She glanced up and saw the majestic hotel. "This is a nice place," she said as Tony helped her down from the carriage.

"Je vous remercie," he said. Emma looked at him askance. "Thank you," he said to her with a smile.

She nodded and they made their way in. The attendant saw him enter and said, "Monsieur votre coffre a été livré à votre chamber."

"Je vous remercie," he responded, then turned to Emma. "Your bags are in the room."

"Wonderful," Emma said, happy her things had made it there.

"Monsieur votre compagnon a un télégramme," called the desk clerk.

Tony stopped and said, "Emma, just a moment. I need to get a telegram from the desk." She nodded and he left her to go to the desk for the envelope. He brought it back and they headed up to their room.

They were on the third floor in a corner room. He opened the door and showed her in. When she entered, she saw a large room with a sitting area and a dining room. He directed her to an inner door, saying, "You'll be in here. This is the room we were using for an office. I've moved the books and papers out of it for you."

She opened the door and found a small clean room.

"Bathroom?" asked Emma.

"Shared," he said ruefully. "We have a key for it. It's down the hall. Be sure to knock first. I can have fresh water brought up for the basin."

"Thanks. I'd like to wash up and lie down. Can we review Philip's room later?"

"Yes, of course. I'll go check on the water now."

"Je vous remercie," she said to him teasingly.

He smiled. "It's great to have a friend here."

She used the washroom down the hall and was happy to see the wash water in her pitcher when she returned to her room. Tony was nowhere to be seen and probably in his room. She closed her door and laid down on the bed thinking, *Telegram. Don't forget to send Jeremy a telegram.*

CHAPTER 67

*E*mma woke and, for a moment, forgot where she was. She looked around and remembered with a smile, sinking back on the bed. *Paris.* She was here on a case, but there was no reason not to enjoy it.

The sun was up, and she felt so much better than she had the previous day. She lay there thinking, *What did we learn yesterday? The curator received a note to meet his friend, owner of the museum. Later the same evening, he went missing. The next day, Tony found the museum empty and all the art removed. A blue color similar to the Vermeer painting was found on the floor of the storeroom. Still, just pieces that need to be organized.* She lay quietly until she heard a knock on her door.

"Emma, breakfast is here," called Tony through her door.

"I'm getting up," she called back. She pulled herself to the side of the bed and took an inventory of any weaknesses. When she didn't notice any, she thought, *I'm finally feeling like myself.*

She stood and washed her face in the basin. She dressed in a black skirt and red shirt with a white lace collar. She pulled her hair into a bun and laced up her boots before leaving her room.

As she entered the main room, she saw the food set up but

no Tony. She left the room and went to the lavatory. On her way back, she noticed a small, nervous-looking man in the hallway. She eyed him curiously, wondering why he was there. He ducked his head and shuffled past her, entering the staircase.

Hmm, something to think about, she thought.

As she entered the room, Tony called from the dining area, "Breakfast is set up over here."

"Thanks, Tony," she said as he pulled out the chair for her. She noticed he continued to wear nice suits; he had developed a style. She smiled, happy he was doing so well.

"I'm starving," said Emma as she settled into eating some of everything: croissants, eggs, bacon, and fruit.

"I did try to get you up last night, but you didn't stir," commented Tony.

"Yes, well, I just needed some extra rest."

Tony started eating also. He finished before Emma and said, "That telegram delivered yesterday was for you."

"Oh. May I have it?" she asked, hoping it was good news.

He pulled the envelope out of his pocket and handed it to her.

She opened it and read silently. *We've gotten him. Zeke is no longer a threat. I'll explain when you return. We miss you. Let us know how Tony is. Love Jeremy.*

"What is it?" Tony asked.

She set the telegram down and looked at Tony, "Tony, Zeke Jones returned to Chicago. Jeremy says they have taken care of him, permanently."

His face went white and said, "Emma, why are you here? I would've thought you'd be in the middle of it. Why aren't you?"

"That's a complicated question. You needed help, and I wanted to be here for you," she explained.

Tony frowned severely and said, "There's more to it than that, isn't there? Emma, I've never seen you without energy, but yesterday you seemed to just fade."

She tried to dodge the second part of the question by saying, "It was a long trip, between the ship and the rail. We also went to the museum."

"Yes, but even then, I wouldn't have expected you to be so tired," he said reasonably.

She would just have to tell him what happened, maybe not all the details, but enough that he was aware she was still recovering. "Tony," she stated, looking him in the eye, "I had surgery a few weeks before I boarded the ship."

"Surgery! Are you okay?" he asked.

"I'm okay now. I was lucky that I was working in a hospital when they found I needed help."

Tony teared up a moment, then something came to him, and grew angry. "Jeremy thought it was okay for you to travel here alone when you were in a weakened state?"

She saw his anger and knew it was because he cared so much for her. She started gently, "Jeremy wanted me out of harm's way because of Zeke's reappearance."

Tony was very silent and then finally said, "So, he made the safe decision to get you away."

"About that," she said, "he didn't tell me until just before I boarded the ship in New York."

Tony saw the humor in what had happened. It was impossible to stop Emma from being in the fray unless she didn't know about it. He laughed out loud at that.

Emma understood the humor and joined him.

"He knows you very well," Tony said.

"Yes," she acknowledged. "He knew I was committed to coming here, and it worked with his plans for Zeke."

"Will you be all right? Can you tell me what the surgery was for?"

Emma turned a bit red, not wanting to admit the full truth. "It was a female surgery, and I was working with the Sisters at the hospital when I collapsed. They immediately took care of me." She saw he was still concerned and said, "I'll be fine."

"Promise?"

"I promise."

Tony looked satisfied and said, "Would you like to move into the living room?"

"Yes," she said, relieved to be moving on to another topic, and followed him into the living room and sat down. She pulled out her notebook to review her notes, then looked up and said, "Tony, what bothers me is why he went out so late and didn't ask you to go with him."

"He felt he was seeing a friend; I don't think he thought there would be any danger. Would you like to review his room?"

She nodded and moved to the room down the hallway from hers.

She looked at him and said, "Do we have a key?"

"Do we need one?" he teased.

"No," she replied, as she reached up to pull a hairpin out and walked over to the door. She knelt in front of the lock, standing after the telltale click. "It's opened."

He smiled and said, "I expected that." He pushed the door open to enter.

As they went in, she could see the room was identical to her own. There were several pieces of furniture: a desk, bed, and dresser. Tony opened the curtains to allow light into the room. It was a bright shiny day and the light flooded all corners of the room Emma looked around, noticing the bed was made, and asked, "Has the maid been allowed in to clean since he disappeared?"

"No. He would only allow cleaning if he was here. I made sure no one was given access in case you needed to examine it."

"Thanks for that," she said absently.

She noticed a large package against the wall and glanced at

Tony. He had opened the closet and was looking around. "Tony, what's that package there?"

"Package?" he asked, stepping out of the closet.

"Yes, over here," she said, kneeling in front of it.

Squatting down next to her, he said, "It looks like a painting. Do you want to open it?"

"Yes, please," she requested.

Tony picked up the picture and laid it down on the bed, then untied the strings holding the brown wrapper closed. "Oh," he said.

"You have seen this before?"

"Yes, as a matter of fact, this is a copy of the Vermeer painting The Girl with A Pearl Earring."

"Why is this one important?" she asked, having to rely on Tony for his expertise.

"It demonstrates the artist's technique for copying Vermeer's. I think Philip saw that. This also gives us the copier's name." He indicated the righthand side of the painting. "It's Charles Allaire."

"Do you know him?"

"Yes, we actually went by his studio. He's very talented; he makes money making copies of other works."

"Interesting. Why would Philip want a copy of a piece of art?"

"Let me look at something," said Tony, moving the picture into the light, looking for something Philip may have seen. He remembered all of the rules for determining if the pictures were fake.

He started talking out loud, detailing his thoughts. "The age of the fame wouldn't be applicable here; the one in the museum was determined to be the proper age. The cracking here is expert and would be hard to tell the difference between an older and newer version of the picture."

She was quiet as she waited for his evaluation.

He continued, "It must be the color. Emma, do you have that example we found in the museum?"

She flipped her notebook back to the aquamarine paint sample. "Yes, here it is," she said.

He took the notebook and compared it to the color used in the picture. "It is an excellent forgery, but the color in this painting is made from more current paints."

"Tony, is it possible Philip noticed the Vermeer in the museum was a fake?"

"The first one we saw was the original, but later when we went back, Philip saw Allaire in the museum storeroom. He was visibly agitated and followed him."

"Did he tell you what he saw?"

"No, he asked me to leave and meet him at the hotel later."

"Do you have any idea what he was planning to do?"

"No, I just followed direction. We often separated to allow us to review more art."

"Tony, we need to go see that artist."

"Yes, I know where his studio is located," said Tony.

"Let's finish this room and we can head that way after."

They continued studying Philip's belongings, finding no other clues.

"Tony, have you seen his notebook or letters?"

"No, but he would probably have taken it with him."

They finished the room and locked it behind them. Tony suggested, "Let's head out. We'll need our coats. It's chilly this morning,"

They headed downstairs to their waiting carriage, heading to Monsieur Allaire's studio.

"Tony, do you think Monsieur Allaire is involved in Philip going missing?"

"I think he might be someone with a piece of this puzzle," said Tony firmly.

Emma fell silent as she watched the scenery passing by.

The area changed as they drove and Tony commented, "We're going into a poor area on the west side."

"I thought he was successful."

"He is, but he's had the space for a long while and I think it keeps him from being too visible."

She watched the elegant homes be replaced by rundown buildings and apartments. The roads also appeared to be less taken care of.

"This is what I mentioned about two sides to Paris. The well off and the not well off," said Tony.

"Yes," she said softly.

When they arrived, they exited the carriage, thanked the driver, and headed toward the doorway of what appeared to be a warehouse. He guided her to the side door, then reached up and banged on it. It was only a moment later when a rather stooped older gentleman opened the door. Funnily, Emma had seen him before this. He was the man in the hallway at the hotel!

"Tony, what a surprise to see you," commented Monsieur Allaire in English.

Emma was watching him carefully and noticed he wasn't surprised to see them. He seemed to be avoiding looking at the painting Tony held. "What can I do for you?"

"You can let us in," Tony said pointedly.

"Both of you?"

"Yes," he said, nodding at Emma.

"Yes, of course." But instead of letting them in, he tried to shut the door. Emma anticipated that move and put her foot in the door to block it from closing. She had also pulled her very large knife out of her hatband. Holding it toward him threateningly, she said, "I think you could step back and allow us in for some questions. You will cooperate, right?"

Monsieur. Allaire looked confused at the little girl with the large knife. He nodded slowly, backing up and letting them in.

"I knew it was a good idea to bring you," muttered Tony out of the side of his mouth as he followed her in.

Emma stayed close to Monsieur Allaire and kept her knife drawn so he would know they were serious. They made their way into a large room full of easels. She assumed this to be the main work area. She couldn't look around much until he was secured. "Tony, I think we should tie him up before we ask our questions."

"Yes," he said, looking around for rope. He saw some piled in the corner, probably used to secure the paper wrapped around the frames. He grabbed a chair and Emma motioned with her knife for Monsieur Allaire to sit down. She watched Tony tie him up and said, "Wait a moment, I know that trick," when she saw how he stiffened his arms. She gripped his shoulders and squeezed so Tony could get the rope tighter around his wrist.

"Tony, also tie his legs to the chair," she directed.

Tony nodded. Once Monsieur Allaire was secure, he backed away.

Emma ran her finger down the length of the knife. "I know you don't want me to use this on you." She was fully prepared to do so if needed.

"No, I want to talk. What's the topic?" he asked innocently.

Tony yanked off the paper on the picture he was carrying. "What about this as a topic?"

"I don't know what you are talking about." He avoided looking at the painting.

Tony continued, anger noticeable in his tone. "This painting has striking similarities in technique to the Vermeer painting. I think Philip Johnson saw you at the museum and thought the same thing we did. You supplied a forgery of the Vermeer to the museum. I think you knew this painting, showing your technique, could give you away."

Emma interrupted, "Tony, he was at our hotel. I saw him in

the hallway. I think he wanted this painting back and he tried to get it from our hotel room."

Tony frown. "Why did you let Philip buy it if you were just going to try to steal it back?"

Monsieur Allaire admitted, "I was careless and did not think when I sold it to him. It wasn't until later when I heard he was authenticating the exhibit, that I knew I'd made a mistake." Emma took a step closer, and he gulped. "Okay, Mon Dieu! I will tell you. Yes, I painted a copy of the Vermeer for the museum and, yes, Philip did see me delivering it."

"Why?" asked Tony.

"The people who originally stole these paintings realized there was no way to escape with the art, much less sell it, so they set up the story that they had recovered the art and became heroes."

"So, Monsieur Martin was involved," Tony concluded.

He didn't want to answer, and Emma nudged him with her boot. "Yes, he was losing money. His museum was not doing well," he said grudgingly.

"Why the duplicate pictures? If he had the originals?"

"He wanted to see if he could fool experts. It would allow him more time to sell for higher values."

"Yes, the authentication would stop any further question about the exhibit," Tony muttered.

"What happened to Philip?" asked Emma.

"I don't know. I just know I told Monsieur Martin that we had not fooled him and he had seen the painting." He shrugged and said, "After that, I was not involved."

Tony looked at Emma and asked, "Do we believe him?"

There was no hesitation in his voice, and he held direct eye contact. "Yes. I think he's telling the truth, at least partially."

"Okay," he said, trusting her.

"But," she said, "I still think he knows more than he's saying. Do you mind if I take over?"

"No, please." He waved at her to start.

Emma stepped closer and said, "Monsieur Allaire, you've told us of your involvement in the forging."

"Copying," he interrupted.

She gave him a look and raised her eyebrows. "Monsieur Martin had to leave in a hurry. What was your role in this?"

"I had no role. I only provided the copy; I was not involved in any of the rest," Allaire muttered.

"It occurs to me that Philip would have been a loose end, a person creating a muddle for this enterprise," commented Emma.

He was quiet and she watched him closely. She went to the big question, wanting to see his reactions if he gave anything away in surprise.

"Charles, where is Philip?" she asked unexpectantly. His eyes darted to the wall and back. He bowed his head and did not respond. She turned immediately to Tony, saying, "That wall."

Tony didn't hesitate and ran over, tapping on it. "It's a fake." He started tearing the facade with his hands. Emma ran over to help. It only took moments to take it down and reveal a door.

Tony reared back once to kick it; it gave but did not open. He kicked it again. The lock flew off and the door splintered. They pushed the debris out of the way and saw the tiny room beyond.

Emma said, "Wait, I have my portable light." She pulled it out of her pocket and lit the small gas lamp. Walking ahead of Tony, she saw a huddled figure against the wall.

Tony ran over to the figure. "Philip." He turned him over. His appearance shocked Tony. He was at least 10 lbs. lighter and appeared to also be dehydrated. He started to untie him, saying over his shoulder, "Emma, get something for him to drink and eat! Hurry!"

Emma left the small room, walked over to Monsieur Allaire, and gripped his neck, saying in a low, threatening voice, "You deserve to be hurt for what you did to that man." He didn't move; he was too scared of her to say anything.

"Where are your food and drink?" she demanded.

"Over there," he said, careful not to move his neck.

She released him and immediately found the baguette and cheese, along with some wine. She ran over to where Tony had moved Philip into the main room. He was coming to, saying, "Tony, I am so glad you found me."

"Tony, get him to eat," Emma encouraged as she tore off some bread, added cheese to it, and opened the wine for him to take a long drink.

He sat eating and trying to gather strength. He had been left in the room with almost no contact and very little food for weeks. The last few days, he had been left completely alone and tied up. After he finished eating, Tony helped him stand and took him to confront Monsieur Allaire. "I have nothing to say to you. You tried to kill me, and you didn't succeed. You did this for money."

Monsieur Allaire was completely defeated at this point.

"It will be prison for you," Philip continued. He sat down; he was still very weak. "There is a schedule of the trip, listing the cities where the art will be shown. We will need to interview some of the rail personnel for storage and location."

Emma watched him, thinking, *Philip will need time to recover.* She looked over at Tony and said, "Tony, you have been in contact with the police about Philip being missing. Could you have them come here to pick up Monsieur Allaire?"

"I can. I will go immediately." He knew Emma could handle herself and didn't stop to question her. He headed out the door, calling, "Emma, lock it up behind me."

"Good idea," she said. After doing so, she returned to the two men. Philip did not want to talk about what had happened to him, but he was curious about other topics. "How did you get involved in this mess?"

"Tony. He knew immediately that something was wrong. He contacted the police, but there was no indication of foul play; they also didn't know you. Tony checked in at the museum and found it abandoned. He knew he needed help and contacted me."

"I appreciate your aid in this. I am not sure I would have made it out alive," Philip said gratefully.

Emma nodded and let the silence settle around them. Much time passed before she heard a pounding on the door. She jumped up and went to answer it, letting Tony and the police in.

As she opened the door, she heard Tony explaining what had happened there. The words forgery, kidnapper, and rideau de mur reached her as they walked to the room. The story unfolded as Philip described the last few weeks. They were pointing at Monsieur Allaire and then at Emma.

"Mademoiselle," the officer said in English. "We have some questions. How did you know the man was hidden in that room?" he asked, pointing at the wall that had been torn down.

"I had a feeling this man was hiding something and, when I asked, he looked in that direction. We investigated and found Philip," she explained.

Philip said, "She is a trained detective. She works with the Pinkertons in Chicago."

The officer knew of the Pinkertons, gave her an appraising look, and thought, *A woman detective?* The officer marked down that information in his notebook. He stopped his writing and said, "We will be taking him in for processing." He motioned toward the officer who had Monsieur Allaire in cuffs. They left with him, saying there would be follow-up questions.

Tony said to Philip, "We have the carriage waiting. We should get you a doctor."

He stood, a bit shaky, but said, "No, I just need out of here. Along with a bath and some more food."

CHAPTER 68

$\mathcal{E}$mma and Tony ignored Philip's objections and went to each side of him, supporting him to the carriage. The ride over was quiet as they each thought about what they had learned. They reached the hotel and helped him inside. Tony assisted him to the lavatory, where he could bathe. After they got him settled onto the couch with a tray of food, he looked like he was feeling better. He asked, "Where do we go from here?"

Emma said, "I think we check in at the rail station and find out where the paintings were shipped. I would assume they had to arrange for the boxes to be loaded into rail cars."

Philip nodded in agreement.

Tony said firmly, "Emma and I will follow up. You need to rest."

"What I need now is not rest. I will stay here and compile my notes for us to review."

"Good idea. Tony, we should get going," Emma said as she gathered her notebook and jacket. They headed downstairs and arranged for a carriage to take them to the rail station. After they arrived, they looked for the office that handled shipping in boxcars. They knew that pictures in that amount and size would need to be on a separate rail car. Approaching the counter, Tony asked for the manager. The man waved him to the side office.

They thanked him and went to knock on the door. Tony called out, "Bonjour."

An older man with dark blond hair walked up, greeting them. "Bonjour, puis-je faire pour vous?" Tony explained the paintings they were looking for.

The manager gave them a surprised look and said, "Oui," as he pulled out his files and confirmed the shipment. "Ils sont sortis il ya deux semaines."

"Pouvez-vous nous dire la destination?" Tony asked.

"Dijon to Lyon, Marseille, and Cannes." He indicated that their tickets had delays scheduled for two weeks at each stop to show the painting locally and continue from there.

"Cela les rendrait maintenant en route vers Lyon," the manager said.

Tony thanked him for the information. They now had a heading: Lyon. He turned to Emma. "Let's go." As they headed to the carriage, he explained what the manager had told him.

Emma nodded and said, "Yes, that confirms it. They are using a tour to change out the painting for the fakes and sell the originals. The artist is lead to believe that their originals will still be returned at the end of the trip."

"Do you expect him to return when the tour is over?" Tony asked.

"No, I think it is an elaborate cover for a long-term theft. I expect he will disappear a very rich man."

They mulled this over and returned to the hotel. As they entered the room, they saw Philip was doing much better. "I guess a few meals made the difference?" asked Tony.

"And lots of water. A bath did not hurt either," Philip said wryly.

As they sat down, he asked, "Did you confirm the stops?"

"Yes, they detailed the locations that the pictures will be on the rail," said Tony.

Philip checked his notes and said, "Okay, he is staying to his schedule, trying to act like nothing is wrong."

"We need to keep it quiet that Monsieur Allaire was arrested and you were found," suggested Emma.

"Yes," they agreed.

"I will notify the police of our plans," said Philip.

"Could we notify authorities at those stops?" asked Emma.

"We could," Philip acknowledged, "but they would not be able to hold Monsieur Martin. They would have to release him since there is no proof that he has done anything wrong."

"What about Monsieur Allaire?"

"They are not sure about him; they think this could just be the work of a sick man. Monsieur Martin is well respected in this community."

"What would make him do this?" asked Tony.

"Money, I think. I sent a note to the bank to ask about the building and ownership. He was way behind on his payments."

"Why handle it this way? Was he involved in the original theft of the artwork?" Tony asked.

"The theft was from his museum initially and, when 'found', it made him a hero. It also made the artist/owners of the art believe he would do anything to protect their paintings."

"Why was the Vermeer included in the show? It seems all the other art is more modern," Tony commented.

"Yes," Philip said, considering this. "I believe the Vermeer is the main prize here. The other works are part of a cover and will get lots of money, but the Vermeer is the one that will allow him to disappear."

"So," said Tony, "we think that, at each stop, he will probably be selling one work of art and replacing it with a copy?"

"I think so," he acknowledged.

"And since the Vermeer is the most valuable piece, it will

probably be the last sale in Cannes," Emma stated, studying at the schedule.

"And from there," finished Tony, "he will disappear."

"Okay, so we go to him, right?" she asked.

Philip and Tony laughed. Philip commented wryly, "Yes, I believe we do."

Tony asked, "Philip if the forgeries are that good, how will we be able to show them to the police?"

"Two things," said Philip. "One, the forgeries will be located somewhere nearby. I assume he wouldn't keep them on location."

"And the second?"

"The second," he said contemplatively, "is based on Allaire's vanity."

"Vanity?" asked Emma.

"Yes, Tony could you bring the Vermeer forgery from my room?"

"I have that out already," he said, indicating the wrapped painting against the wall by the door.

Philip did not look toward the painting. "No, not that one. There is another one. Pull up my mattress, you will see it."

Tony got up to retrieve it. He brought it back to the room and uncovered it. "You had the picture from the museum!"

"Yes, that day I told you I would join you later at the hotel, I had seen Allaire and knew he might be up to something. I found this in the storeroom."

"What made you take it?" asked Emma.

"Instinct, Allaire's behavior, and my wanting to protect Monsieur Martin."

"Which is it the original or the copy?" asked Emma.

"Let's take a look," Phillip said.

"Where do you want it?" asked Tony.

"Over here on the table. Emma, open the curtains," directed Philip. "Tony, take a good look and tell me what you see."

Tony looked at it again, marveling at the detail. "The cracking in the aged paint is amazing; the colors, though a different medium, pass for the original at first glance." He looked at Philip and asked, "What am I looking for?"

"It is a tiny thing, but you are looking for something that should not be there. Mr. Allaire is a very vain man and, when I saw this in the storeroom at the museum, I knew I had to take it and evaluate it. They really should hire better security," he said wryly.

"Taking the painting was what got you targeted? Then why go when Monsieur Martin called that night?"

"I'd thought we were friends. I hoped he wasn't involved or, at the very least, I hoped to talk him out of his plans."

"And when you got there?"

"He was waiting, I tried to talk to him, but he kept demanding to know where I had taken the painting. I wouldn't tell him; he had men hiding in the shadows. We didn't talk much after that," he said ruefully. "Next thing, I woke up in that tiny room."

"So, what did you see on the painting?" asked a curious Emma.

"Look here," he said, pointing to a faintly-stroked AA, barely distinguishable.

"What is it?" Emma asked, squinting.

Tony smiled when he located what Philip was referencing. "Allaire's initials."

"Good eye, Tony," offered Philip, proud he had seen it. "That's it exactly, and that was the reason I knew they were forgeries."

Tony said, "I had thought it was the color blue; it is not an exact match to Vermeer's blue."

"Tony, I knew you were perfect for this work. Yes, that is also another tell, but most people don't know to look for it. It will be easier to show the authorities the initials."

"So, we need to get to Monsieur Martin and locate the forgeries?" asked Tony.

"Yes," said Philip." I have arranged for tickets. We will keep these rooms and take smaller bags with us. We will go by train first to Dijon and then Lyon. Train travel should put us in Lyon while the exhibit is there."

"When does the train leave?" asked Emma.

"We leave at 4:00pm."

She looked down and saw it was 2:00pm and said, "Let's get packed and meet here in twenty minutes?"

They nodded, looking at each other, and then headed to their rooms. Philip had arranged for a carriage to the train station. He exited his room and saw Tony but not Emma. "Is Emma not ready yet?"

"She needed to send a wire in the lobby. We'll meet downstairs."

They joined her there as she was finishing up her message. It contained an update of her plans and that they had found Philip. She also sent her relief and gratitude that Zeke was caught, as well as confirming her return in another one to two weeks.

They left the hotel and took a carriage to the train station. On the way there, Emma tried to see everything. Philip saw her straining out of the carriage and promised, "Emma, we'll show you around as soon as we return."

She smiled. "That would be wonderful."

They reached the station and found their cabin. They would need just the one due to the fact the trip to Dijon would only take a day. They settled in and Philip said, "We'll be getting off at Dijon and going to the museum there."

CHAPTER 69

They spent a pleasant morning on the train and got organized as they entered the station at Dijon.

The museum they were looking for was located in one of the grand mansion houses. Philip had the address and gave it to the carriage driver.

They stopped in front of one of the more imposing buildings —beautiful and so much older than anything Emma had ever seen. They paid the driver and approached the entrance. There was a painted sign turned toward the wall. Tony turned it toward them and read it out loud. "It says it's a limited one-week exhibit." It was an open museum and seemed quite popular.

They entered the door and asked for the curator, giving his name and title. Philip did not know him but hoped he would be able to tell them something about Monsieur Martin's behavior.

They waited for a moment when a man with black hair and dark brown eyes came up, saying, "Je comprends que vous êtes ici pour me voir à propos d'une exposition antérieure?"

Philip nodded, glad he was open to discussing an exhibit not currently featured, but they needed privacy. "Oui est-il quelque part où nous pouvons parler?"

The man looked at him consideringly and said, "De cette façon s'il vous plait."

They followed him and entered a rather large office filled with stuffed furniture, an imposing desk, and lovely artwork on the walls.

"S'asseoir s'il vous plait," he offered, gesturing to the seats.

They sat. The curator started, "Vous avez mentionné votre nom est Philip?"

"Oui. Et voltra nom?" asked Philip.

"Claude Bernard. Je te connais vous avez authentifié les peintures qui étaient dans notre exposition la semaine dernière."

Philip's eyes widened, surprised the man knew his previous work authenticating paintings. He went on to explain that he had been tricked and the paintings were being switched out as they were sold.

Mr. Bernard looked at Emma and Tony. "Would you like me to switch to English? So that we may include your companions?"

"Please."

"So, tell me what we can do to prevent this theft from continuing. I am ready to help. People like this man make our business difficult," said Monsieur Bernard.

"Do you have additional storage other than the pictures on display?" asked Philip.

He frowned and said, "Now that you mention it, he did ask if we had an offsite storage location beside the one here."

"Do you?" Philip pressed.

"Yes, we do. We change out our displays and have a controlled area for the works of art not on display."

"We believe he is keeping the forgeries at those offsite locations," said Tony.

"It is empty now, and they have made their way to Lyon for the next part of the exhibition," said Mr. Bernard.

They nodded and Emma asked quietly, "Can we ask you not to mention our visit to anyone?"

"Oui, of course." He was also thinking out loud. "I might also have the person who purchased the picture that was replaced with a copy."

"Who was it?" Emma asked.

"That is hard. It is a political thing for me. If you allow it, I will look into this while you go after Monsieur Martin," he requested.

Philip studied him, then looked at Emma, knowing she would see something he didn't. She saw his gaze and nodded that he should continue forward. He turned back and said, "Okay, we have a deal."

"You will contact me about your progress?" Mr. Bernard inquired.

"We will and please let us know the progress here," stated Philip firmly.

"One more thing. Do you know the museum curator at the museum in Lyon?" asked Tony.

"I do. He is an honest man. He will work with you once he realizes he is involved with a criminal. I will write you a letter of introduction," Mr. Bernard said.

"Thank you so much. We're heading out by train this evening," said Philip.

"I will have it to you at the station before you leave," he promised.

"Thank you so much."

"No, thank you. We must stand together to stop people like this."

"Agreed." They all shook hands and left the office.

They didn't have much time, but they did take a moment to eat a nice dinner before heading back to the train.

The promised letter of introduction arrived just prior to them leaving. Philip read it as they discussed their learning on the trip to Lyon. He put it down and asked, "How do we want to handle this? It could be confrontational if we go straight to the museum."

"We'll need support before we go. We should talk to the local police and explain the situation. We should also get the curator to meet us there," suggested Emma.

"Agreed. We don't want anyone hurt, but we want to prevent any more theft," said Philip.

They arrived in Lyon late at night. They agreed to stay at a local hotel and go to the Sûreté in the morning. They met early and went straight there, asking for an officer who could speak English; it was getting complicated, and they needed to make sure there were no misunderstandings.

The Sûreté looked at them and said, "I will have to confirm this information with the office in Paris."

"Yes, I understand, but we need to move as soon as possible," Philip said and remembered the letter. He took it out of his pocket, handing it to the officer. "This might help."

The Sûreté read the letter and said, "I will still send the note to Paris, but with this, we can contact the curator to come over." He looked behind him and called, "Julian, I will need you to ask Jules Borde, the museum curator, to join us for a talk. You must keep it very quiet and do not wear your uniform. Pretend to be a friend and hand him this letter."

"I will change and head over now."

The officer directed them to a conference room down the hall. "You may wait in that room there; I will also get the note to the Sûreté in Paris."

Once they entered the room, Tony asked, "What do you think, Emma?"

"I think we have to trust that he's doing as he says. We have no reason not to at this time."

"That's true," he agreed. All they could do is wait.

It turned out that it didn't take long, A knock sounded at the door and a man they assumed was the curator appeared.

"Bonjour, I am Jules Borde, the curator for the museum," he said in very hesitant English. "I have read that you must speak with me and I cannot tell anyone about this."

They introduced themselves and went over everything in detail with Mr. Borde.

"You are sure that Monsieur Martin is involved in this, this criminal enterprise?" he asked, surprised he had such a man's exhibit in his museum.

"We are," stated Philip firmly.

"Before you come into my museum with such accusations, I will need proof."

Tony looked at Philip and said, "I think I can do that." He had the Vermeer with him and removed the paper to reveal it. There was a gasp from Monsieur Borde. "But that is the Vermeer we have in the museum exhibition. How do you have this?" he asked incredulously.

"It is not an original. This is a copy that was made to replace the original," explained Philip.

"How do I know this is a copy and not the actual picture?"

Philip understood that this man did not want to be involved in something nefarious, so he was responding defensively. He acted calmly, pointing to the addition of Allaire's name. Mr. Borde knew that name and how talented he was at forgery. "I will need to check the painting in my museum, but I am believing more and more that we have a criminal running an exhibit there."

At that moment, the Sûreté entered and said, holding a telegram, "Mr. Boarde, I can also confirm that Monsieur Allaire is in prison awaiting trial for kidnapping and attempted murder of Monsieur Johnson."

Monsieur Borde looked resigned and said, "It looks like we need to work fast and get these people out of my museum."

"Agreed. Can you tell me if you have another storage location Monsieur Martin was using?" asked Tony.

"There is," he acknowledged and shared the location.

"Do you think it's watched?" asked Tony.

"I think he would have a person assigned," the Sûreté said, looking at Monsieur Borde. "We can handle that. You will need to go to the museum with Monsieur Johnson and his group to confirm the paintings."

"Can you send an officer with us as well, to stop him from leaving?" asked Emma.

"I will need one of you to come in and identify the forgeries," stated Mr. Bernard.

Tony said, "It will have to be Emma. She's the only one of us he doesn't know."

"That's right, she would go unnoticed," confirmed Philip.

When they arrived at the museum, Tony and Philip waited outside with the officer. Others were guarding the back entrance. Emma went in and was being walked around the new exhibit with Monsieur Borde. "There it is over there," he said to her.

"Let's not rush," she cautioned.

"You are right. Let's look at some of the other paintings." She went to each one, using her observation skills to find the added initials. She made a mental note which one had been replaced. "If you'll notice," she said, trying to keep it brief, "this painting has Allaire's initials. We need to move on, or we'll be noticed." She had seen Monsieur Martin in the room with them. He seemed to be taking special notice of her.

"Yes," Monsieur Borde said, feeling troubled but trying to be nonchalant. "We have another exhibit going on I think you would like to also see." He escorted her to the next exhibit. That seemed to relax Monsieur Martin, and he went back to studying the book he was holding.

Emma reached the window and sent the prearranged signal. It was the right time and there were few people in the exhibit. The officers came into the back room as Tony and Philip were escorted in the front door. Monsieur Martin looked incredulous at the sight of Philip. "But you are dead!" He didn't seem to notice the police officers arriving.

"Turns out Allaire is better at forgeries than he is at murder. You should have gotten a professional," commented Philip in a dry tone.

Monsieur Martin looked at a loss, not understanding the conversation he was trapped in. An officer tapped him on the shoulder, and he jumped. "What?"

"You will need to come with us," the officer said in French.

He didn't seem to know how to respond.

"Emma, did you find the painting that was forged?" inquired Philip.

She nodded toward the wall across from them. "It's that one."

Monsieur Martin blanched at the identification, stuttering, "I don't know what you are talking about. These are not forgeries and, if they are, I was not aware."

At that moment, the lead officer entered and said, "We have the other forgeries; they are secure and the gentleman watching them is in custody."

Monsieur Martin kept arguing that he didn't know what they were talking about.

"We will need to take custody of the painting and shut down this exhibit," stated the officer.

Monsieur Borde said, "I understand. We will have them taken down."

"I will leave several officers here to help you. The other paintings are being delivered to the station."

They took Monsieur Martin down to the station and placed

him under arrest. He just didn't seem to believe that his operation was over and that his well-thought-out plan wasn't going to work. When they arrived, they escorted him to the interrogation room, where he kept arguing they were wrong and he wasn't aware of any of this.

The Sûreté let him talk, not asking any questions. Another Sûreté came over and whispered, "The room is set up for your convenience."

Feeling he was finally being treated with the respect he should have been given all along, Monsieur Martin stood and wrinkled his nose at them as he passed. *I knew I was smarter than these people. I will be released soon,* he thought as he moved to the next room. What he did not expect to see was the art from his exhibition lined up around the walls. It was not just his art; the forgeries were also there next to their originals. *They think they have me,* he thought. *I can explain this.*

The Sûreté started with their questions. "Monsieur Martin, can you tell me why you have two of each painting?"

Feeling very much in charge, he said, "As any seasoned museum curator will tell you, you need to have copies on hand in case one of the originals is on loan to another gallery or a private party."

"Hmmm, that is an explanation," he said as he slowly reached into his pocket. "Except that I have a wire here from Paris that states Monsieur Allaire has said he was paid for forgeries and further implicates you in Monsieur Johnson's kidnapping and attempted murder."

"Bah," Monsieur Martin said loudly. "Allaire is a villain. Whatever he did, he did of his own volition."

"Hmmm, that may be," commented the Sûreté, "and I might have given you the benefit of the doubt. But then I received another wire from the gallery curator in Dijon. It was sent to Monsieur Johnson; I hope you don't mind if I read it aloud."

"Please do," said Philip.

"It says here that the original of that painting," he pointed to the one standing on its own, without a copy, "was sold to a city official. The official says he was unaware that his provenance was falsified. I believe, if we also check with the artist, that this work of art is on loan and not for sale."

"Well, mistakes could have been made. I thought I sold him a copy not an original," he blustered.

The Sûreté looked down on him from his imposing height. "A man with your experience could not tell a copy from an original?"

"Allaire is very good," he said lamely, for the first time looking defeated. That seemed to finally make Monsieur Martin stop talking. They took him out of the room for further processing.

The officer jotted down Emma, Tony, and Philip's statements.

"What will happen to the art?" asked Philip.

The officer looked up from his notes and said, "It will be held until the trial, along with the originals and forgeries. We will notify the owners of the situation and the location of their art. Thank you so much for your help in capturing this man. What do you believe the plan was?"

"My theory was that Monsieur Martin had planned to sell the originals along the route and replace them with the forgeries," said Philip.

"How would that have worked with the Vermeer, since you had the forgery?"

"Interesting question," said Philip. "I have thought about that; it would have to be the last one sold. I think he didn't plan on returning. You will probably find out that he let go of his Paris apartment."

"So, just disappear," the officer stated.

"He would have had plenty of money," said Tony.

"Do you plan to stay in Lyon? We have some wonderful buildings and museums to view," the officer asked with a smile.

"I think we will stay for a few days and then head back to Paris; I owe someone a tour there," Philip teased as he looked at Emma.

CHAPTER 70

The Sûretés arranged a hotel for them and they stayed
for three days. While they waited to give testimony,
they toured and saw La Basilique Notre Dame de Fourviére.
Emma read that Fourvière is dedicated to the Virgin Mary, to
whom is attributed the salvation of the city of Lyon from the
bubonic plague that swept Europe in 1643.

Next was the Vieux Lyon, the largest Renaissance district of
Lyon. There are three distinct sections: Saint Jean, Saint Paul,
and Saint Georges. In the Middle ages, the Saint Jean quarter
was the focus of political and religious power. The Cathedral of
St. Jean, seat of the Primate of Gaul, was a good example of
Gothic architecture.

The Saint Paul section, predominately Italian banker-
merchants in the 15th and 16th centuries, had moved into
wonderful urban residences called hôtels particuliers.

Lastly, they saw the Cathedral Saint-Jean-Baptiste. It was
founded by Saint Pothinus and Saint Irenaeus, the first two
Bishops of Lyon, located in the heart of Vieux Lyon, and backed
up to the Saône river.

After they had completed their final statements to the police, they caught the train back to Paris. It would take a full day, but they were eager to return. When they arrived at the hotel, they found a message for Emma from the local police. They wanted her to meet with them. "I wonder what this is about," said Emma.

"I am sure it's okay," stated Tony. "We can head over together and ask in the morning."

"Yes," agreed Philip.

Emma thought about that and said, "You know, I'll go on my own. I'm okay."

"If you're sure," said Tony.

"I am," she stated.

They started to head up to their room but were stopped by the manager. "I would like to accompany you to your room. If you do not mind."

Philip frowned but said, "Yes, that would be fine."

As they were finally entering their room, they were surprised at what they saw. Numerous paintings lined the walls. "Where did these come from?" asked Philip.

The manager spoke from behind them. "Monsieur, all of Paris heard what you have done for our artists. This is their thanks. Some of our best artists are sending their work to your museum. On loan," he cautioned, with a chuckle.

As Tony and Philip immediately began looking at each painting, the manager silently exited. Emma was sitting quietly and said, "I think we should all head home. I think it's time."

"But I have promised to show you Paris," protested Philip.

"I know, but I want to get back. I have responsibilities there," she said.

"Okay, I will start the arrangements," Philip promised. It turned out that they did have time to see the sights; it would take at least four days to organize the paintings for shipment. They took her to see the Arc de Triomphe, a massive triumphal arch that Napoleon Bonaparte commissioned in 1806 after his great victory at the Battle of Austerlitz.

Next, they saw the royal residence and the Palais du Louvre had been hosting the Louvre Museum since 1793. Lastly, they saw the Notre-Dame de Paris, the location of Napoleon Bonaparte's coronation in 1804.

Emma took a carriage to the Sûreté. They had heard about her experience with Pinkerton and wanted to spend some time showing her one of their methods called signaletics or bertillonage. This method identified an individual by measurements of head and body, shape formation of the ear, eyebrow, mouth, and eye. It also included markings such as tattoos, scars, and personality characteristics. They applied this information onto cards that included photographs. The cards were systemically filed and crossed indices so they could easily be retrieved. Emma took lots of notes to share with Cole and Jeremy. She thanked them for their time.

The ship pulled into the port in New York, and Emma was the first person waiting for the plank to be lowered. She took off at a run and was in Jeremy's arms before anyone else could leave the ship.

"Welcome home, Emma," Jeremy said as he kissed her forehead and held her tight.

Notebook Mysteries

Unexpected Outcomes

KIMBERLY MULLINS

ABOUT THE AUTHOR

Kimberly Mullins is the author of series of books titled "Notebook Mysteries". Her stories are based on historical events occurring in 1800's Chicago. She holds a BS in Biology and a MBA in Business. She lives in Texas with her husband and son. When she is not writing she is working as a Process Safety Engineer at a large chemical company. You can connect with her on her website www.kimberlymullinsauthor.com.

Photo Credit: Blessings of Faith Photography

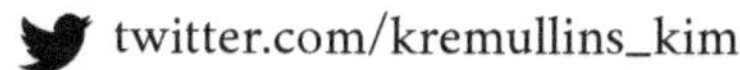 twitter.com/kremullins_kim